Last Days of Summer

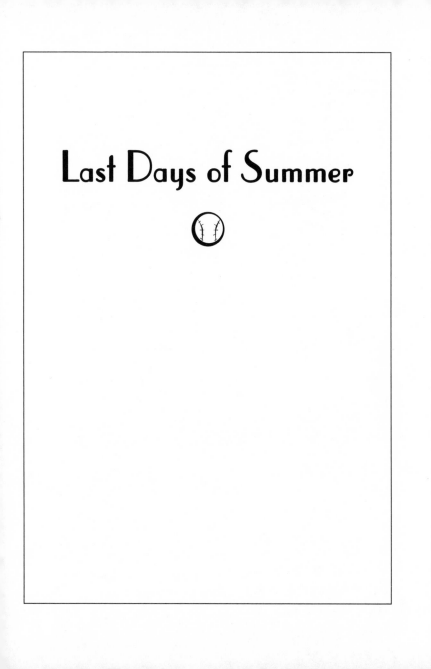

Also by Steve Kluger

Fiction
Changing Pitches

Non-Fiction
Lawyers Say the Darndest Things
Yank: World War II From the Guys
Who Brought You Victory

Stage Plays
Bullpen
Cafe 50's
Pilots of the Purple Twilight
After Dark

Teleplays
Yankee Doodle Boys (with Glen Brunswick)

Screenplays
Almost Like Being in Love
Bye Bye Brooklyn (with Glen Brunswick)
Once Upon a Crime

Last Days of Summer

A NOVEL BY

Steve Kluger

AN AVON BOOK

AVON BOOKS, INC.
1350 Avenue of the Americas
New York, New York 10019

Copyright © 1998 by Steve Kluger
Interior design by Jean Cohn/Design-a-roni
Visit our website at **http://www.AvonBooks.com/Bard**
ISBN: 0-380-97645-5

Library of Congress Cataloging in Publication Data:
Kluger, Steve.
    Last days of summer / Steve Kluger.
       p.   cm.
     I. Title.
  PS3561.L82L37   1998   98-11225
  813'.54–dc21   CIP

First Bard Printing: June 1998

BARD TRADEMARK REG. U.S. PAT. OFF. AND IN OTHER COUNTRIES, MARCA REGISTRADA, HECHO EN U.S.A.

Printed in the U.S.A.

FIRST EDITION

QPM   10   9   8   7   6   5   4   3   2   1

For my father—
who never had a hero when he needed one

Last Days of Summer

⚾ Prologue

THE WHITE HOUSE

November 26, 1936

Dear Joseph:

Please allow me to express my deepest gratitude for the dollar you contributed to my campaign. Although I have indeed considered lowering the voting age as you suggest, I am afraid I would have to draw the line at eighteen. Nine is out of the question. I wish it weren't. In any event, I am touched by your support.

Mrs. Roosevelt joins me in thanking you for your kind words. I hope that the next four years will justify your continued faith in us.

Yours very truly,

Franklin D. Roosevelt

Franklin D. Roosevelt

It's funny how the years have changed everything about Brooklyn geography. Time was when uptown meant Nathan's—if you were in the mood for an orange pop, a neurotic hot dog, and some front-line scuttlebut from a lonesome GI—or the old Paramount, where Veronica Lake once sold war bonds and kisses, and nearly financed the entire Normandy invasion herself. The business district was really the Citizen-News building, where if you hung around long enough and practiced your eavesdropping you might learn that Bataan wasn't just the name of a movie; and downtown, of course, was Flatbush, where on the Fourth of July the 433rd Infantry marched from Grand Army Plaza to Anzio with only an Irving Berlin cadence pointing them in the right direction.

Slugger Banks Whips Iowa City 5–0

SPRINGFIELD, ILL., May 14—Nineteen-year-old rookie sensation Charlie Banks propelled the Springfield Bluejackets to an easy win over Iowa City here, with a solo haymaker in the second inning and a slammer at the bottom of the eighth. The volatile third baseman has become something of a local legend since early April, when he failed to make the squad cut during tryouts but was issued a uniform regardless after refusing to get off the team bus.

Brooklyn is where I grew up. It's where I learned what a storm trooper was, what an egg cream was, what "flak attack" meant, and what rubbers were used for outside of keeping your feet dry. It's where I discovered the true market value of a steelie versus an aggie and the queasy sounds your stomach made whenever you saw a hundred thousand hobnail boots goose-stepping through the Pathé News. It's where any kid could tell you that "Captain Colin Kelly shot a tiger in the belly, then he sent the ship *Haruna* to the bottom of the sea" but not know the capital of Michigan. It's where the nearest you were likely to get to heaven was smelling the popcorn at Luna Park, or seeing a real-life Dauntless dive-bomber—blue

4

with white trim—taking off from the Navy Yard, or falling asleep with your blackout curtains drawn tight while Glenn Miller played "Moonlight Serenade" over the radio, live from the still waters of the Glen Island Casino ("mecca of music for moderns"). Brooklyn is also where I learned that I was a kike, that my second-to-best-friend was a Nip, and that my father was never coming back home.

"Nana Bert, is my Dad there?"

"He's busy, dear. We're going to Monte Carlo, but with all those Germans, you can't get a reservation. Call him after the eighteenth."

Banks Downed by Food Poisoning; Goes 5-For-6

JOPLIN, MO., June 24—The Racine Rocket lost his bid for 38 consecutive hits this afternoon when an attack of food poisoning brought about by a tin of tainted anchovies caused him to ground into a double play against Joplin in the eleventh inning after having hit safely in his first five at-bats.

"I thought they were sardines," mumbled a sheepish Banks as he was carried off the field with a fever of 104. Asked where he had learned such stamina, the nineteen-year-old third-sacker retorted, "In the 3 C's [Civilian Conservation Corps]. Unless you were dead, you kept going."

After the divorce, my mother moved us from a largely Hasidic community in Williamsburg to an old brownstone at the corner of Bedford Avenue and Montgomery Street, where the mailboxes in the vestibule presaged the special fabric out of which my adoles-

5

cence was to be woven. "Corelli. Verrastro. Fiore. Bierman. Di Cicco. Fusaro. Delvecchi. Margolis." This told me all I needed to know. Of course, as the newly appointed resident Jew, I couldn't be entirely certain what recreational activities the neighborhood was willing to offer, but I had a pretty decent hunch that bleeding was among them. Not that my mom or my Aunt Carrie did much to promote my cause: they openly lit Shabos candles on San Gennaro Day, walked to *shul* through the Our Lady of Pompeii street festival, and helped feed the Italian-American War Widows with a tray of stuffed derma and potato knishes. The day we unpacked, I figured conservatively that I had a week left to live; one look at Lenny Bierman and I pared the estimate by half. But I was determined to fit in.

"Get it, Margolis? Sheenies walk on that side of the street."
★SPLAT!★

Banks Clips Association's Top Tomato

CHICAGO, ILL., December 18—On a ballot that surprised absolutely no one, the Midwestern Association today unanimously voted Charles Banks the 1937 Henry Chadwick Award, marking only the second time in the league's 61-year history that the honor has gone to a rookie. (Turkey Mike Donlin, in 1898, was the first.) Twenty-year-old Banks was notified via telegraph at his home in Racine, Wisconsin, and purportedly wired back, "Who in Hell is Henry Chadwick?" Springfield Bluejackets officials have turned down several lucrative offers for purchase of the rookie's contract, including a bid from the Brooklyn Dodgers which purportedly involved the

---

By the time I turned twelve, the Dodgers made me vomit. There was a popular misconception floating about the borough that they were lovable losers; for my money, one might just as easily have dispensed with the adjective altogether and developed a much clearer rotogravure of the truth. They had neither brains nor breeding—forgivable shortcomings in and of themselves if perhaps they had owned even one shred of talent. But they didn't have that either. What they had was a hartebeest at first named Dolph Camilli, a hop-o'-my-thumb at short they christened Pee Wee and thought it cunning, and something at third base called Cookie Lavagetto. Nobody had the balls to ask why. Then there was Craig Nakamura's idol, Leo Durocher, who plainly belonged behind bars—at a precinct house or an animal sanctuary, the need to distinguish was purely moot and predicated solely upon space availability. All things considered—and given the way my luck was running—about the last thing I needed was a bedroom window that overlooked Ebbets Field. And the only hurdy-gurdy in Flatbush.

> *Leave us go root for the Dodgers, Rodgers,*
> *They're playing ball under lights.*
> *Leave us cut out all the juke jernts, Rodgers,*
> *Them Dodgers is my gallant knights.*

Of course, it never would have occurred to me that my father's lifelong passion for the damned team might have had something to do with my utter loathing for them; this, after all, was 1940, and we hadn't heard about pop psychology in those days. The only thing I knew for sure was that I wasn't going to be finding any heroes in Brooklyn. So I looked where I could—but the results were kind of disappointing.

April 9, 1940. I have decided to turn to a life of crime. My dad was supposed to take me to Coney Island but he never called back, my left eye is black-and-blue again, the Japanese say they're only borrowing Nanking temporarily but nobody believes them, and Hitler is beginning to scare the holy heck out of me.

I am lurking behind a post in the Metropolitan Avenue subway station on the Canarsie Line, casing my first heist: the cherry swizzle jar at the newsstand run by this crusty old blind guy with a tin cup and a half-dead beagle. Sentiment would compel me to admit in retrospect that he was really a kindly old curmudgeon—were it not for the fact that in truth he was the meanest bastard who ever lived. "Dirty mocky" was not without the realm of his considerable prosaism; "Have a nice day" clearly was. Therefore, I have little compunction about moving in on the kiosk and making a big deal out of buying *The Brooklyn Eagle*—strictly as a diversionary tactic to throw the old fart off the scent—while my left arm snakes its way toward the swizzle shelf.

"Paper."

"Two cents. Get outta here." Hot damn! This is gunna work! As I covertly wrap my fingers around the sacred licorice, a train hurtles through the station and, seeing no real advantage to stopping, continues on its way to Montrose, Morgan, DeKalb, and Hell. Eventually the platform is once again shrouded in ersatz silence. Broken shortly.

"And get your fuckin' hand outta the jar."

Needless to say, I've never gone near a cherry swizzle since. But the newspaper was another story.

FINAL

The Brooklyn Eagle

TWO CENTS

VOL. LXXVI....No. 6,242   TUESDAY, APRIL 9, 1940   Cloudy, 48-53

GERMANS OCCUPY DENMARK, ATTACK OSLO; NORWAY DECLARES WAR ON GERMANY; HITLER CLOSING IN ON SCANDINAVIA; DODGERS LOSE OUT ON CHARLIE BANKS

GIANTS SIGN TEMPERAMENTAL THIRD SACKER

By Bert Hochman
Special Wireless from The Polo Grounds

NEW YORK, Tues., April 9—The New York Giants today announced that they have purchased the contract of third baseman Charlie Banks from the Springfield Bluejackets (Midwestern Assoc.), putting an end to a bidding war that, by late last night, included the Chicago Cubs, the Washington Senators, the St. Louis Cardinals, and the Boston Bees.

Banks, 22 and a native of Wisconsin, has been a favorite topic in sporting pages across the country ever since his arrival in Springfield three years ago, both for his sustained batting average of .369 and for a notorious freedom with his fists "whenever anybody gives me lip or such other good reasons." Although he has monogrammed virtually every minor league batting title with the initials "C.B." and has most recently been awarded the A. G. Spaulding Cup, perhaps the greatest testament to his abilities came late last summer from no less a personage than former New York governor Franklin Delano Roosevelt, who called the right-hander "America's Secret Arsenal." When informed of the President's comments, rookie Banks replied, "The President of what?"

More realistically touting the busher as "the new Roger Bresnahan," Giants manager Bill Terry speculates that Banks will be worked into the lineup during tomorrow's opener at the Polo Grounds, eventually splitting third base with current sacker Mel Ott who, on hearing the news, reportedly groaned, "I can't wait."

In a related story, the Brooklyn Dodgers denied that they had expressed any interest in acquiring the rookie first, despite earlier reports that indicated they were determined to keep the Giants from getting their

Continued on Page Six

10

1940

Juvenile Detention Center of the Borough of Brooklyn
1215 Bushwick Avenue
Brooklyn, New York

To: Capt. E. LaFontaine
From: Sgt. F. Kahane
Subject: The Margolis Kid

1. He won't eat dinner. Says he wants brisket on rye bread. We tried to fool him with roast lamb, only it didn't work.

2. Claims to be suffering from a variety of ailments that mandate his immediate release. These include appendicitis, heart attack, diphtheria, polio and gonorrhoea (which he pronounced correctly). Actually, we think he has a slight fever—this has been regulated with Bayer aspirin and orange juice.

3. Still hasn't identified the boys who attacked him, and won't even admit that it happened. Says he was run over by a vegetable truck. Judging by the severity of the beating, we're pretty sure the Bierman brat was involved, but we have no way of corroborating without the kid's help.

4. The mother and the aunt were notified and have been waiting in reception since 3:30 this afternoon. We believe it would be inadvisable to let them see Joseph for several days, or at least until his facial lacerations have healed somewhat. Both are apparently unaware of the repeated assaults on the boy; on such occasions, he's told them that he fell off his bicycle. Note: Mrs. Gettinger (the aunt) has now determined the religious affiliations of all receiving personnel and will only speak to Sgt. Greenberg.

5. We have telephoned the father several times at his residence in Manhattan. The housekeeper advised that she had given him the message, but as yet we have not heard from him.

6. We asked the kid if he wanted to tell us why he did what he did, and were informed, "You bulls can't keep me in this creep joint forever. Not unless you want your lamps put out." Considering that he's only twelve, we felt it polite to treat the threat with the same sort of respect it's accorded in the movies; as such, Lt. Frierson (who sounds more like Edward G. Robinson than anyone else on staff) warned him, "Yeah? Well, if you don't start singing, you're going up the river." It didn't work. All he did was bribe us with the Maltese Falcon.

7. We've contacted Don Weston in Psychology, who's interviewing the kid in the morning. In the meantime, I'd be careful about drinking the water.

I Must Not Pee in the Reservoir
BY JOEY MARGOLIS

I must not pee in the reservoir. I must not pee in the reservoir. I must not pee in the reservoir.
I must not pee in the reservoir. I must not pee in the reservoir. I must not pee in the reservoir.
I must not pee in the reservoir. I must not pee in the reservoir. I must not pee in the reservoir.
I must not pee in the reservoir. I must not pee in the reservoir. I must not pee in the reservoir.
I must not pee in the reservoir. I must not pee in the reservoir. I must not pee in the reservoir.
I must not pee in the reservoir. I must not pee in the reservoir. I must not pee in the reservoir.
I must not pee in the reservoir. I must not pee in the reservoir. I must not pee in the reservoir.
I must not pee in the reservoir. I must not pee in the reservoir. I must not pee in the reservoir.
I must not pee in the reservoir. I must not pee in the reservoir. I must not pee in the reservoir.
I must not pee in the reservoir. I must not pee in the reservoir. I must not pee in the reservoir.

I must not pee in the reservoir. I must not pee in the reservoir. I must not pee in the reservoir.
I must not pee in the reservoir. I must not pee in the reservoir. I must not pee in the reservoir.
I must not pee in the reservoir. I must not pee in the reservoir. I must not pee in the reservoir.
I must not pee in the reservoir. I must not pee in the reservoir. I must not pee in the reservoir.
I must not pee in the reservoir. I must not pee in the reservoir. I must not pee in the reservoir.
I must not pee in the reservoir. I must not pee in the reservoir. I must not pee in the reservoir.
I must not pee in the reservoir. I must not pee in the reservoir. I must not pee in the reservoir.
I must not pee in the reservoir. I must not pee in the reservoir. I must not pee in the reservoir.
I must not pee in the reservoir. I must not pee in the reservoir. I must not pee in the reservoir.
I must not pee in the reservoir. I must not pee in the reservoir. I must not pee in the reservoir.
I must not pee in the reservoir. I must not pee in the reservoir. I must not pee in the reservoir.
I must not pee in the reservoir. I must not pee in the reservoir. I must not pee in the reservoir.
I must not pee in the reservoir. I must not pee in the reservoir. I must not pee in the reservoir.
I must not pee in the reservoir. I must not pee in the reservoir. I must not pee in the reservoir.
I must not pee in the reservoir. I must not pee in the reservoir. I must not pee in the reservoir.
I must not pee in the reservoir. I must not pee in the reservoir. I must not pee in the reservoir.
I must not pee in the reservoir. I must not pee in the reservoir. I must not pee in the reservoir.
I must not pee in the reservoir. I must not pee in the reservoir. I must not pee in the reservoir.
I must not pee in the reservoir. I must not pee in the reservoir. I must not pee in the reservoir.
I must not pee in the reservoir. I must not pee in the reservoir. I must not pee in the reservoir.
I must not pee in the reservoir. I must not pee in the reservoir. I must not pee in the reservoir.
I must not pee in the reservoir. I must not pee in the reservoir. I must not pee in the reservoir.
I must not pee in the reservoir. I must not pee in the reservoir. I must not pee in the reservoir.
I must not pee in the reservoir. I must not pee in the reservoir. I must not pee in the reservoir.
I must not pee in the reservoir. I must not pee in the reservoir. I must not pee in the reservoir.
I must not pee in the reservoir. I must not pee in the reservoir. I must not pee in the reservoir.
I must not pee in the reservoir. I must not pee in the reservoir. I must not pee in the reservoir.
I must not pee in the reservoir. I must not pee in the reservoir. I must not pee in the reservoir.
I must not pee in the reservoir. I must not pee in the reservoir. I must not pee in the reservoir.
I must not pee in the reservoir. I must not pee in the reservoir. I must not pee in the reservoir.
I must not pee in the reservoir. I must not pee in the reservoir. I must not pee in the reservoir.
I must not pee in the reservoir. I must not pee in the reservoir. I must not pee in the reservoir.
I must not pee in the reservoir. I must not pee in the reservoir. I must not pee in the reservoir.
I must not pee in the reservoir. I must not pee in the reservoir. I must not pee in the reservoir.
I must not pee in the reservoir. I must not pee in the reservoir. I must not pee in the reservoir.
I must not pee in the reservoir. I must not pee in the reservoir. I must not pee in the reservoir.
I must not pee in the reservoir. I must not pee in the reservoir. I must not pee in the reservoir.

I must not pee in the reservoir.   I must not pee in the reservoir.   I must not pee in the reservoir.
I must not pee in the reservoir.   I must not pee in the reservoir.   I must not support Fascist Spain.
I must not pee in the reservoir.   I must not pee in the reservoir.   I must not pee in the reservoir.
I must not pee in the reservoir.   I must not pee in the reservoir.   I must not pee in the reservoir.

INTERVIEWER: Donald M. Weston, Ph.D.
SUBJECT: Joseph Charles Margolis

Q: What happened to your face?

A: Jack Dempsey knocked me out in three rounds. It was in all the newspapers.

Q: You don't trust me, do you?

A: Nope.

Q: You want some candy?

A: No.

Q: You want a drink of water?

A: No.

Q: You want a cigarette?

A: I'm twelve. Almost. On June 8th.

Q: Lots of kids your age smoke cigarettes.

A: Not me. How about a brandy instead?

Q: I don't have any.

A: That figures.

Q: Does your mother smoke?

A: No. But she can drive.

Q: How about your father?

A: He's an aviator. He built the *Spirit of St. Louis* with Lindbergh and the Curtiss Robin with Wrong Way Corrigan, and sometimes he takes me flying over the—

Q: Your father owns a textile plant.

A: Right. I forgot.

Q: Do you like your father?

16

A: Yes.

Q: Why?

A: Don't know.

Q: How come he wouldn't have lunch with you?

A: I think he had to talk to some people about nylon in his office. And Nana Bert always says he's not there at home.

Q: Who's Nana Bert?

A: His wife. They live on Fifth Avenue.

Q: Does that bother you?

A: Not much, I guess.

Q: What did you do when they told you he wasn't coming?

A: I ordered a shrimp cocktail and a steak. The maitre d' is Kenny and he calls me boychik. He went to the yeshiva with my Dad. And he always lets me say things like "Put it on my tab."

Q: Then you urinated in the reservoir?

A: Not yet. First I clipped a goldfish from the five and dime. I ate it.

Q: How much of this are you making up?

A: All of it. How come?

Q: Joey, do you think maybe you got into trouble so you'd get caught and they'd call your father?

A: You mean negative attention?

Q: Uh—yes.

A: Wouldn't work. Even the police couldn't get him to come over.

Q: You don't think so?

A: Nope. Nylon. But he's taking me to the World's Fair. He promised.

Q: What happened to your face?

A: Bank holdup. I want to be like Jimmy Cagney in *Each Dawn I Die*. "Stay out of my way, copper."

Q: Do you really?

A: No, but stuff like that scares the heck out of you guys.

Q: What about your mother?

A: She boils my underpants.

Q: I beg your pardon?

A: You heard me. On the stove. Aunt Carrie almost ate a sock once.

Q: Do you like her?

A: Aunt Carrie?

Q: Your mother.

A: I love her. A lot.

Q: She says you don't get along too well at school.

A: That's because Mrs. Hicks had a nervous breakdown. I gave it to her by accident.

Q: How?

A: I found the sacrifice fly rule in the Bill of Rights. She didn't believe me, but I proved it. Then they took her to the hospital.

Q: Do you mind if I show you some pictures?

A: No.

Q: All right. Now what do you see?

A: A Rorschach blot.

Q: Joey—

A: Okay, okay. Center field at the Polo Grounds. This is the bleachers and that's the ball that Charlie Banks hit into them on April 10th. He's the only one who ever did that. Even DiMaggio in the '36 Series couldn't. Only Charlie.

Q: You sound pretty proud.

A: I am.

Q: What happened to your face?

A: My head got caught in a mechanical rice picker.

Q: Take a look at this one. What do you see?

A: Third base. That's where Charlie lives. Over here is right field, and this is the plate. You know what happened there on April 19th?

Q: Charlie Banks hit three home runs.

A: How did you know that?

Q: Doesn't everybody?

A: Not in Brooklyn. I *hate* Brooklyn.

Q: I don't blame you.

A: You don't?

Q: Who cut you up like that? Was it Lenny Bierman?

A: He called me a kike first. I told him Charlie Banks was my best friend, but he didn't believe me.

Q: How come?

A: I was lying.

Q: Let's try another one.

Q: Okay, what do you see?

A: What do *you* see?

Q: Uh—I think it's the Polo Grounds again. Right?

A: Are you humoring me?

Q: No. Why?

A: Because it's a sideways map of Wisconsin. This is Racine where he was born.

Q: Charlie Banks?

A: You bet.

Q: It wasn't just Bierman, was it? Joey?

A: No. Delvecchi too.

Q: What are you going to do about it?

A: Don't know yet.

Mr. Charles Banks, NY Giant
c/o Third Base
The Polo Grounds
Coogans Bluff, NY

Dear Mr. Banks,

I am a 12 year old boy and I am dying of an incurable disease. It is a horrible one. I have had to spend most of my life in hospitals and in bed with high fevers and very white skin. This is because I have no more corpusles, which you may remember is what provides you with antibodies. I am also paralyzed. Sometimes I am racked by so much pain that I cry out in the night and say things like "Dear God. Dear God."

The reason I am writing is because I read in a magazene once where Babe Ruth visited a dying boy in a hospital, and although he provided him with an autograph which he had asked for, what the boy really wanted was for the Babe to hit one out for him. Well he did, and the Lukemia went away like that. You do not have to come and visit me, but I would appreciate it if you would hit one out. All you have to do is point to left field or wherever makes you comfortable and then say "This is for my friend Joey Margolis" (on the radio if possible) and then swing.

I hope you can do this soon because I don't think I will be around much longer.

Your friend,
Joey Margolis

Mr. Joseph Margolis
236 Montgomery Street
Brooklyn, New York

Dear Friend:

Many thanks for your letter and the kind words contained therein. I am enclosing my picture with the autograph you requested.

Keep on slugging.

Best wishes,
Charles Banks

Mr. Charles Banks, NY Giant
c/o Third Base
The Polo Grounds
Coogans Bluff, NY

Dear Mr. Banks,

I am a 12 year old boy and I am blind. This is a terrible thing. But I was not always blind. In the old days I used to be able to swim in the creek and build log cabins and greet each day like it was a new adventure, the way boys have done since the dawn of time. Then one day my eyes started to fill up with mucus and the sunshine went away forever.

The reason I am writing is because I read in this magazene where Lou Gehrig once visited this blind boy in a hospital and promised he would hit one out for him. And when he did, that boy (who had been listening on the radio) was heard to cry out "I can *see*! I can *see*!"

Mr. Banks, it would do me alot of good if you would hit one out for me the way Iron Horse did that other time. I would not even ask you to make a special trip to the plate for it. You can pick one you were going to hit out anyway and just say ahead of time (on the radio) "This is for my friend Joey Margolis."

I must stop writing now. It is so very very dark.

Thank you.

> Your friend,
> Joey Margolis

Mr. Joseph Margolis
236 Montgomery Street
Brooklyn, New York

Dear Friend:

Many thanks for your letter and the kind words contained therein. I am enclosing my picture with the autograph you requested.

Keep on slugging.

Best wishes,
Charles Banks

INTERVIEWER: Donald M. Weston, Ph.D.
SUBJECT: Joseph Charles Margolis

Q: You didn't think it was going to *work,* did you?

A: I was just warming up. This is a tough one. If I only knew where he lived.

Q: Is that a new cut over your eye?

A: Don't remember.

Q: How did it happen?

A: I fell in front of the "A" train. Can we look at some more baseball pictures?

Q: Sure.

Q: What do you see?

A: A midget lying on his back with a hard-on.

Q: Where did you learn to talk like that?

A: "The Street, see? That's where I grew up. The Street. Now they're gunna make me swing for it." Guess what? I live upstairs from the Green Hornet. He thinks I'm the Shadow. We send messages in code up and down the fire escape on heat-resistant string like in *Gangbusters*.

Q: How come?

A: Nazis take no prisoners.

Q: That sounds pretty serious.

A: You bet it is. Know that old lady who owns the clock store on Sullivan Street?

Q: Mrs. Aubaugh?

A: Don't turn your back on her. She's a saboteur.

Q: She has a wooden leg!

A: That's where she keeps the grenades. I tried to send a warning to the Hornet, but the string broke and it fell through the bars onto a German courier. Now they're wise to us.

Q: Tell me about the inkblot.

A: It's the flag pole.

Q: Where?

A: Over the Giants clubhouse in deep center. Me and Charlie always stand next to each other with our hats over our hearts when they play The Baseball Song.

Q: "Take Me Out to the Ballgame"?

A: "O Say Can You See".

Q: Where's your father?

A: Over there. In the stands.

Q: Is he rooting for the Giants?

A: For Brooklyn.

Q: Does that bother you?

A: Only when he brings Nana Bert.

Q: How often does he do that?

A: Not since I hit her with a foul ball. It was Charlie's idea.

Q: You don't like Nana Bert much, do you?

A: She has long red fingernails. Aunt Carrie says with claws like that she could climb the Chrysler Building. My Dad is bringing her with us when he takes me to the World's Fair. Maybe the Trylon'll fall on her.

Q: Have you ever been out of Brooklyn before?

A: No. Afraid.

Q: Of what?

A: Smokes, what if I look back over my shoulder and turn into a pillar of salt? That's what happened to Lot's wife.

Q: I remember.

A: Then stop laughing. It isn't funny. When Charlie Banks takes me on a road trip with him—

Q: Joey, listen to me. Charlie Banks doesn't even know who you are. And he's not going to take you on any road trip.

Bureau of Vital Statistics
964 Marquette Street
Racine, Wisconsin

Dear Bureau of Vital Statistics—

My name is Joseph Margolis Banks and I am eight years old and I am doing a project for my school where we have to draw our family tree. Since my father died last year and can't help me my teacher Mrs. Hicks told me I should write to you. The only thing I know is that his family came from Racine and I have a cousin named Charles who was born in 1917 and knew my dead father.

Please help me find him.

Very truly yours,
Joseph Margolis Banks

Mr. Joseph Margolis Banks
236 Montgomery Street
Brooklyn, New York

Dear Joseph:

Thank you for your letter. I am glad that your teacher told you to write to us, so that we can help you learn to use the friendly services provided to you by our government. I was surprised to find out that you are only eight years old, because we usually hear from older boys and girls!

Most of the time, we need to know a little bit more about your family before we can help you—such as your father's first name, which you forgot to give us. There are many Banks families in Racine, but I am happy to tell you that only one of them had a Charles born in 1917. (By the way, our records show that your father Herbert is still alive, but since receiving your letter we have changed that. We've also added your name to his family. You see? Sometimes you can help us as much as we help you!)

Charles lives at 615 Riverside Drive, New York, New York, which practically makes you neighbors! I believe that he is some sort of an athlete, so you can be very proud of him. You and he still have a Cousin Ivy, who recently moved to Des Moines; Charles also had an older brother named Harlan, who died of a concussion seven years ago. I am so sorry.

I am enclosing your full family tree, and hope that it helps you to get good marks in school!

Sincerely,
Elsie McKeever
Archivist

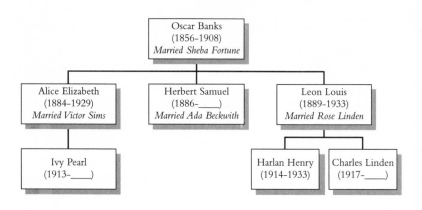

INTERVIEWER: Donald M. Weston, Ph.D.
SUBJECT: Joseph Charles Margolis

Q: Oh, my God. This is mail fraud!

A: You haven't heard the half of it yet. I also found out that he gets his hair cut at a place called Popo's and he drives a Reo with a radio in it and he can almost play "In the Mood" on the alto sax and Harlan used to call him Chucky. Elsie McKeever's a lousy security risk. Can I have an inkblot?

Q: You know, if you were seven years older they could put you in jail!

A: But you'd get me off, wouldn't you? You're my mouth-piece.

Q: Joey, how long do you think you can get away with this?

A: Until Charlie takes me on a road trip with him.

Q: I see.

A: You don't believe me, do you?

Q: Why don't we look at some inkblots?

A: Forget it. I'll ask the Green Hornet.

28

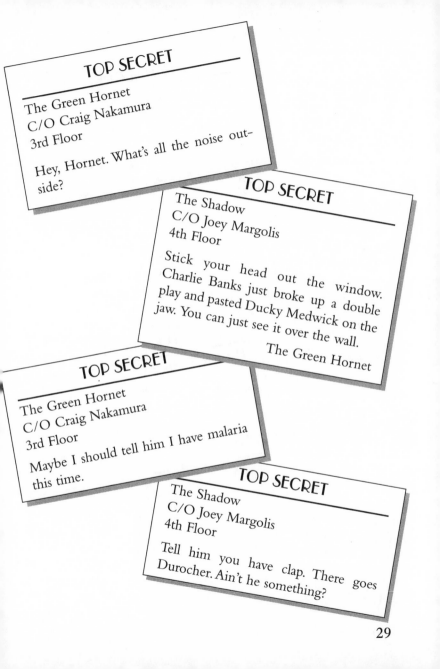

TOP SECRET

The Green Hornet
C/O Craig Nakamura
3rd Floor

Hey, Hornet. What's all the noise outside?

TOP SECRET

The Shadow
C/O Joey Margolis
4th Floor

Stick your head out the window.
Charlie Banks just broke up a double
play and pasted Ducky Medwick on the
jaw. You can just see it over the wall.

The Green Hornet

TOP SECRET

The Green Hornet
C/O Craig Nakamura
3rd Floor

Maybe I should tell him I have malaria
this time.

TOP SECRET

The Shadow
C/O Joey Margolis
4th Floor

Tell him you have clap. There goes
Durocher. Ain't he something?

29

TOP SECRET

The Green Hornet
C/O Craig Nakamura
3rd Floor

You're screwy in the head. What's clap?

TOP SECRET

The Shadow
C/O Joey Margolis
4th Floor

Beats me. Mrs. Aubaugh is down at Atlantic Beach signaling U-boats. She has a Morse lamp in her leg. Want to go catch her?

TOP SECRET

The Green Hornet
C/O Craig Nakamura
3rd Floor

The string broke again. Use your walkie talkie.

TOP SECRET

The Shadow
C/O Joey Margolis
4th Floor

Uh-oh. She's got us surrounded.

Alexander Hamilton Junior High School

— SEMESTER REPORT —

STUDENT: _Joseph Margolis_ TEACHER: _Janet Hicks_

ENGLISH	A
ARITHMETIC	A
SOCIAL STUDIES	A
SCIENCE	A

Neatness	A
Punctuality	A
Participation	A
Obedience	D

Teacher's Comments:

Joseph remains a challenging student. While I appreciate his creativity, I am sure you will agree that a classroom is an inappropriate forum for a reckless imagination. There is not a shred of evidence to support his claim that Dolley Madison was a Lesbian, and even fewer grounds to explain why he even knows what the word means. Similarly, an analysis of the Constitutional Convention does not generate sufficient cause to initiate a two-hour classroom debate on what types of automobiles the Founding Fathers would have driven were they alive today. When asked on a subsequent examination, "What did Benjamin Franklin use to discover electricity?" eleven children responded, "A Packard convertible." I trust you see my problem.

Finally, there is the matter of Joseph's growing infatuation with Rachel Panitz. Though I have nothing against puppy love, per se, he is at an age when boys tend to hide feelings of romantic attachment behind acts of overt hostility. In short, I am unable to stop him from throwing things at her, such as erasers, paper clips, fountain pens, and lightweight textbooks. Frankly, I haven't heard of anyone's being shelled that badly since the Germans attacked Gallipoli. Perhaps you can have a word with him in this regard.

Janet Hicks

Parents' Comments:

As usual, I am very proud of Joey's grades. I too was unaware that Dolley Madison was a Lesbian. I assumed they were all Protestants.

Thank you for writing.

Ida Margolis

Mr. Charles Banks, NY Giant
615 Riverside Drive
New York, NY

Dear Mr. Banks,

I am a 12 year old boy and I have just enlisted as a drum-mer in the marine corpse. The reason for this is because I read the newspapers all the time, and you don't even have to have an education to see that this Hitler is no laughing matter. No sir. So even if it means that I have to die at a very young age, I have made up my mind that I will go down fighting for God and my country just to keep the world safe for democracy.

I am writing because me and the other boys are shoving out for Montazuma and Tripoli and other places where fighting is already fearce, and we are not expected to come back alive. Anyway last night we were in our bunks won-dering how many more sunsets we would get to see, when all of a sudden the Sarge said "Gee, wouldn't it be great if Charlie Banks could hit but one more before we go off to lay down our life?" Everybody shook their head yes includ-ing the general, and being the youngest I got to write the letter, the same way I always have to do KP from being only 4 ft. tall and everybody can beat you up if you don't.

Mr. Banks, I read in this magazene once where Tris Speaker visited an army barracks and promised all the boys there that he would hit one out for them before they got shot up. So I would appreciate it if you would come to the plate sometime during Saturday's game with Saint Louis and point to one of the outfields and say "This is for my friend Joey Margolis" (please do this on the radio). Then all you have to do is hit one over the wall.

Thank you so very much.
God Bless America.

> Your friend,
> Joey Margolis

Mr. Joseph Margolis
236 Montgomery Street
Brooklyn, NY

Now look you little pisser. You write one more letter like that last one and your going to *wish* you were
dying from an incurable disease. Because if there's a
war—and there better not be as long as that dime store
New Dealer keeps his damn nose where it belongs—
there's going to be a lot of guys scared to death who
figure that if they're lucky, maybe they get to come
back with all their parts. That's if they come back at all.
So you just think about that before you pick up another pencil, you understand?

If I was your old man I would take a hair brush to
your butt and fix it so you would not be able to sit
down again until you were old enough to vote.

Charles Banks
3d base

P.S. And how did you get my home address anyway?

Mr. Charles Banks
615 Riverside Drive
New York, NY

Dear Mr. Banks,

You can go to Hell. My old man is a submarine commander who could knock your block off.

Do you know what would have happened if a Brooklyn policeman or somebody got ahold of my mail and found out I was writing to a Giant? The pokey probably, that's what. So don't give me any of your lip. Juvenile Hall was bad enough.

Anyway, nobody asked for your damned autograph. I never even heard of you before. And even if I did, you can bet that I've got more important things to do with my life than waste my time with a bully who just because he gets caught trying to steal home would pop a pitcher in the mouth. And you're supposed to be the new Roger Bresnahan? I guess that shows you can't believe everything you read in the papers. Even Roosevelt.

You're just about the cheapest kind of sport I ever heard of. And I hope you break both your legs the next time you slide into second base.

> Your arch foe,
> Joseph Margolis

P.S. Who are you calling a dime store New Dealer? Did *you* ever end a Depression?

Dear Kid,

Whoa.

In the first place, nobody held a gun to your head to fib about being blind and etc., which means if you get caught you shut up and take your medicine like a man.

And in the second place, I never slugged Derringer on account of getting picked off, as that is the nature of the game. I slugged him on account of calling me a cocksucker which is a whole different matter. You better learn how to get your facts straight before you go shooting off your mouth.

Charles Banks
3d base

P.S. What were you in Juvenile Hall for? I signed baseballs there once. Some little shit swiped a rubber from my wallet but left the fin and the picture of Lucille Ball. Was that you?

Dear Mr. Banks,

This is from *the Brooklyn Eagle* on April 24.

Banks Starts Another One

New York Giants third baseman Charlie Banks incited yet another brawl over what appeared to be a routine call during a doubleheader with Cincinnati yesterday afternoon at the Polo Grounds. The showdown began in the sixth inning of game one, when Redlegs hurler Paul Derringer attempted a pickoff at third base and caught Banks, long noted for his short fuse, in a rundown between the bag and home plate. Upon being called out by plate umpire Lucchesi, Banks promptly charged the mound and left Derringer with a split lip that later required four stitches. There appears to have been no provocation for the rookie's latest display of on-the-field fisticuffs

---

Don't tell *me* to get my facts straight.

> Joseph Charles Margolis
> (but the Charles gets
> changed because of you)

P.S. They locked me up in the Joint for assault with a deadly weapon but had to let me go because the bullets were made of bubblegum. I am a fugitive from a chain gang. So you'd better not get in my way.

Dear Fujitive,

Nice way to finish the damn sentance. ", although an unnamed Cincinnati outfielder admitted that Derringer may have uttered an obscenity that was misinterpreted by Banks." Misinterpreted my ass. He called me a cocksucker. How many different ways are there to interpret *that*?

I'm inclosing one last picture. Don't write to me again.

Charles Joseph Banks
(looks like we *both* got burned)

Dear Mr. Banks,

Your middle name isn't Joseph, it's Lindon because of your mother's father. You were born in Racine, Wisconsin, on August 7, 1917, and you're 5'11 1/2" and 181 lbs., and your father was the Vice President of Racine Produce Incorporated and your mother wrote for a newspaper and you bat right and throw right. Except when you were a Springfield Bluejacket and you batted left in three games. So don't try to pull any more fast ones. And stop sending me your damned picture. Didn't Harlan teach you any manners?

Joey Margolis

Dear Arch-Foe,

1. I batted left in *four* games at Springfield. The reason why people think it is only three is because the fourth one hit the Waterloo pitcher in the nuts and they do not like to write about such things in the newspaper, but pretend it didn't happen instead. Even though you could hear him screaming "shitfuckpiss" all over Illinoise.
2. "Lindon" doesn't have an "o" in it but an "e". Linden.
3. It is six feet even now. Practically. 5'11-15/16" with a haircut.
4. Who in Hell is Harlan?

Now go find yourself a new idle. I don't want to hear from you anymore.

Charlie Banks
3d base

Time Magazine

Roper Poll Results:
The Five Most Admired Men and Women of 1940

1. Franklin D. Roosevelt, *Chief Executive*
2. Jesus Christ, *Savior*
3. Ginger Rogers, *Actress*
4. Eleanor Roosevelt, *First Lady*
5. Charlie Banks, *Third Baseman*

Dear Mr. Banks,

Nobody ever said you were my idol. You couldn't even get in front of Ginger Rogers, and all *she* ever did was have big bosoms.

Know what really browns me off? At school we had to write this English assignment called "An American Hero" and mine was going to be about my father—except his secretary Molly said, "I'm sorry honey but he's all booked up." Then Nana Bert said "He's sleeping, dear. Call him in October, dear. We're going to Monte Carlo, dear." So I went and wrote it about you instead. I even clipped one of your baseball cards from the five and dime so I wouldn't have to get paste on the ones I already have. No wonder I got an F.

And you can forget about the home run. I only needed one because I'm a short Jew and Lenny Bierman isn't. Somehow he thinks you're my best friend, and I ran out of ways to stall him. Thanks for nothing.

Joseph Margolis

P.S. Harlan was your brother from 1914. What kind of a dope do you think I am?

Racine Rocket Shatters Own
Record With Solo Shot

THE POLO GROUNDS. Third baseman Charlie Banks today ripped the longest home run ever hit out of Coogan's Bluff, measuring 519 feet and breaking the same record he set last month by a full three yards. Asked why he bothered, considering the Giants' 9-0 lead over the Cubs going into the inning, the Wisconsin-born righthander replied, "I was bored."

Dear Kid,

Let's see Ginger Rogers do *that*.

I'll tell you what gets under *my* hair. All over the world right now is guys who would give their right arm to get a letter back from me, some of them even grown people who think I am their God. A previous example: "Dear Mr. Banks, We would like you to come to our town for Charlie Banks Day and accept the key to our city" (from some place in Iowa I never heard of and wouldn't know what to do with their damn key anyway), or this one: "Dear Mr. Banks, Although I had never been a baseball fan until you began to play, I would like to thank you for making me feel young again" (from Tenesee which is that long skinny thing next to West Vagina). Then there's you: "Dear Charlie, Piss off."

You got no kick coming. Go bug DiMaggio.

Chas. Banks
3d Base

P.S. You take the Charles Banks 3d Base card back to the 5 & Dime and tell them your sorry.

P.S.2. "Somehow" he thinks I am your best friend? Where did he hear that from? A Nazi spy? J. Herbert Hoover? Hetta Hopper? You could not tell the truth unless you thought you were prevaricating. And didn't I tell you not to write to me anymore?

P.S.3. Who said I had a brother named Harlan?

THE WHITE HOUSE

Dear Joey:

Thank you for your most recent letter. Addressing your points in order:

(a) While I agree that Neville Chamberlain has not been especially effective in containing the Nazi aggressor, I hardly think there is any evidence to suggest that he is collaborating with them.

(b) The President is fully aware of the Reich's air base in Bolivia. How did *you* find out about it?

(c) We are not particularly concerned about running against Wendell Willkie in November, either. But thank you for your encouragement.

(d) Joey, Holland is of no practical use to the Germans, and is therefore all but impervious to attack. There would be no advantage to Hitler's crossing its borders unless it were to antagonize the entire Western Hemisphere. Furthermore, even in such an implausible scenario, Belgium would be the far more viable target; however, that is not likely to happen either.

I hope this puts your mind to rest. At least for the remainder of the week.

Cordially as always,
Stephen T. Early
Press Secretary

Germans Launch "Lightning War" on Low Countries

Holland and Belgium Under Siege

ANTWERP, Friday—The Wehrmacht today dispatched 500 bombers on a series of strafing raids over Belgium and Holland, eliminating the last few pockets of peace in Europe.

Calling the assault "shameful," President Roosevelt denounced Hitler's aggression as "wanton and unprovoked," but denied—at least for the moment—that a mandatory draft would be enacted in order to put the U.S. on a tentative war footing.

Brooklyn, however, rebuffed the newest Nazi threat sensibly and without panic. Several local restaurant owners have removed hamburger and sauerkraut from their respective menus and have replaced the items with liberty steak and pickled cabbage. Mayor Fiorello LaGuardia has not yet responded to a petition that would require other Borough eateries to follow suit.

INTERVIEWER: Donald M. Weston, Ph.D.
SUBJECT: Joseph Charles Margolis

   Q: What's the matter?
   A: Cheesed off.

Q: At your father?

A: No. At Steve Early.

Q: President Roosevelt's Steve Early?!?

A: Yeah.

Q: What position does *he* play?

A: You're humoring me again.

Q: I'm sorry. Why are you cheesed off at Steve Early?

A: He wouldn't listen to me about Czechoslovakia or Austria. Now he says Holland is nothing to worry about either.

Q: How do you know that? From the newspaper?

A: No. He told me so.

Q: Of course.

A: You think I'm slap-happy, don't you?

Q: I didn't—

A: You want to read the letter?

Q: If you'd like—

A: Here.

Subject hands interviewer an envelope and a sheet of paper.

Q: Oh, my God.

A: See?

Q: How long has this been going on?

A: Since 1937. He apologized when the *Panay* got sunk, 'cause I told him that was gunna happen too. See, right after Nanking—

Q: He calls you Joey....

A: Right after Nanking—

Q: He calls you Joey *twice*—

A: Charlie Banks calls me "Kid". I hate it when he does that.

Q: Then why don't you tell him so?

A: Because.

Q: Because why?

A: Just because.

Q: What do you see?

A: C-Crosley Field in Cincinnati. The game where Charlie hit two grand slams in a row. W-we all waited for him at the plate after the second one and then jumped on him when he got there. But—but I was the only one he hugged back. M-my Dad calls him a loser. How come I don't believe him anymore?

Q: We can stop now, Joey. Do you have a handkerchief?

A: N-no.

Q: Here. Use mine.

A: Thanks.

Q: Know what *I* see?

A: What?

Q: A Rorschach blot.

A: You mean I was *right*?

Q: I'm beginning to wonder....

TOP SECRET

The Shadow
C/O Joey Margolis
4th Floor

Be on the alert, Shadow. Mrs. Aubaugh closed early today. We think she's going to set fire to the Navy Yard. When she lifts up her leg it turns into a blowtorch.

Any word from Banks yet?

TOP SECRET

The Green Hornet
C/O Craig Nakamura
3rd Floor

No. Maybe I shouldn't have said the part about Ginger Rogers and the bosoms.

TOP SECRET

The Shadow
C/O Joey Margolis
4th Floor

Know what your problem is, Joey-San? You never know when to keep your mouth shut. What did you tell your mom about the black eye?

46

The Green Hornet
C/O Craig Nakamura
3rd Floor

That I got clipped by a moving van. What did you tell yours?

The Shadow
C/O Joey Margolis
4th Floor

That I fell off of Grant's Tomb. We got lucky. Bierman doesn't like Irish kids either. You should see what he did to Chip Reilly. How much would you pay me if I told you how to put the fix on Banks?

The Green Hornet
C/O Craig Nakamura
3rd Floor

A hundred dollars.

The Shadow
C/O Joey Margolis
4th Floor

Here. This was in today's Daily Mirror. Read the last part. You know what to do. Try something messy with pus in it this time.

Man About Town

by Winchell

Merman Kayos MacKay

The latest shot in the Ethel Merman-Hazel MacKay feud was fired yesterday when the Merm snapped up the title role in Cole Porter's new tuner *Panama Hattie,* checking in at the 46th Street in October. According to the rumor mill, the part was scripted with MacKay in mind when Broadway wags predicted that Merman's current wow, *DuBarry Was a Lady,* might run into next season.

Battle lines were first drawn four years ago when MacKay landed a small role in Merm's *Red, Hot and Blue!,* held a high C for sixteen bars, and the walls came a-tumblin' down. By the next a.m., the boys on the aisle had dubbed her "the new Ethel Merman." The old one didn't agree.

"I've got nothing against her," said Eth at the Stork Club shortly after MacKay was fired. "She's a talented dame."

Meanwhile MacKay—who's not a fiery-tempered redhead for nuttin'—continues her engagement with the Benny Goodman Orchestra at the posh Manhattan bistro Tuxedo Junction. Her on-again/off-again romance with New York Giants rookie sensashe Charlie Banks appears to be back on track—at least for now. Can we blame her? Sech muscles!

Miss Hazel MacKay
c/o Tuxedo Junction
5 West 49th Street
New York, New York

Dear Miss MacKay,

I am a 12-year-old boy and I have gangreen in both of my legs. I used to play third base like my hero Charlie Banks, but if they have to amputate I will only be 2½ feet tall and nobody will ever let me near an infield again.

The reason I am writing to you is really two reasons.

1. I wrote to Charlie Banks at his house on Riverside Drive (Mayor LaGuardia got me the address when he visited me in the hospital) and I asked him if he could hit a home run for me the way Babe Ruth used to do. Well I guess he thought I was a fibber or something because when he wrote me back he called me a "little pisser" and told me never to write to him again.

2. The other reason is because when my fever came down to 105°, the first thing I heard was you singing "Give Him The Ooh-La-La" on the radio. So you are good luck to me.

Miss MacKay, I do not want to lose my legs. Since Charlie Banks doesn't like me very much, could you instead sing a song for me the next time you are on the Chase and Sanborn Hour? It would make me so happy.

Your friend,
Joey Margolis

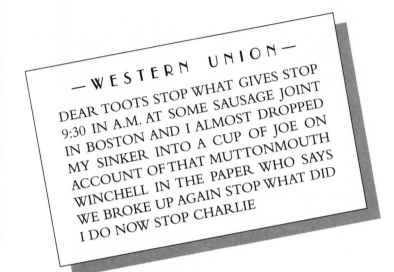

—WESTERN UNION—

DEAR TOOTS STOP WHAT GIVES STOP
9:30 IN A.M. AT SOME SAUSAGE JOINT
IN BOSTON AND I ALMOST DROPPED
MY SINKER INTO A CUP OF JOE ON
ACCOUNT OF THAT MUTTONMOUTH
WINCHELL IN THE PAPER WHO SAYS
WE BROKE UP AGAIN STOP WHAT DID
I DO NOW STOP CHARLIE

—WESTERN UNION—

YOU OUGHT TO BE ASHAMED OF
YOURSELF STOP IF BABE RUTH CAN
MAKE THE TIME TO VISIT A SICK CHILD
SO CAN YOU STOP NOT THAT YOU'RE
BABE RUTH STOP DON'T EVER CALL
ME AGAIN STOP HAZEL

50

Dear Chiseler,

Look up in your dictionary the word cheat. Next to it you will probably find a picture of your face. Also swindler and phony and double-crosser and blackmaler and fake.

One thing you better wise up to PDQ (pretty fuckin quick) is that you don't ever get something you don't earn just on account of asking. And earning it takes alot more than making up some load of crap about dying or getting snot in your eyes or whatever the Hell. Ask that Noodlemouth in the White House. He wanted something for nothing too. Just because everybody felt sorry for him from polio and his brother or somebody was Theodore. Know where he was headed for? Nowhere. And he would of gotten there safe and sound too, if it wasn't for his wife. On account of she was the one who nearly killed herself making people want to vote for him. She was the one who climbed into the coal mines from worrying that the guys down there might someday not come back up alive. She was the one who went into the slums and talked to the Negroes in person and tried to get them a better deal even though you would of thought that her husband heard of Lincoln and all, what with both of them being Presidents. FDR is a waste of my time. Eleanor is okay I guess.

Read the newspaper kid. And not the *Brooklyn Eagle* either which it is clear to me is only good for a laugh. Poland's gone. So is Denmark. France is halfway there. And the Brits were damn lucky to get off of Dunkirk

Beach last week with their butt in one piece. So you can bet that if Mr. Franklin Delano Biscuithead isn't careful, there is a good chance we will be eating sour kraut in November instead of turkies and etc. Up in Cooperstown NY there is a place they call the Hall of Fame. Maybe you heard of it. In it you will find C. Mathewson from Factoryville PA who so what if he had a fade-away? He went to fight in The World War though he did not have to, and breathed some gas that somehow turned into TB and he died. When he was still practically young. And you think people will call you special just on account of getting a home run hit for you? You kick that around for a while and if you start feeling a little lousy, good.

Now look. I know your full of shit and you know I know your full of shit but my girl doesn't know how full of shit you are yet and in the meantime she just had dinner with Tyrone Power who she hates but told the Herald Tribune about it anyway just to burn my ass. So one way or another we're going to figure out a way for you to get me out of this mess. If it works I don't put the slug on you. If it doesn't you better hit the dirt running because you don't get much of a head start. You owe me one, Bucko.

Chas. Banks
3d Base

P.S. And what the Hell do you know about Roger Bresnahan anyway? You weren't even alive yet.

Dear Mr. Banks,

Big deal. You weren't alive yet either. They got him for a couple thousand dollars from the Baltimore Orioles and people called him the Duke of Tralee. He was the only one who knew how to catch Matty the right way and if you turn out to be even half the man he was, you'll be lucky. But I doubt it.

Another thing. If you ever call Roosevelt a Noodlemouth or a Biscuithead again, you'll wish that you never left Springfield, Illinois, which by the way doesn't have an "e" on the end of it. I mean it, Charlie. How do you know I'm not really 8 feet tall? How do you know I don't have fists of iron? You don't scare me. Did you ever get an inauguration? Did you ever tell Hoover he was an "ass hole"? Do you have an Oval Office? You bet you don't. You're just some dumb ball player. Who won't hit a home run for me.

Know what I wish? I wish that I played third base for the New York Giants and your last name was Margolis and that you lived in Flatbush next door to the Hitler Youth. Then we'd see how fast you'd be writing to *me*. Only I'd have my secretary send you a greeting card or some such that said "Many Happy Returns" even if yours said "Help". Maybe you think I'm just some knucklehead, but I don't have enough time in my life to worry about Bierman *and* Delvecchi *and* The Third Reich and neither would you. Okay, I guess I shouldn't have said those things about the Marine Corps and KP and all, and it was probably a dumb thing to do and if it was I guess I'm sorry. But smokes, Charlie. How many times can I tell my Mom I fell off my bike?

Joey Margolis

P.S. When are we going to Tuxedo Junction to see Hazel?

Dear Iron Fists,

How does a week from never sound?

Maybe you didn't get me. We aren't going *any-where*. Your going to sit your ass down and pick up a pencil and tell her you made it all up. Then your going to put it in an envelope and mail it. Loud and clear?

So don't get the wrong idea and think we are friends. Or anything like it. The only reason I am even writing back is on account of it being 2:00 in the a.m. in Philly and they just traded my roommate Gridley Tarbell to the White Sox, a fate I would not wish on a dog. (That is the same team that gave us the 1919 World's Series and people like Eddie Cicotte and Swede Risberg and Chick Gandil and Al Capone.) I asked Mr. Terry if I could room with Jordy Stuker who is even worse at 5 card stud than Gridley was, and Mr. Terry said yes. So instead he gave me Carl Hubbell by saying "He will be a good influence on you Charles."

The Good Influence never says "shit" and he only plays bridge and he eats hot dogs with a *fork* and he right now is fast asleep in the next bed in this damn hotel room but he is still talking anyway. I think he is giving an interview—he just said "Couldn't of done it without the team." Oh, yeah? Let's see how fast he wins another 200 games with a towel in his mouth. Stuke would of been a much better deal all the way around. He can fart the first part of "God Bless America" good enough to sing along with it, and he also thinks Lucille Ball is going to marry him. Even though she won't answer any of his letters, including the one with the malt balls in it.

You don't know everything Kid. Maybe you think you do, but batting averages and etc. are only the gravy on the tip of the iceberg. There are other things that count for alot more: like Churchhill and Anshluss and Kristal Nacht and people who are always on your side no matter what. The trouble with you is thinking because your a Jew you have got the World Market cornered on hard knocks which really hands me a laugh from not noticing you doing anything about it. If you ever once found the guts to stand up for yourself, you would realize that it doesn't matter if your a Cathlic or a Gentle or one of those people from India with holes in their farhead. I don't take *any* of that crap serious which is how come I know your full of it. But I'll tell you something. Third base belongs to *me*—nobody else—and anyone who tries to take it away better be ready for a good fight. You included.

So maybe it's time you found a place of your own in the infield. You need alot of work. And it's a cinch your old man isn't minding the store.

> Charles Banks
> 3B

P.S. And by the way. Your not suppose to put quotion marks around asshole. And there's no space in the middle. Two can play at this one, Kid.

P.S.2. How do you know about Harlan?

P.S.3. Don't waste your time writing back. I found another place to move to and only 3 people in the world get the address. Your not one of them.

Miss Elsie McKeever
Bureau of Vital Statistics
964 Marquette Street
Racine, Wisconsin

Dear Miss McKeever,

I do not know if you remember me, but I wrote to you in April and you helped me find my family.

I have some sad news. My Cousin Ivy got hit by a train and died. She was very close to our Cousin Charlie and we sent him a telegram on Riverside

Drive, but Western Union says he doesn't live there anymore. Do you know where he moved to?

Thank you.

Very truly yours,
Joseph Margolis Banks

Mr. Joseph Margolis Banks
236 Montgomery Street
Brooklyn, New York

Dear Joseph:

Of course I remember you! And I am so sorry to hear about your cousin. We have, of course, changed our records to reflect her unfortunate passing.

I have checked with the post office and am happy to report that Charles is now living at 227 West 94th Street, Apt. 14-A, New York, New York.

My deepest sympathies to both of you and the rest of your family. Please let me know if there is anything else I can do.

Sincerely,
Elsie McKeever
Archivist

Charlie Banks
227 West 94th Street
Apt. 14-A
New York, New York

Dear Charlie,

Who *says* my father isn't minding the store? He's a United States senator and he's taking me to the World's Fair on Sunday. Inside the Perisphere there's a ride that shows you what the future looks like. I hope you're not in it.

Joseph Margolis

TOP SECRET

The Shadow
C/O Joey Margolis
4th Floor

This is great, Joey-San. You've got him on his toes. Whatever you do, don't write to him again. Keep him guessing.

TOP SECRET

The Green Hornet
C/O Craig Nakamura
3rd Floor

Then how can he take me on a road trip with him? Don't be a sap, Craigy.

The Shadow
C/O Joey Margolis
4th Floor

Didn't you see The Brooklyn Eagle? It says that Hazel MacKay and Errol Flynn were spooling spaghetti at Luchows. We've got it made. Any minute now he'll blow. And I don't mean maybe. I have to go. A dive bomber crashed at Floyd Bennett Field. We think Mrs. Aubaugh shot it down with her leg.

Dear Kid,

Do you hire people such as Flash Gordon and The Batman to follow me? I would report you to the FBI for knowing such things as West 94th Street and thinking I have a brother named Harlan and etc., except for the part of me that thinks maybe you are working for them. Maybe your not really short and 12. Maybe your really 38 and look like Rock Nuteny or somebody. I dropped two pop-ups today due to wondering.

Now look Iron Fists. She changed her telephone number again so when I called and said I Love You, I was really talking to a pissed off Negro with a dick.

And when I stood under where she lives and played "In the Mood" on my sax, instead of her opening the window to listen like she always does, all I got was hit in the face by a shoe.

Okay. Maybe I said some things in my previous letters that I shouldn't of. But the Mirror says that Clark Grable saw her show twice last night so I am running out of time. I will give you one more chance to tell her the truth. Otherwise I will have to break your neck.

Charlie Banks

P.S. Your old man must punch one Hell of a time clock on account of being a sub commander *and* a senator, huh? Gotcha you little goop.

P.S.2. But at least he took you to the Worlds Fair, right?

P.S.3. The way I figured it on the train to Philly, you are still not telling me why they put you in the Juvenile Pokey for three reasons: (a) you are punishing me (which if you are good luck and fuck you), (b) they are going to send you to the chair for it (but your still a miner so I doubt it), or (c) you think that whatever they put you there for was the worst thing in the world and your ashamed (which is the way *every*body in there feels). Since it couldn't be (b) and it better not be (a), chances are it is probably (c), so I am inclosing something from my own scrap book, which if you show it to anybody I will pull your arms off.

This is me when I was 15 yrs. old before I had stats. In the back ground is the mess hall at Father Flanagans. They sent me there for armed robbery after I stuck up a candy store with a pop gun, even though all I got out of it was two sticks of spearamint gum and some Hershey Kisses.

Your not the first one to get in trouble, you know? And it's nothing to feel bad about.

Dear Charlie,

You never held up anybody in your life. That's a picture of Mickey Rooney in *Boys' Town* just after Spencer Tracy yelled at him for the first time and he was going to run away, except there was lunch. You must be pretty stupid even for a ball player if you think I would fall for that one. I saw it nine times, not counting once when it was playing with *The Roaring Twenties* only they threw me and Craig out of the theater before Bogey even croaked. And all we did was accidentally sneak in through the fire door without paying. Brooklyn stinks.

Nana Bert didn't want to wait in line for the Perisphere because of her high heels and also because they were having dinner with the Shiffmans at Twenty One and had to leave. So instead they put me on a ferris wheel but I got stuck at the top when it broke. The only thing I could see when they got into their limou-

61

sine was Nana Bert's fingernails. But my Dad gave the ferris wheel guy $20 for me to take a cab home in case I ever got down again. Instead I bought some dirty postcards and took the subway.

My Mom said I could go to Tuxedo Junction with you to see Hazel as long as you're the real Charlie Banks and not just some imposter who wants to kidnap me because of my father's money. Aunt Carrie says we don't know if you have any diseases and besides you're goyim.

So how come you won't let me go?

Joey Margolis

P.S. My Dad makes parachutes for the Army and stockings for girls. If you tell anybody that, I'll say you're making it up.

P.S.2. They sent me up the river for peeing in the reservoir. So what?

Dear Joey,

Come to think of it, that's the most disgusting thing I ever heard in my life. You ought to be ashamed of yourself. Don't they have crappers on Montgomery Street?

The reason you can't go with me is because (1) your not suppose to get a prize for being a liar and (2) I don't even *like* you yet. But me being your hero and all, it's only fair if I give you one piece of advice. But this is the only one:

We were in Boston when the Hitler Boys took France, and in the meantime it was raining in Bean Town. Next to our hotel was this library and since there wasn't anything to do except count the damn raindrops or slug your roommate (or in my case watch Carl Hubbell stand in front of a mirror like he was posing for a statue which come to think of it he probably was), I went in there looking for an encyclopedia because they always have pictures of naked girls from Argentena or wherever the Hell it is they keep jungles nowadays. Only thing is, in Boston they lock up their encyclopedias like they were a fuckin treasure or something, and so instead I found a copy of maybe the only real book I ever read in my life, which is by the writer named Chas. Dickens and the name of the book is *David Copperfield.* Since I don't have a Mass. library card, I checked it out the other way (meaning under the old sweater) which is always safe since the lady at the desk was old and skinny with white hair and if you are wearing a raincoat, half the time they think you are going to open it and wave your dick in their face or pull down your pants and make a bowl movement on the floor. So they leave you alone.

This Dickens is really something, you know? The reason is because if you ever tried reading the truckload of crap that they like to pass off as books (meaning *Jane Air* and *Ivenhoe* and so forth) you can stop wondering why the world is getting so fucked up and how come there is no more Austria and etc.—because the *real* problem is that nobody knows how to say what is on their mind anymore. It is like trying to get a turnip out of a stone. That's how come when I was your age David Copperfield was my idle. "Chapter One—I am born." A man can relate to that kind of thing.

The second reason I rooted for Copperfield was because of what kind of ringer he had to go through before he got what he got. It looked like every time you turned around he was always getting thrown out of somewheres or having the shit knocked out of him again or taking crap from losers like Miss Murdstone who he really should of pulled her tongue out to get her off his back. But you know what he did? Nothing. He kept his mouth shut, all the time knowing that what he was really doing was keeping score so that when the time was right he could turn around and boot them all into next week. He had them fooled too. Like:

> *Miss Murdstone looked at me and said "Generally speaking I don't like boys. How d'ye do, boy?" Under these encouraging circumstances I replied that I was very well.*

Now doesn't that make you wonder how he could of held it in like that without sticking a fork in her eye? Me, I don't think I could of pulled it off, which is how come some nights when I couldn't sleep for thinking I'd never make the squad cut or get to Springfield or even just get the Hell out of Wisconsin, I'd make myself David Copperfield just to see what I would of done different. Like:

> *Miss Murdstone looked at me and said "Generally speaking I don't like boys. How d'ye do, boy?" Under these encouraging circumstances I replied "Kiss my ass".*

So think about that the next time Nana Bert makes monkey-eyes at you.

Charlie

P.S. How did you wind up in that kind of soup anyway?

Dear Charlie,

Nana Bert is 43. My father met her at a party when she had on a skinny black dress with leopard spots on it. The kind that if she was wearing it on the beach at Coney Island instead, they would have arrested her for being naked. After that a process server came to our house at 11:00 at night and made my mother sign some papers. Then my Dad married Nana Bert and told us to leave and my Mom threw his shirts down the incinerator. All we had left of him was this little statue of his head that he gave my mother for an anniversary present once.

Aunt Carrie took it outside and put it against the garbage cans to keep them from falling over in the wind.

The only good part about moving was that when you stick your head out of my window you can see the right field part of Ebbets Field and people like Cookie Lavagetto and Pee Wee Rockhead Reese and other Dodgers who I used to throw up from even looking at until I swapped nine Chick Hafeys for a slingshot. Now I can draw blood whenever I want to. One time I plugged Dixie Walker, Tuck Stainback and Jimmy Ripple all in two innings, and they almost had to call the game off because they couldn't figure out where the marbles were coming from. So watch your step. I could probably reach third base if I wanted to the next time you play here.

Can I go to Tuxedo Junction now?

Joey

INTERVIEWER: Donald M. Weston, Ph.D.
SUBJECT: Joseph Charles Margolis

Q: Let me see your nose. How did *that* happen?

A: Bierman slugged me. Then Delvecchi kicked me in the stomach.

Q: You mean you're not going to tell me you fell off the Woolworth Building?

A: I don't have to. They're not allowed to beat me up anymore.

Q: Says who?

A: Charlie Banks. I told you so.

Q: Joey—

A: They had me and Craig on the ground—

Q: Craig?

A: Nakamura. The Green Hornet. His father owns the fruit store downstairs. He's 12 too.

Q: What was Charlie Banks doing in Brooklyn?

A: Hazel went dancing with Joel McCrea on Tuesday night. It was in all the papers. I guess Charlie couldn't take it anymore. Craig was right.

Q: So he broke up the fight?

A: Better. He lifted Bierman up into the sky with one hand and told him to scram. Then he said to me in front of everybody, "When I come over for dinner, you'll tell me if this gentleman needs to be reminded."

Q: That ought to do it.

A: You bet it did. Now I scare the heck out of them. This is *fun.*

Q: Don't be a sore winner. Then you went to see Hazel?

A: Not yet. First we went to the store to get a steak for my eye, but all they had were pork chops and they aren't kosher. Aunt Carrie locked herself in the bedroom when we brought it into the house, even though my Mom told her it doesn't count as long as no one's eating it.

Q: If you're making all of this up, you're doing a very good job.

A: I'm not making it up. *Then* we went to see Hazel. At Tuxedo Junction. I got to wear my serge suit and my smoked glasses. She was singing the funny valentine song in a shiny blue dress. Boy, is she snakey. Her bosoms are bigger than Ginger Rogers'. No wonder he likes her.

Q: Did you tell her the truth?

A: Charlie wouldn't let me order a scotch on the rocks and say "Leave the bottle" the way Bogey does. But he bought me a Coca-Cola and let me say "Put it on my tab" and—

Q: Joey? Did you tell her the truth?

A: Uh. Well, I started to. Does that count?

Dear Miss MacKay,

Thank you so much for inviting me and Charlie to watch your show. And especially for singing the ooh-la-la song to me. I feel so much better and it's all because of you.

> Your friend,
> Joey Margolis

P.S. I'm sorry I had to wear the smoked glasses. Bright light still hurts my eyes.

Dear Joey,

Knock it off.

By the way, the smallpox routine needs work. Your delivery was okay, but you could use a good director—the fainting bit went out with two-reelers. And if you ever do an encore, it'd be a smart idea to remember which leg is supposed to be the one with palsy.

I'll make a deal with you. We'll tell Charlie that you 'fessed up, and I won't spill the beans as long as you keep him in line. Okay?

> Fondly,
> Hazel

TOP SECRET

The Shadow
C/O Joey Margolis
4th Floor

I <u>told</u> you the thank-you note was a goopy idea. Why did you have to push your luck?

TOP SECRET

The Green Hornet
C/O Craig Nakamura
3rd Floor

And how. You think I can trust her?

TOP SECRET

The Shadow
C/O Joey Margolis
4th Floor

What choice do you have? Just don't tell her about Mrs. Aubaugh and the leg. I don't want to split the reward three ways.

Man About Town
by Winchell

Extra Innings for MacKay and Banks

If the way to a man's heart is through his stomach, slinky songbird Hazel MacKay's next big number might just be "O, Promise Me". Table-hopping across Gotham this week, MacKay the Giant killer and smokin' third-sacker Charlie Banks were spotted looping linguine at Delmonico's, spooning spumoni at the Rainbow Room, and chewing cheesecake at Lindy's. According to sources, the often star-crossed pair had eyes only for each other, even when our Romeo dropped a $20 bottle of Cordon Lafitte on Juliet's foot. Watch those grounders, kid!

Dear Winchell,

You forgot the Stork Club. That's where I saw you squeezing the titties on that cash register girl while your wife was out peeing.

Mind your own fuckin business.

Chas. Banks
3d Base

Alexander Hamilton Junior High School

STUDENT: Joseph Margolis   TEACHER: Janet Hicks

ENGLISH	A
ARITHMETIC	A
SOCIAL STUDIES	A
SCIENCE	A

Neatness	A
Punctuality	A
Participation	A
Obedience	F

Teacher's Comments:

I had hoped that Joseph would return from summer vacation ready to apply himself in a more cooperative fashion. Instead, one week after a history lesson in which I properly assessed President Roosevelt's National Recovery Act as an utter failure, I received a letter from press secretary Stephen Early suggesting that I might wish to re-evaluate my position. It was not necessary to wonder which of my students had "turned me in," so to speak.

Mrs. Margolis, I am not accustomed to criticism from the White House. Especially when I fully intend to vote for Mr. Willkie in November. Furthermore, my authority as a teacher has begun to deteriorate. I suggest we schedule a conference as soon as possible.

Joseph's attachment to Rachel Panitz seems to have matured beyond the point of physical assault. Unfortunately, he has now taken to leaving love letters in her lunch bag, most of which run along the lines of "You don't smell half as bad as you used to" and similar heartfelt sentiments. Although Rachel continues to remain unmoved, this only seems to be encouraging him.

Janet Hicks

Parents' Comments:

The boy got seven A's. What more do you want—blood?

Carrie Gettinger
Joey's Aunt

BOOK REPORT
BY JOSEPH MARGOLIS

HELD FOR RANSOM
A NEW SKIPPY DARE MYSTERY STORY
BY HUGH LLOYD

Kidnapped, and in the hands of a ruthless gang of crooks, ten-year-old detective Skippy and the son of a millionaire almost give up. A thrilling story with tense drama in every chapter.

I did not like *Held for Ransom* by Hugh Lloyd for three reasons:

1. It is the same Skippy Dare story as in *Prisoners in Devil's Bog* and *Among the River Pirates,* except that the bad guys have different names. Also, in this one Skippy gets thrown out of an airplane, which he did not do in the other ones.

2. Only a grownup who is screwy would let a kid get in trouble with crooks, no matter *how* much he just wanted to help. But Inspector Conne lets Skippy get caught by spies all the time, like they are dumb enough to think that a 10-year-old boy with a shortwave radio just showed up by accident.

3. How come Skippy Dare doesn't know any Jews? In *Footprints Under the Window* by Franklin W. Dixon, there's the Hardy Boys (Christian), Phil Cohen (Jewish), Tom Wat (Chinese), Tony Prito (Italian), and Chet Morton (fat). Aren't all men supposed to be created equal? Not to Skippy Dare.

In *Mein Kampf*, Hitler says the exact same thing, only out loud. He thinks there are three kinds of people in the world. The ones who own everything, the ones who sweep the floors and do the laundry for the ones who own everything, and the ones who get shot. If you don't believe me, ask London. How would you like to wake up at 2:00 in the morning to go to the bathroom, but just when you flush the toilet your house blows up? They call it the Blitz. And it happens every night. "This is Murrow. America, can you hear me?"

I think we need to have a classroom discussion about Fascists who write books like this for kids. Hugh Lloyd isn't the only one. Mark Twain stinks too. Remember what he said about Negroes and Indians?

I did not like *Held for Ransom* by Hugh Lloyd.

Alexander Hamilton Junior High School

To: All Students
From: Herbert Demarest, Principal
Re: Mrs. Hicks

I know you all join me in wishing Mrs. Hicks a pleasant trip to the Caribbean. Although her leave of absence was a sudden one, we can expect to see her cheerful smile again in time for Hallowe'en.

In the meantime, Mrs. Adeline Diehl will be taking over her classes. Let's all do our best to make Mrs. Diehl feel welcome.

Dear Charlie,

I need to write a hundred word essay on Huey Long for our substitute teacher Mrs. Diehl, and I want to do a good job because this one cries. But I was only eight when Huey Long died so I wasn't paying attention, except for the part about calling him "Swordfish". What should I say?

Joey

P.S. Are you still sore at me?

P.S.2. When are you coming over for dinner? You promised.

Dear Joey,

There are two chances I am coming over for dinner. Fat and slim. The only reason I said I was going to was to scare the piss out of that fartmouth who had his hands around your neck and the other one who was standing on your buddy's head. And it worked, didn't it? Your damn lucky I batted you home from third—now don't jinx the dirt. *Your* the one who said you were going to tell Hazel the truth. Instead she was almost ready to call the New York Times and get them to invent a new charity for you. You bet your ass I am still sore. Check with me again in 1978.

And stop sending me your damn Re-Elect FDR handouts. All I use them for is toilet paper. Two terms was bad enough—your not *suppose* to get 3. Yeah, he's not going to dope us into the Big Smoke over there, is he? Not much he isn't. That's why he just started drafting us. No wonder you like him. He's a bigger double crosser than you are.

We will be leaving tomorrow for our last road trip of the season. We will be in Cincy for 5 days and Saint Louis for another 5 and then Chic. for 4. You can write to me at Crosley Field and Sportsmans Park and Wrigley in those places.

Charlie

P.S. It wasn't "Swordfish", but "Kingfish". And start with "Huey Long was a sack of shit." How many words does that leave left?

P.S.2. What kind of a Jew are you anyway? I thought you were suppose to have long pieces of hair all the way down your face.

P.S.3. I guess you saw in the papers that Hazel wants to be my girl again. This time she says it's because of you. I don't know what you said to her but I guess this makes us even.

Dear Chucky,

I told her to put up or shut up. Then I pushed a grapefruit in her face like Cagney did to Mae Clark. Girls like that.

I saw a picture in the *Tribune* of the fuckin Reds game. You probably know which one it was. You had your knuckles in Ernie Fuckin Lombardi's teeth and it was just before the front one fell out. Charlie, I'm not saying I'm on Lombardi's side or anything, but I don't think he did it on purpose. His fuckin butt just got in the way of the fuckin ball is all. I mean, they didn't give you a fuckin error or anything so I don't get it.

Joey

P.S. There are three kinds of Jews. The ones with side-locks are Orthodoxes. They wear long black coats and sing scary songs and they aren't allowed to ride roller coasters. Second is Conservative like Aunt Carrie and third is Reformed like me and my Mom. After that comes Lutheran I think, but I'm not sure.

Dear Iron Fists,

I don't know what they teach you in that school of yours or whether you are too busy pissing into our drinking water to listen, but I would bet that the old 10 commandments show up sooner or later, and you will notice that nowhere in it does it say anything about some Red son-of-a-bitch sticking his ass into the middle of a routine throw to first just on account of blowing all of their previous chances and merely wishing to stay alive. So go gripe to E. Lombardi. Maybe if he learned how to run.

Cincy is the shit hole of the world and if you ever get on a tour or something and Cincy is a part of it, if I was you I would ask them to change my plans and send me somewhere else. Even Hell. The thing they call downtown is on this river, the Cincinattie I think, and if you want to get a good education in smell, just wait until it is the summer and 95 degrees and 2:00 in the a.m. while you are trying to sleep, and the Noodlehead up there who is in charge of the weather decides it is time to send a breaze into your hotel room. Jordy Stuker, my new roommate after I started bowing to Carl Hubbell and calling him "Pius The First", is also a rookie but he grew up in Kansas and Cleavland so he has been to this area before and brought nose plugs. Only that means you have to breathe that shit in through your mouth and no thank you ma'am. You probably need a picture post card of this place like a third foot, but I'm sticking one in anyway. Smell it and see what I mean about Cincy. I drew an arrow on the front pointing to where our hotel is, only you really can't see it on account of the Court House being in the way. Tomorrow we play one more in this arm pit before we can lam out of here to Saint Louis which come to think of it is not a whole Hell of alot better.

One other thing. Mr. Terry has this saying he says all

the time, especially in Spring Training. That's when all of these pitchers show up from California or Oragon or wherever the Hell pitchers go over the winter and spend the first two weeks of March throwing crap. It's always the same story—they try to get fancy and wind up pitching ten times as many balls as they normally got to, saying it's because they are trying to find their form. Well all they are really trying to do is hide the fact that they are a lot fatter than they were in September. Anyway that's when Mr. Terry steps in and says "Boys, remember one thing. Less is more."

Bucko you only need one "fuckin" per letter unless it's a long one and then you can use 2.

Charlie

P.S. I am inclosing a button that says NO THIRD TERM-ITES. Wear it in good health. They are giving them away all over town. Also ones with your buddy's face on them and a big X through it. Maybe Cincy isn't so bad after all, even with the stink.

P.S.2. And by the way Big Shot. I dare you to tell me what Christy Mathewson's real knickname was on account of not being The Big Six like everybody thought. And don't waste your time cheating because it's not in any books.

P.S.3. Ever wonder how fast you can run? Call me Chucky again and find out.

Dear Charlie,

Matty's real nickname was Gunboots. They gave it to him at Bucknell when he was still playing football in college.

And I don't care *why* you said you were coming over for dinner. You still said it. And a promise is a promise. Didn't Harlan tell you that you're always supposed to keep your word?

Joey

═══════════○═══════════

Bad Day at Black Rock for Banks

═══════════○═══════════

ST. LOUIS, Wednesday—The Cardinals' 13-2 rout over Bill Terry's "unstoppable" Giants here today was stamped by an historic three errors on the part of New York's self-proclaimed Messiah, third baseman Charlie Banks. A two-out shot by the Redbirds' Johnny Mize in the second went right through the rookie's legs, a soft liner off the bat of Country Slaughter in the fourth hit the kid on the instep and bounced out to short left, and backstop Mickey Owen's routine pop-up in the seventh landed on his head.

Somebody's been staying up past his bedtime, Mr. Terry.

═══════════○═══════════

Downtown St. Louis at night. Sportsman's Park, home of the Cardinals, can be seen at left.

How do you know about Harlan?

Charlie

Joseph Margolis
236 Montgomery Street
Brooklyn NY

Folies Bergere: Lilo Freneau and her two greatest assets. Ooh-la-la.

When are you coming over for dinner?

Joey

Charlie Banks
c/o Third Base
New York Giants
Sportsman's Park
St. Louis, Missouri

Dear Toots,

I checked with Stuke who once went out with a Jewish girl and the only thing he could tell me about what they eat was kreplak and kugel and kishka and kanushes. Is he putting me on or is this really food? Because it sounds like stuff I built a barn with when I was 14.

I do not think this is a very good idea. The only thing I know about Moses is him coming down from the mountain with the commandments and saying "The good news is I got him down to 10. The bad news is adultery is still in." Also, when I took the kid home with the pork chop, the Aunt kept looking at me like she wanted me to fall out a window. What the Hell is a shagits?

I miss you.

Charlie

P.S. And what are those round yellow things that float in soup? Stuke forgot.

Dear Goodlookin',

Three hints: (1) the round yellow things are called matzoh balls, (2) never ask for milk if there's meat on the table, and (3) *don't* talk about Moses. I'll walk you through it when you come home.

Call me the minute you get in, even if it's 3:00 in the morning. I'm tired of looking at your picture in the newspapers and pretending you're here. I'll be in rehearsal until Friday—they asked me to replace Ethel Merman in *Panama Hattie* for two weeks over Christmas. (The bitch is going on vacation.) Otherwise, I'm all yours.

I love you.

-H-

P.S. I checked with Rabbi Weiss at Temple Beth-El. A shagitz is a non-Jewish male. It also means "abomination." Thanks, Rabbi.

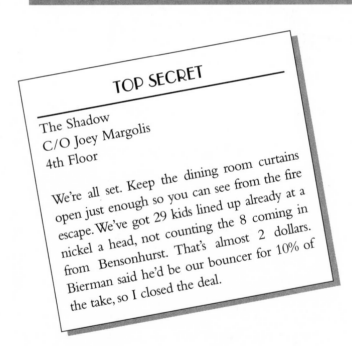

TOP SECRET

The Shadow
C/O Joey Margolis
4th Floor

We're all set. Keep the dining room curtains open just enough so you can see from the fire escape. We've got 29 kids lined up already at a nickel a head, not counting the 8 coming in from Bensonhurst. That's almost 2 dollars. Bierman said he'd be our bouncer for 10% of the take, so I closed the deal.

INTERVIEWER: Donald M. Weston, Ph.D.
SUBJECT: Joseph Charles Margolis

Q: What happened next?

A: He asked my Mom for more soup and another yellow meatball. She got a big kick out of that. Then she taught him how to say the blessing over the candles. He looked kind of funny in a yarmulke.

Q: Your buddy's a good sport.

A: Aunt Carrie didn't think so. She kept getting him mixed up with Cookie Lavagetto. On purpose. So when she was giving him brisket, he asked her for a bacon cheeseburger instead. She had it coming.

Q: Did you tell him about Harlan?

A: After dinner he took me to the soda shop for an ice cream cone and when I dropped it he got me another one.

Q: Did you tell him about Harlan?

A: Uh. I sort of didn't. And he forgot to ask. We were blowing paper wrappers from straws at an old lady's ass.

Q: Joey?

A: Well, smokes. If I told you that I had to knock off your Cousin Ivy just to get your address, what would *you* do?

Q: I'd probably kick your butt halfway to the Bronx.

A: See?

Q: But maybe I wouldn't.

A: Honest?

Q: Not if I'd just bought you two ice cream cones when I didn't have to. Who hit her ass first?

A: I did. Can I go now?

Dear Joey,

Thanks for the phone call buddy. And also for coming clean about Harlan. It's too bad your Archive Lady doesn't work for the Germans. With a mouth that big we would know what they were planning before *they* did.

If I was you, I would not worry too much about getting shortchanged in the old man department because you got a terrific 2-for-1 deal with your mother. It's like not being able to field for shit but hitting 65 over the wall—some guys can't have everything but what they got is Hall of Fame. Besides I never met anybody before who could make chocolate cake without any crums. Only level with me. Did your Aunt Carrie think I had flies or something? And how come she kept calling me Oy?

Harlan was my big brother. He was the best friend I ever had and the only one I ever loved until Hazel. When he got hit in the head from a pitch he hung on for 4 days before he died. That's what kind of a kid he was.

You don't play games with things like that, Joey. Especially when it hurts peoples feelings. So from now on your going to have to be a Tough Guy on your own. Because I think this is the end of the line.

Charles Banks
3d Base

Dear Charlie,

Like you've got room to talk Banks. What about Derringer and Medwick and that guy from St. Louis who you even left fingerprints on? Paul Derringer only called you a cocksucker. Bierman cut my face with a Coke bottle while Delvecchi held me on the ground and it took three weeks to heal and I had to tell my mother I fell off my roller skates even though I don't have any. And all because you wouldn't hit a home run for me. Who else was I supposed to call, my father? "Nana Bert, this is Joey. Can you ask my Dad to come over and slug Lenny Bierman?" "Joey Who, dear?" Maybe if I had a big brother like Harlan, but why do you think I've been writing to *you*?

You know what I think you should do? What I think you should do is go to that place in Iowa and take the key to their city only instead of coming home you should lock yourself in and then lose it. And the how come is because you're no ball player. You're just some guy who got to dress up like a New York Giant and play in the same place as Mathewson. And Turkey Mike Donlin. And Doyle and Bridwell and McGinnity and McGraw. Almost like you deserved to be there. Well you want to know a secret, Charlie? You're better than all of them. Only they were guys. You're an "ass hole". IT WAS ONLY A FUCKIN HOME RUN. YOU HIT THEM ALL THE TIME.

Maybe I do need a lot of work. But guess what. You need a lot more. So go to Hell.

Joey Margolis

P.S. Don't ever say you're my hero. Save that for the phonies who got fooled.

Dear Joey,

If your wondering how come this is over 2-1/2 weeks late it is because I started to write it six times and wound up crumbling it up and tossing it across the room instead from wanting to drive to Brooklyn again, this time for purposes of seperating your head from your shoulders and then throwing it into Buttermilk Channel. The only reason you are getting the dignity of a reply at all is from being on a smoker to Michigan due to a hunting trip with some of the boys, and at 75 miles an hour I figure you are pretty safe from whatever I might decide to do to you if I start getting sore all over again. Anyway, with Jordy Stuker setting up a farting contest at the other end of the car (in front of nuns), there's already a couple of people on my list ahead of you.

You are beginning to make a mess out of my life. I don't know if it is an accident or if you are really one of Durocher's boys after all, but I am going to have to ask you to knock it off. Maybe you heard our last game of the season on the radio. The four strikeouts? I have never had four strikeouts in my life. Especially off of a marshmellow like Higbe, who no matter what they say could not find bullshit in a meadow, never mind about finding the plate. Only instead of sending things out into the Harlem River which is what I usually do, I four times landed on my ass. Because of Mathewson. Who in case you haven't guessed by now was *my* hero. And until you shot off your mouth I never thought about him and me working out of the same park before. And was he still keeping an eye on things from Up There? Because if he was, was he saying "Boy that Banks is something isn't he?" or was it more like "What is that potatoe head doing on 155th Street?" Your a pretty cheap kind of sport yourself on account of making me think about such things. I even have a note stuck to my mirror that says "Charlie, do not send this Kid anymore letters." Except all that reminds me to do is go out and buy stamps.

Joey, either you and me are going to have to call it quits right here, or else we're going to have to get a couple of things straight between us. And since it's probably too late for the first one and it is pretty clear at least to me that neither of us wants that anyway, we better talk business on the second, on account of the way it looks now, I think we are stuck with each other. So here goes. And remember—you started it.

1. We are always square with one another. If I ever find out you lied to me again, you can start hanging around Pee Wee Rockhead Reese or whoever else because for my money I never even heard of you. Don't jinx the dirt.
2. You will start listening to what I have to say and not give me lip when I tell you something that is for your own good. This is not because I am Charlie Banks and not because I play 3b for the NY Giants, which I do, but because I am older than you.
3. Don't ever call me "Banks" again. Or "Mister".

You call me Charlie or whatever other knick-names we come up with. As long as none of them are Chucky. And if you ever tell me to "Go to Hell" again, you will be alot shorter than you are now.

4. I will try to remember that you are only 12 and therefore there are things you have not learned yet and do not deserve to get chewed out for from not knowing. I already have made this mistake a couple of times and I will try not to do it again. But I'm not promising anything.

5. If you ever catch me doing something I shouldn't of, like socking some guy who maybe it wasn't their fault or saying somebody is a Noodlehead who happens to be one of your idles like that Meatball in the White House, you get equal time. This means you can sound off and tell me where to put it if you think I've got it coming. Only if I was you I wouldn't make this part a habit. Because I'm not just older than you, I'm bigger too.

6. You will stop putting quotion marks around ass-hole with a space in the middle. It really pisses me off when you do this.

7. We each get to say whatever we want that bugs us about the other one. This is not for purposes of being a wise-guy but for fixing it before other people notice. I get to start: you talk too much Bucko. Give somebody else a chance once in a while, for crying out loud.

8. If anybody ever really hurts you, you tell me and I will take care of it. Your still going to have to fight most of your own battles by yourself. But not all of them.

9. You will always remember that you are probably somebody very special. I do not know this for a fact yet, but nobody ever made me strike out 4 times before. Especially Higbe.

10. This will be signed and waiting for me when I get back from Michigan.

_____   _____
Me   *You*

Can I get a hit now?

Charlie

P.S. And I will still be thinking of you on Tuesday when I vote for Willkie.

FINAL | The Brooklyn Eagle | TWO CENTS

VOL. LXXVI....No. 6,336   WEDNESDAY, NOVEMBER 6, 1940   Cloudy, much colder

IT'S ROOSEVELT AGAIN!
FIRST THIRD-TERMER IN HISTORY; 429 ELECTORAL VOTES SO FAR

THE WHITE HOUSE

November 23, 1940

Dear Joseph:

Stephen Early has passed along your October 30th letter for my reply.

First, allow me to express my thanks for your diligent efforts on my behalf. The forty-seven votes you were able to secure for me in Brooklyn counted for a great deal. In an election such as this one, each of them is precious.

Second, I was most impressed with your state-by-state analysis of the electorate—particularly since you were 16 votes closer to the truth than the Gallup poll was. I consider myself fortunate to have you in my corner. I would be in substantial trouble had you decided to endorse my opponent.

Mrs. Roosevelt joins me in sending our good wishes for the upcoming holiday season and beyond.

Yours very truly,

Franklin D. Roosevelt

DEC. 16, 1940

DEAR CHARLIE,

*Blessed be the child who
   shall lead mankind.*

   *May the words of Jesus
      illuminate your Christmas.*

JOEY

P.S.   "The alphabet we'll always have,
        But one thing sure is true,
        With FDR the New Deal's in,
        And that means PDQ."

P.S.2. Here is your damned contract.
       But I know a lawyer so don't pull
       anything funny.

DEC. 21, 1940

DEAR JOEY,

Let each candle on the Menorah
light up your heart.

Happy Hanukkah.

CHARLIE

P.S.   "Woodrow pulled the whistle,
        Calvin rang the bell,
        Franklin gave the signal,
        And the country went to Hell."

        Lend–Lease my ass.

P.S.2. What's a Menorah?

P.S.3. Almost gave up on you. Guess I
        should of known better, huh?

P.S.4. Happy 1941. From your buddy.

1941

Alexander Hamilton Junior High School

Via Messenger

To: Charles Banks

From: Herbert Demarest, Principal

Re: Joseph Margolis

It has come to my attention that you have taken a proprietary position with regard to one of my students, Joseph Margolis. While I appreciate the attention you've given the boy in light of his absent father, and whereas the other children have been duly impressed by the occasional presence of a celebrity on our grounds, I believe that there are one or two points we will need to clarify. At 1:20 this afternoon, Joseph delivered an oral book report on *David Copperfield,* along with a few extemporaneous observations of his own. By 1:25, he'd been sent to my office.

Mr. Banks, with all due respect, what kind of smut are you *teaching* this kid?

Mr. Herbert Demarest
Alexander Hamilton Jr. High
2236 Bedford Avenue
Brooklyn NY

Dear Mr. Demarest,
   Did *you* ever read the damn book? "Yes ma'am,"
"No ma'am," "Please pop me in the kisser again
ma'am." Is that how you want him to grow *up*?

                              Chas. Banks
                              3d Base

Alexander Hamilton Junior High School

Via Messenger

To: Charles Banks

From: Herbert Demarest, Principal

Re: Joseph Margolis

Thank you for your interest in the boy's well-
being. However, since I would not presume to
tell you how to bat, why don't you leave his
education to me?

Mr. Herbert Demarest
Alexander Hamilton Jr. High
2236 Bedford Avenue
Brooklyn NY

Dear Mr. Demarest,

Then why don't you give him "Withering Heights"? At least Heathcoat knew how to kick some ass.

Chas. Banks

3d Base

Dear Joey,

If your trying to make a monkey out of me your doing a good job. The only reason your principle did not throw the book at us was on account of bluffing him like I have not done since Whit Wyatt nailed me to a 3 and 1 and then threw a curve ball from thinking I was going to bunt. Like I would ever bunt. From now on when I teach you things, some of them are suppose to stay between us. David Copperfield is one of them. I will tell you what the other ones are when they happen.

We get to Florida in the early A.M. and start Spring Training at 11:00. I don't know what they are trying to prove, for even our uniforms won't be here yet. Carl Hubbell is already getting a head start by doing push-ups in the isle, but only when he thinks Mister Terry is looking. So we threw his clothes off the train some-where around Baltimore. Let's see how many people take him serious when he is pitching in his under pants.

Right now we are in the middle of a Carolina. Stuke thinks it is still the North one but Mel Ott thinks it is the South. So they bet on it. (At dinner there was a round thing under Stuke's gravy. He thought it was a Lima Bean and Ott thought it was a dime. They bet on that too. Whatever it was, it had legs.) I will be glad when we get out of this part of the South due to Gone With The Wind and etc. They still do not like us down here, though you would think after 80 years they would grow the fuck up.

Stuke finally stopped wearing black from Lucille Ball marrying that Cuban guy in November. Instead he paid a bookie $30 for Veronica Lake's address and sent her a telegram when we stopped at Richmond. But she didn't send one back yet, even though he told her what train we were on. He says he will give her two more days and then he will ask Rita Hayworth. But first he needs to find another bookie.

Hazel will be keeping a glim on you until I get back. So don't try to get away with anything.

Charlie

P.S. Tell your mother thanks for the pointy coconut things, even though nobody here knows what they are.

P.S.2. We heard on Murrow that there's this new gang

in D.C. called America First. Their saying is "Keep Our Ass Out of Wars That Do Not Belong To Us" or such words that you can say on the radio. What do you think? Maybe I should join up huh? You can bet they did not send an invite to Mustard Mouth in the White House. By the way, Stuke started calling Goring and Mussolini The Two Little Pigs. We are taking a vote on who the third one should be. So far Tojo has 8, Stalin has 6, and FDR has 2 (I got to vote twice due to coming up with the idea in the first place).

P.S.3. Your wrong. If Bogey would of wound up with Ida Lupino instead, he wouldn't of got his ass shot off on the mountain. Go back and see it again if you want proof. And stop calling yourself Mad Dog Earle. Your principle will think it was my idea.

Gangland Killing in Brooklyn

BROOKLYN, Monday. An unidentified man was shot and killed on Sunday night as he was exiting a reputed house of prostitution in Sheepshead Bay. The assailant was believed to have been driving a silver 1938 Dusenberg touring car, which reportedly reduced its speed as it approached the victim. Eyewitnesses then heard two shots ring out before the auto sped off. Police believe that the murder bears the all-too-familiar markings of mob-related retaliation as a result of the recent

Dear Charlie,

This was in today's *Eagle*. It happened practically around the corner. The longer we stay here the scarier it gets, with innocent children getting pumped full of hot lead and buildings burning down with children in them (maybe even from sabotage), and children who walk to school in the morning but disappear before they get there and nobody ever sees them alive again.

Me and Craig are almost the only two of us on our block who aren't allowed to go to camp this summer—him because of tilty eyes and me because of not being Gentile. The only other kids who will be here are the ones with police blotters who knock off juke joints and trip old ladies for money and once in awhile shoot a cop. So I guess we will hang around with them and learn a few things. Like how to open a fire hydrant and make it look like we are just trying to cool down from the 112° heat when what we're really doing is pointing it at the jewelry store so the water can blow out the window and we can loot. Come to think of it, if I go on a road trip with you this summer I will probably be a lot safer than I am here.

The lady from the Giants sent the tickets for Opening Day. Craig and my Mom are going, but Aunt Carrie says if she lets you invite her places, the next thing you know she'll be eating ham on Yom Kippur. I don't know what she's going to do, but you shouldn't have told her that Pete Reiser was a chowdermouth. I think it only made her like him, especially since she knows he will be playing against you on Opening Day. This is all I need. An Aunt who reads box scores.

I figured out a way to make bathtub hooch, which I'm going to sell to the speakeasies if I don't get my lamps put out first.

Mad Dog Earle

P.S. I hope you have a good time at America First. When we get in the war and I am in a fox hole in Germany shooting Rommel, I will write you letters. By the time you get them I'll probably be dead, but at least you won't have to pick up a gun yourself. Traitor.

P.S.2. I even gave my old radio and some bubblegum and sweaters without holes in them to Bundles for Britain. I'll bet that you didn't give them anything except maybe smelly socks. Double traitor.

P.S.3. What if your bat boy gets sick or something and can't go on the road? Won't you need to get somebody else instead?

Dear Mad Dog,

"If" is a funny word. Sometimes it is a tough one like "If I work really hard" and sometimes it is an easy one like "If I sit on my butt and wish for it" and sometimes it is a word you can blow out your ass like "If I go on a road trip with you." Guess what. If you had tits you could float. That doesn't mean your going to do that either.

First of all Sheepshead Bay is not practically around the corner, it is half way to New Jersey. Second of all you do not own a whorehouse (yet). Third of all the only scary thing about your block is that you live on it. And by the way, don't get any funny ideas about our bat-boy. He is a good kid. And if he one day falls on the ground with bubbles coming out of his mouth due to arsenic or etc., your going to be in big trouble.

They are making us play Sarasoda for 5 days in a row and the hotel they gave us only has 3 walls. There use to be 4 but one of them blew off in the Hurricane of '38 and they keep forgetting to put it back. Me and Stuke are sharing our room with two tree snakes and a cotton rat but only until Rita Hayworth gets here.

Charlie

P.S. Britain got enough bundles from us already, such as bailing their ass out of France in 1918 and picking up the tab for it. We do not need to give them anything else. Maybe if they paid their bills once in a while.

P.S.2. Your too easy to piss off. You should watch that.

TOP SECRET

The Shadow
C/O Joey Margolis
4th Floor

You rock-head. Did you really think he was going to fall for that? You're slipping, Shadow.

TOP SECRET

The Green Hornet
C/O Craig Nakamura
3rd Floor

Okay, wiseguy. Then how do we get him to think I'm in terrible danger?

TOP SECRET

The Shadow
C/O Joey Margolis
4th Floor

We can introduce him to Mrs. Aubaugh. But when she points her leg at him, he better duck. Where are our seats?

TOP SECRET

The Green Hornet
C/O Craig Nakamura
3rd Floor

Behind home plate. Aunt Carrie is practicing saying things like "Throw the bum out". This could gum the whole works. What if he puts the slug on her?

TOP SECRET

The Shadow
C/O Joey Margolis
4th Floor

So what? Your aunt could knock out Joe Louis in two rounds. Do you think he could get me Mel Ott's autograph? They're worth 4 Charlie Bankses.

TOP SECRET

The Green Hornet
C/O Craig Nakamura
3rd Floor

Craigy, I want to go on a road trip with the Giants.

TOP SECRET

The Shadow
C/O Joey Margolis
4th Floor

You're going to, Joey-San. But you have to make him think it was his idea.

106

Mrs. J. Hicks
Alexander Hamilton Jr. High
2236 Bedford Avenue
Brooklyn NY

Dear Mrs. Hicks,

Please excuse Joseph Margolis and Craig Nakamura from school tomorrow due to watching me and the team kick the crap out of Brooklyn.

> Very truly yours,
> Chas. Banks
> 3d Base

Alexander Hamilton Junior High School

To: Charles Banks

From: Herbert Demarest, Principal

Re: Joseph Margolis/Craig Nakamura

Your absence excuse has been duly received and accepted. In the future, please telephone me directly about such matters. I can't put a note like this in the boys' files—only a handful would understand. Mrs. Hicks is not one of them.

Temple Chizuk Amuno
1243 Parkside Avenue • Brooklyn, New York

Mr. David Margolis
900 Fifth Avenue
New York, New York

Dear Mr. Margolis:

Congratulations on your son's upcoming thirteenth birthday. In accordance with the traditions of our faith, as well as the calendar of our synagogue, we have scheduled his Bar Mitzvah for Saturday, October 25, at 10:00 a.m.

Joseph's Bar Mitzvah instruction will commence in early May, and will continue once a week thereafter. As the father's participation is of singular significance, we are able to offer evening lessons Monday through Thursday in order to accommodate your workday schedule.

Please let me know of your availability so that we may begin preparing Joseph for his passage into manhood.

Respectfully,
Rabbi Morris Lieberman

Rabbi Morris Lieberman
Temple Chizuk Amuno
1243 Parkside Avenue
Brooklyn, New York

Dear Rabbi Lieberman:

My wife and I expect to be out of the country from Labor Day through early November. However, we will be with you in spirit.

Our very best to you and Mrs. Lieberman.

> Very truly yours,
> David Margolis

DM:mm
[Dictated but not read]

Giants Whip Brooklyn 7-1 in
Home Opener at Polo Grounds

BROOKLYN (N.)

	ab	r	h	po	a	e
Reiser, cf	4	0	1	4	0	1
Walker, rf	4	0	1	0	0	0
Camilli, 1b	4	0	0	11	1	0
Medwick, lf	3	0	2	0	0	0
Lavagetto, 3b	3	0	0	0	1	0
Herman, 2b	3	0	1	2	3	0
Reese, ss	3	0	0	3	4	0
Phelps, c	3	1	1	3	2	0
Casey, p	2	0	0	1	2	0
Total	29	1	6	24	13	1

NEW YORK (N.)

	ab	r	h	po	a	e
Brunswick, lf	3	1	2	1	0	0
Demaree, cf	4	1	1	1	0	0
Ott, rf	4	1	2	2	0	0
Stuker, 1b	3	1	0	12	0	0
Whitehead, 2b	3	1	2	3	3	0
Banks, 3b	4	0	2	4	2	0
Witek, ss	3	1	1	1	4	0
Danning, c	4	1	2	3	0	0
Hubbell, p	4	0	0	0	0	0
Total	32	7	12	27	9	0

Brooklyn 0 0 0 0 0 0 0 1 0—1
New York 3 1 0 1 1 0 1 0 x—7

Runs batted in—Ott, Banks 3, Danning 2, Phelps.
Two-base hits—Medwick. Three-base hits—Witek, Demaree. Home runs—Danning, Phelps. Double plays—Lavagetto, Herman, Camilli; Whitehead, Witek, Stuker. Left on bases—Brooklyn 5, New York 5. Bases on balls—Off Casey 4, Off Hubbell 1. Struck out—By Casey 2, Hubbell 1. Hits—Off Casey 12 in 8 innings. Wild pitches—Casey. Winning pitcher—Hubbell. Losing pitcher—Casey. Umpires—Goetz, Reardon and Conlan. Time of game—2:11. Attendance—42,653.

Q: Wow.

A: That's not all. Every time he came to the plate he'd turn around and ask us what he should do. Everybody saw it. Even on the radio. They thought we were really short coaches.

Q: I heard. You even made the papers.

A: We *did*?

Q: The *Telegram*. I saved it for you. So what did you tell him?

A: I said he should look for the inside fastball since that's what Hugh Casey likes to throw at him. Craig just told him to give the bat to Mel Ott so we could see some *real* hitting.

Q: That wasn't very smart.

A: And that's a fact. But the only reason Craig lives dangerously is because that's what the Green Hornet would do.

Q: What about Aunt Carrie?

A: She watched the whole thing through teeny binoculars. When Pistol Pete Reiser came up, she called out a blessing on his head and said he was a mensch.

Q: Bet it pissed him off.

A: Bet it didn't. He hit the first pitch to left field. But whenever Charlie batted she went to the ladies' room.

Q: And your mom?

A: She made him noodle kugel but I think he saved it for later. If he ate it before the game he wouldn't have been able to stand up. How come my father doesn't like me?

Q: Hey, now. Nobody ever said that.

A: He won't go to my Bar Mitzvah. Smokes, that's about the worst thing you can do to *any*body. Aunt Carrie says that

Job had it easy with locusts. He could have known my father instead.

Q: Joey—

A: Well, *some*body's got to stand up for me. I'm not allowed to get Bar Mitzvahed by myself, for Pete's sake. Am I?

Q: Don't you have any uncles?

A: No. Only a cousin in San Diego. But he's nine.

Q: Come on, Shadow. You've been in tougher spots than this before.

A: Well, I do have *one* idea.

Q: I figured you would. And I'll bet I know what it is.

A: Then don't tell anybody.

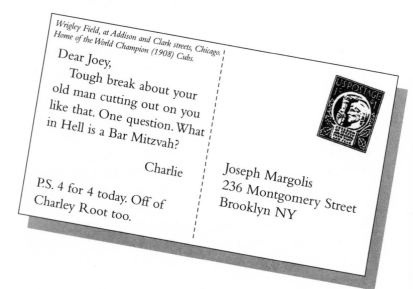

Wrigley Field, at Addison and Clark streets, Chicago.
Home of the World Champion (1908) Cubs.

Dear Joey,

Tough break about your old man cutting out on you like that. One question. What in Hell is a Bar Mitzvah?

Charlie

P.S. 4 for 4 today. Off of Charley Root too.

Joseph Margolis
236 Montgomery Street
Brooklyn NY

Dear Charlie,

For some reason Jews think that you're old enough to be a man when you turn 13, even though you're still not allowed to drink Scotch or smoke cigars or play pool or pack a heater or kiss girls like Rachel (even on the side of her face). So what's the point? But they still make a big shindy out of it. You get to go to Temple on the Sabbath and be up on the stage with your Dad in front of everybody and open the Torah (which is just a Bible on one really long piece of paper rolled up onto two sticks). Then you read out loud from it and run the whole service by yourself, just like you were the Rabbi or somebody. Remember the time Carl Hubbell got to be temporary manager when Mr. Terry had the squirts from anchovies? It's the same thing.

Big deal anyway. At least I don't have to ruin the whole summer by learning Hebrew. The only bad part is not getting presents because Jewish relatives know how to give presents better than anybody. Most of the time it's handkerchiefs or books about birds or a subscription to *Natural Wonders,* but once in awhile a good one sneaks in like a typewriter or a wireless receiver or new marbles with mostly glassies or The Shadow's Secret Code Book.

Craig wants to know if he can come with you the next time you have dinner with Leo Durocher. He's not trying to be a pain in the ass so don't get sore at him. Craig is one of those people who goes around singing about "Murgatroyd Darcy, a broad from Canarsie, who went 'round with a fellow named

Rodgers, while doing a rumba or jitterbug numba" and all the rest of that crap. It's a very popular song in Brooklyn. Everybody sings it except me. Know why? Well you don't need an education to figure out what rhymes with "Rodgers," do you? I hate them all. Craig doesn't. I think he'd lick the sidewalk if Durocher or Babe Herman or Ducky Medwick walked on it. Me, I'd rather get my face bashed in first.

Joey

Dear Joey,

There you go again. Your the kid who got that Pumpkin Mouth in the White House to write you back and thank you himself for getting him elected (though you will one day look back on this and think it was the worst mistake you ever made) and also got Chas. Banks 3d Base to call you a Chiseler before he even knew who you were. But just because your old man does not know a good thing when he's got one means you cannot have a Bar Mitzvah???? I don't think so.

I will show you how easy this is.

Charlie

P.S. Tell Craig I would not have dinner with Leo Durosher if he had the whole Hall of Fame stuck up his ass. Come to think of it, I would not have dinner with Craig either. Let him ask his buddy Mel Ott.

P.S.2. Aunt Carrie showed up at Ebbets Field for both of our Lady's Day games with The Team You Hate And Would Rather Get Your Face Bashed In First Than Even Say Their Name. I do not mind her telling P. Reiser how to hold a bat or even calling him Darling for good luck, on account of knowing it is only to get my goat. But his average goes up 20 points every time she is here and some of the boys are starting to look at me like it is my fault. Also, how come she never has to go to the crapper until I am on deck?

P.S.3. Uh-oh. Who's Rachel?

Rabby Morris Lieberman
Temple Chizuk Amuno
1243 Parkside
Brooklyn NY

Dear Rabby Lieberman,

I am writing because I think you are giving Joseph Margolis a raw deal. Even though I am a Protestant and would not know a Tora from a rats ass, fair is fair. And just because the kid's father does not even have the ABC's of a 50¢ whore on New Years Eve does not mean you have to take it out on the kid by not letting him get a Bar Mitzvah or presents such as glassies that come with the deal. Okay maybe you've got Moses and we've got Jesus. So what. They are both dead. And all we have left of either one of them is the 10 commandments which are the same for all of us.

This is a kid who can pull off anything. Including not needing anybody to stand up for him on account of being able to do it all by himself. But if your church still thinks that a father or somebody like him should be put into the lineup, who says it has to be a relative???? There's plenty of other guys who would do it for him PDQ without even asking how come.

Do not cross him, Rabby. He knows the President.

Charles Banks

Temple Chizuk Amuno
1243 Parkside Avenue • Brooklyn, New York

Mrs. Ida Margolis
236 Montgomery Street
Brooklyn, New York

Dear Mrs. Margolis:

I received the attached, somewhat incomprehensible letter this morning. While no one was more dismayed at the father's apparent lack of interest than I was, I am sure you can understand that I could not possibly permit a Gentile to participate in a Sabbath service, regardless of how deeply felt his intentions may be.

Please assure the boy that I am doing my best to locate a solution to this rather unfortunate turn of events.

> Respectfully,
> Rabbi Morris Lieberman

Dear Rabbi Lieberman,

There is something you should know. Charlie Banks wants to convert. We have been talking about it for a long time, though it is still supposed to be a secret due to Hitler and others like him. And because it is not very safe to be Jewish these days, I think he is very brave. When I told him the story about Pharaoh and the Red Sea, he got a funny look on his face and all he could say was "That's for me." Then he bought a Star of David for his house, just like Hank Greenberg who is his idol. (In case you don't know, Mr. Greenberg plays for Detroit and they call him Hammerin' Hank and he hit 41 home runs last year and his Rabbi was in Time Magazine.)

Anyway, Charlie thought that my Bar Mitzvah would be good practice for him so that when he begins to study with you next year he will already have a head start. Besides, how many people in our temple are batting .367?

Joey Margolis

Man About Town
by Winchell

MacKay Platter Hits the Sky

Steamy songstress Hazel MacKay remains on top of the world and on top of the charts for the third week running with her latest series of Bluebird recordings, *"I Get a Kick Out of You" and Other Old Friends,* a collection of love songs made popular by that ever-piping brass calliope Ethel Merman.

Word of MacKay's razzle-dazzle reached the Merm at El Morocco where she was sipping a Singapore Sling. "Is she still around?" asked Eth. "I heard she got tired of doing my old material and quit. It's like eating yesterday's hash anyway."

MacKay's only comment: "These songs are timeless. Especially when they're sung properly."

Friday Night Late
(and I miss you)

Dear Goodlookin',

I was on my way to the club when that loud-mouthed cow crossed the street right in front of my taxi. I offered the driver double the meter if his brakes should happen to fail.

Joey sat through both shows tonight and by 11:30 he'd learned all the fills to "This Can't Be Love". So I brought him up onstage with me and we did it as a duet. The kid's a born ham. Five encores. I'm either going to have to kill him or put him in the act.

I loved your letter to Lieberman. One suggestion: if you ever hear from him again, try to avoid bringing up the rat's ass and the 50¢ whore. Sometimes they get funny about that. By the way, stop worrying. You're thinking of a Bris. And they don't try to cut it off—it's a lot less dramatic than that.

Guess who loves you?

-H-

P.S. I read in the *Daily News* that there's a Charlie Banks fan club in Philadelphia composed entirely of attractive young women. If they show up at your hotel, call me. I'll take it from there.

Dear Toots,

You heard wrong. I tried 4 of the girls in the Philly fan club and they are not *that* attractive. (Only kidding!!!!!!) But Pitt. would be a lot prettier if you were here.

Be careful about letting the kid sing with you on account of the next thing you know you will be eating dinner at his house and getting the Third Degree from the Aunt and taking him to places such as Coney Island and writing him letters when you should be practicing instead, and half the time you will not even know why your doing it. He is like an earthquake. When it happens you can't stop it.

I will remember about not cussing out a Rabby again, just in case. But I think he knows the score now and Joey will get his Bar Mitzvah even without that thing he calls a father. The Rabby just needed to be straightened out.

Guess who loves you back.

Charlie

P.S. Stuke says he is going to marry Jean Harlow. Would you please tell him she croaked? He thinks I am making it up due to being jealous.

Temple Chizuk Amuno
1243 Parkside Avenue • Brooklyn, New York

Charles Banks
227 West 94th Street, Apt. 14-A
New York, New York

Dear Mr. Banks:

I have discussed your letter in depth with Rabbi Cohen and Cantor Rosenfeld, and though such a concession is irregular—to say the very least—we believe that the special circumstances involved permit us to accept your offer.

As the adult male responsible for standing beside Joseph as he becomes a man, you are requested to work with him informally on his Torah and Haftorah readings throughout the summer, whenever time will permit. Copies of both are enclosed. (I trust you are familiar with Genesis 6, v. 9—the story of Noah.) During the ceremony itself, your recitation from the Scriptures will be divided equally between the two of you:

אֵלֶּה תּוֹלְדֹת נֹחַ נֹחַ אִישׁ צַדִּיק תָּמִים הָיָה בְּדֹרֹתָיו
אֶת־הָאֱלֹהִים הִתְהַלֶּךְ־נֹחַ: וַיּוֹלֶד נֹחַ שְׁלֹשָׁה בָנִים אֶת־
שֵׁם אֶת־חָם וְאֶת־יָפֶת: וַתִּשָּׁחֵת הָאָרֶץ לִפְנֵי הָאֱלֹהִים
וַתִּמָּלֵא הָאָרֶץ חָמָס: וַיַּרְא אֱלֹהִים אֶת־הָאָרֶץ וְהִנֵּה
נִשְׁחָתָה כִּי־הִשְׁחִית כָּל־בָּשָׂר אֶת־דַּרְכּוֹ עַל־הָאָרֶץ: ס
וַיֹּאמֶר אֱלֹהִים לְנֹחַ קֵץ כָּל־בָּשָׂר בָּא לְפָנַי כִּי־מָלְאָה
הָאָרֶץ חָמָס מִפְּנֵיהֶם וְהִנְנִי מַשְׁחִיתָם אֶת־הָאָרֶץ: עֲשֵׂה
לְךָ תֵּבַת עֲצֵי־גֹפֶר קִנִּים תַּעֲשֶׂה אֶת־הַתֵּבָה וְכָפַרְתָּ אֹתָהּ
מִבַּיִת וּמִחוּץ בַּכֹּפֶר: וְזֶה אֲשֶׁר תַּעֲשֶׂה אֹתָהּ שְׁלֹשׁ מֵאוֹת
אַמָּה אֹרֶךְ הַתֵּבָה חֲמִשִּׁים אַמָּה רָחְבָּהּ וּשְׁלֹשִׁים אַמָּה

Although formal instruction is usually held on a regular basis, we recognize your obligations as a professional baseball player and are willing to work our schedule around yours. Please advise us in this regard.

One more thing. In order to ensure that we do not get off on the wrong foot, I would appreciate your addressing me as Rabbi. "Rabby" is intensely annoying.

Respectfully,
Rabbi Morris Lieberman

Dear Kid,

You did it to me again, didn't you? One minute I am telling your Rabby what a swell guy you are and how you deserve a break and etc. and the next thing I know he sends me something you and me are suppose to read together that looks like a cat with a broken leg walked across the paper. "I trust you are familiar with Genesis 6 v. 9 the story of Noah." Yeah. It rained and everybody died.

This did not happen all by itself. What did you tell him?

Charlie

Dear Charlie,

Rachel Panitz is this girl with dark brown hair who sits three seats in front of me and to the right, close enough for spitballs and shmoogies and other things. Craig thinks she is stuck up but I don't, even though the only time she ever looked at me was when she was giving a book report about what an "ass hole" Tom Sawyer was, which is probably because I hit her in the back of the neck with a jar of paste. A little one. Craig says I'm afraid to talk to her but every time I think I'm going to, I wind up gluing her bicycle tire to the playground or something stupid like that instead. The funny thing is that she never squeals on me to Mrs. Hicks. Not even when she found the centipede in her tuna fish and the note I thumb tacked on her banana. She just pretended it didn't happen and then traded bracelets with Kathy Fine. I don't get it. Sometimes I wish she would haul off and slug me. At least it would mean she knew who I was.

Joey

Dear Joey,

What did you tell the Rabby? I am not going to ask you again.

Charlie

TOP SECRET

The Shadow
C/O Joey Margolis
4th Floor

Gulp. Shadow, I think you went too far this time.

TOP SECRET

The Green Hornet
C/O Craig Nakamura
3rd Floor

I don't take nothin from nobody, see? They couldn't break me at Sing-Sing and they're not gunna break me here.

How come, Craigy? What did I do?

TOP SECRET

The Shadow
C/O Joey Margolis
4th Floor

Didn't he make you promise not to lie to him anymore?

125

The Green Hornet
C/O Craig Nakamura
3rd Floor

I didn't. I lied to the Rabbi. That's a whole other thing.

The Shadow
C/O Joey Margolis
4th Floor

Joey-San, I think you just double-crossed God. How many seats are in a temple?

The Green Hornet
C/O Craig Nakamura
3rd Floor

About 800. But only half of them get used.

TOP SECRET

The Shadow
C/O Joey Margolis
4th Floor

Smokes. At fifty cents a head maybe we <u>could</u> make this work. Jiminy Crickets. Did you just hear that bang? It sounded like a Krupp mortar.

TOP SECRET

The Green Hornet
C/O Craig Nakamura
3rd Floor

It was thunder, Hornet.

TOP SECRET

The Shadow
C/O Joey Margolis
4th Floor

It was Mrs. Aubaugh. Reloading. I have to go.

Dear Charlie,

Maybe I had to pull a few strings. But you started it. If you hadn't sent him that letter then he wouldn't have written one to my Mom and I wouldn't have found out about it so it's your fault.

Anyway, he sort of thinks you want to convert. But you really don't have to. What you can do is act like you changed your mind after it's over. How is he going to know if we don't tell him? I *promise* this is the last thing I'll ever ask you to do except take me on a road trip with you.

Joey

P.S. My mother says we're not supposed to say anything to Aunt Carrie for as long as we can get away with it. She has a weak heart and this could finish her off.

Dear Joey,

Your a real pip, you know that? Okay here's what is going to happen.

1. Your going to learn this Hebrew thing front-wards and backwards so many times that your going to dream about it. And then
2. Your going to teach it to me. And you better do it fast before I change my mind which could be any minute.
3. I will handle the English. If you can call that English.

4. Remember that I am only doing this because your in a real jam this time. And I promised you that you would not have to fight the big ones by yourself anymore.

5. If this Rabby really thinks I am going to convert he must be a lot bigger lunkhead than he sounds even with his $10 words such as "irregular" and "obligations". I do not even know anything about being a *Protestant*.

We only have 5 months to pull this off and I will be on the road half the time. So I'm warning you Bucko. You think your teacher gives you a hard time? You haven't worked with *me* yet. Ask Stuke. The only reason nobody can figure out how to beat our double play is on account of me keeping him there past 3:30 in the A.M. until we got it right, even though all we had to see by was part of a moon and a flashlight that didn't work. Which is probably why he acts the way he acts due to getting hit in the head all night.

Hazel has a saying that she says and it goes "Be careful what you ask for, for you may get it." Know what? You got it.

Charlie

P.S. And if we pull out of this mess in one piece, don't think I will be giving you a type writer or a wireless or etc. You will be lucky if I do not push you off a cliff. This is what happens when you jinx the dirt.

P.S.2. Go ahead. Put quotion marks around asshole with a space in the middle again. Your living on borrowed time anyway.

"Lucky" Lindy Pilots
America First

DES MOINES, Saturday. Charles A. Lindbergh, the aviator who captured the imagination of an entire world when he became the first man to fly non-stop from New York to Paris in 1927, has emerged as the most visibly rising force behind America First—the rapidly growing isolationist movement organized to keep the United States neutral throughout the duration of the European war. Lindy's outspoken rhetoric has already drawn fire from the White House as a result of a recent rally in Iowa, when he cautioned America's Jews to shut up or else. "Because of Jewish ownership and influence in our motion pictures, our press, our radio and our government," he warned, "if war comes, they will be blamed for it." President Roosevelt called the former hero "an irresponsible nincompoop."

Many recall that, among the accolades bestowed upon him by the world's leaders, Lindbergh was decorated by Hitler himself during a visit to the European capitals after his

THE WHITE HOUSE

Dear Joey:

Thank you for your most recent letter. I can assure you that America First is sponsored neither by Communists, by neo-Fascists, or by Mrs. Aubaugh. But we'll keep an eye on her, just in case.

Naturally we are monitoring the Manchurian situation closely and remain convinced that the Japanese have no desire to become embroiled in a world war. However, we are also attempting to preserve the rather fragile peace that presently binds our two countries. Suggesting that Kurusu and Nomura are a couple of sneaks would only complicate things.

Fala had a mild cold. Nothing to be concerned about. (But thanks for asking.)

My regards to your mother and your aunt.

> Cordially as always,
> Stephen T. Early
> Press Secretary

Dear Charlie,

It's a good thing you didn't join America First, because right now all of my Charlie Banks stuff would be in the trash can with my Lindbergh newspapers and magazines and other "Lucky Lindy" junk that the garbage man is going to burn tomorrow.

The first line of the Hebrew goes like "Ay-leh toldos Noach." When you get to the "ch", you're supposed to say it from the back of your mouth on the top, like when you have a sore throat and it itches.

And stop talking to me like you were my drill sergeant. I'm not one of those guys you shot gunboats with in China. I said I was sorry, okay? Jinx your own damn dirt.

Joey

Dear Joey,

I got gigged $50 today and it is all your fault. In the 4th inning in Saint Louis, G. Mancuso for the Cardinals tripled when Bobby Carpenter threw him a fast ball by mistake due to farting at the same time and losing his edge. Then Mize came up, who does not like to hit until he has wasted a good 20 minutes fouling them off, which meant that me and Mancuso were standing on 3d Base for a while with nothing to talk about on account of we have maybe swapped two words with each other in our whole life and both of them were fuck you. So instead I

132

practiced the "ch" but accidentally wound up spitting a mouth full of snot onto Mancuso who thought I did it on purpose. Then both of the benches cleared and when it was over they made me cough up $50 due to starting it. I had a peach of a time. Thanks for nothing. What else I had was a split lip from G. Mancuso who still does not believe me—and the only reason I am not going to tap him on the conk tomorrow is from all of a sudden being able to play "In the Mood" on my saxaphone without any mistakes. (I hope this does not mean I need to get pasted in the mouth whenever I wish to play it again.) But I am still out $50. This is because the NY Giants do not really make their nut from the gate but from handing out fines for breaking rules that nobody but a dead man could follow anyway. We are not suppose to play poker. We are not suppose to have intercourse. We are not suppose to be awake after 10:00 in the P.M. And etc. Mel Ott says that the only two people in the world who could score 100 on the list are God and Carl Hubbell. And God is a maybe.

How come nobody ever told me that Noah was a pain in the ass? "Make thee an ark of gopher wood, with rooms shalt thou make the ark and thou shalt pitch it within and without with pitch." Well no kidding. What *else* is he going to build the damn boat with? Bricks? And while we are here, how come it doesn't say anything about where all those animals were suppose to shit? Do they want us to think they held it in for 40 days? And this one. "The length of the ark 300 cubits, the breadth of it 50 cubits, and the height of it 30 cubits." What in Hell is a cubit? I am warning you. If there is math in this, you can forget it.

When we see the Rabby on Monday, let me do the talking.

Charlie

P.S. You should of burned the Lindbergh stuff a long time ago. Anybody with money can do what he did. If he was flying Wrong Way Corrigan's 25¢ crate instead, he would not of even made it to Ellis Island. Did you hear that FDR called him a nincompoop? What a laugh. That's like you calling somebody a Big-Mouth.

P.S.2. Burge Whitehead broke his finger in a crap game so they made Stuke play 2d Base today on account of he owned the dice. It was suppose to teach him a lesson, but don't you know he pulls off the first unassisted triple play since Wamby did it in the 1920 Series. If he was not a picnic to live with before, now he will need a kick in the ass on a regular basis just to remind him that he still pisses and etc. like everybody else.

P.S.3. And who ever said anything about gunboats and China?

134

Charles Linden Banks

The Racine Rocket

THIRD BASE, NEW YORK GIANTS

Born: August 7, 1917   Ht. 5'11½"   Wt. 181   BR   TR
Racine, Wisconsin

		G	AB	R	H	2B	3B	HR	Avg.
SPRINGFIELD	**1937**	95	408	106	134	28	14	27	.328
	1938	90	393	111	155	26	11	29	.394
	1939	98	416	127	160	31	11	32	.385
	TOTALS	283	1217	344	449	85	36	88	.369
NEW YORK	**1940**	120	511	143	173	40	17	38	.339
	TOTALS	120	511	143	173	40	17	38	.339

What's Charlie Banks got that Superman hasn't? Try 31 triples, 68 doubles, and enough haymakers to feed most of the horses in the Midwest. And that ain't hay! Beats the heck out of Kryptonite, doesn't it?

Born in Wisconsin, Charlie Banks was an only child whose father was the vice president of Racine Produce, Inc., and whose mother wrote a society column for the *Milwaukee Sentinel*. Though hard-hit by the Depression, he fought back against malnutrition by joining the Merchant Marine and sinking three Japanese gunboats along the Yangtze River. (Where do you think those muscles came from, folks!) Soon he drifted on to Hong Kong, where he earned his cleats on a rundown ball field across the street from a waterfront saloon. The rest is history. A devout Protestant who attends church regularly, Charlie shrugs off his success on the basepaths by insisting, "God is my umpire."

He likes making spaghetti, hunting for deer, and devoting his spare time to humanitarian causes. His dislikes include Dodgers, Reds, and Cardinals. And we don't mean maybe. Mr. DiMaggio, watch out!

Dear Joey,

1. The gunboats and Merchant Marines and muscles on the Yangtze Riv. happened in 1926. I was 9.
2. I never got malnutrated in my life.
3. The only thing I told them about China was that their noodles make me barf. They came up with the rest of it by themself.
4. I did not even know what cleats *were* until I got to Springfield. Up until then we played in our toes.
5. It also says that I did not have a brother, and nothing about Harlan getting dropped by a foul ball or etc. So do not believe what you read. Except when it is from me.

Charlie

P.S. How's this for a pisser? "And God saw the earth, and behold it was corrupt." Like this is news.

Temple Chizuk Amuno
1243 Parkside Avenue • Brooklyn, New York

Mrs. Ida Margolis
236 Montgomery Street
Brooklyn, New York

Dear Mrs. Margolis:

It might be a wise idea were someone to suggest to Mr. Banks that there is a significant difference between the

Torah and the *Daily News.* One of them is open to conjecture and the other is not. Furthermore, the story of the great flood provides the moral foundation upon which the entire human race has been built. Whether or not Noah had "a couple of loose spark plugs under the hood" is both anachronistic and moot. (It also happens to be blasphemous, but blasphemy is the least chargeable offense I encountered all afternoon.) Then too we must consider whether Mr. Banks is even remotely capable of grasping the nuances of the Hebrew tongue; when he attempted to pronounce "Noach," he nearly drowned Cantor Rosenfeld. This does not bode well for October. Similarly, it is Joseph's opinion that he open his Bar Mitzvah speech "with a few laughs to loosen them up"—more specifically, that worn-out routine chronicling Moses' descent from the mountain with the Ten Commandments, concluding with the epigram "Adultery's still in." Given the manner in which the two of them recited the punch line in unison, I gather that Mr. Banks and your son are a well-suited match. So, however, are Laurel and Hardy.

On the other hand, I cannot recall when I last encountered a boy quite as eager to meet the challenge of his Bar Mitzvah as Joseph appears to be. Most of the time we have to bribe them. For this reason alone, I recommend that we proceed as planned. I will do the best I can—and we'll leave the necessary miracles to God.

Respectfully,
Rabbi Morris Lieberman

Jordy Stuker, 1st Base
c/o The New York Giants
Polo Grounds
New York, NY

Dear Stuke,

Betty Grable lives at 12217 Bentley Avenue in Los
Angeles, California. After she got rid of Jackie Coogan
she had dinner with Cary Grant a couple of times and
once with Victor Mature. But right now she doesn't
have a boyfriend, even though she went to see the Harry
James Orchestra three times by herself so there may be
somebody in the band who she likes. Also, she's four
years older than you in case this is a problem.

Charlie told the Rabbi that he looks like the Smith
Brothers and then he asked him for cough drops. I
should have told him that Rabbis never think anything
is funny. If they laugh they get fired.

Did you talk him into it yet?

Joey

Dear Sprout,

I've been putting the pressure on him for 3 weeks
and he's still not ripe. I thought I could get him to cave
in before our Boston-Cincy-Chicago swing in the middle of the summer, but you know what a hard-head he
is. Once he says no, forget it. I'll keep trying, tho.

Thanks for the dope on Betty. I sent her $22.73 worth
of roses (all I had in my pocket) & also a telegram to

Victor Mature (collect) saying she never wants to see him again. Didn't know she was old, tho. She doesn't *look* 25.

I had a shoulder to shoulder talk with your buddy & set him square on the right way to handle a rabbi. Usually he doesn't listen to me, but he went 1-for-4 and I have the first unassisted triple play in 21 years. (Did I mention that?) So you can stop worrying. I'll make sure he fixes whatever he broke.

Stuke

Rabby Morris Lieberman
Temple Chizuk Amuno
1243 Parkside
Brooklyn NY

Dear Rabby,

Behold. I am sorry if I pissed thou off.

That better?

Chas. Banks
3d Base

P.S. Here is something else I just found. "And the Lord said unto Noah, of every beast thou shalt take to thee seven and seven, each with his mate, male and female, to keep seed alive on the face of the earth." If this means what I think it does, you and me are going to have a little talk. He's still a *kid,* for Christ's sake.

Alexander Hamilton Junior High School

To: All Seventh Graders

From: Mrs. Hicks
Mr. Demarest

Re: Summer Assignment

We are proud to announce that Alexander Hamilton Junior High is one of 200 schools chosen to participate in Mrs. Roosevelt's national essay contest. This year's competition is entitled "If My Father Were President." You are encouraged to be as creative as possible, but within certain limitations. The last time we did something like this, six fathers were spies, nine were gangsters, and one of them was Orville Wright. Mrs. Roosevelt has neither the time nor the patience for this kind of nonsense.

Papers should be neatly handwritten on ruled paper, and should not be longer than 500 words. They will be due on the first day of school in September.

Have a wonderful summer!

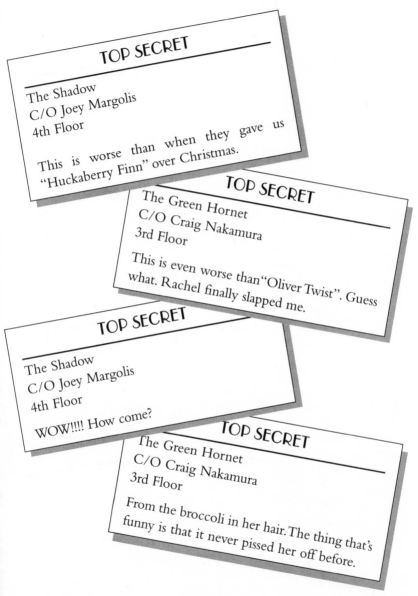

TOP SECRET

The Shadow
C/O Joey Margolis
4th Floor

This is worse than when they gave us "Huckaberry Finn" over Christmas.

TOP SECRET

The Green Hornet
C/O Craig Nakamura
3rd Floor

This is even worse than "Oliver Twist". Guess what. Rachel finally slapped me.

TOP SECRET

The Shadow
C/O Joey Margolis
4th Floor

WOW!!!! How come?

TOP SECRET

The Green Hornet
C/O Craig Nakamura
3rd Floor

From the broccoli in her hair. The thing that's funny is that it never pissed her off before.

141

TOP SECRET

The Shadow
C/O Joey Margolis
4th Floor

Did you talk to her?

TOP SECRET

The Green Hornet
C/O Craig Nakamura
3rd Floor

Not yet. But I will in September. Swear to God. Hope to die. Crossies twice. What kind of President is your dad going to make?

TOP SECRET

The Shadow
C/O Joey Margolis
4th Floor

Beats me. I was going to have him put the chop on Mrs. Aubaugh from being a hit man before he got elected, but now we're not allowed to do that. What about you?

TOP SECRET

The Green Hornet
C/O Craig Nakamura
3rd Floor

Don't know. You think she did it because of the broccoli or because she likes me?

142

IF MY FATHER WERE PRESIDENT
BY JOSEPH MARGOLIS

If my father were president, I think he would be a very good

I think my father would make a really good president because

If my father shot Nana Bert then he might make a good president, but only if

How the Hell should *I* know what kind of a president my father would make? Most of the time I don't even know where he *is.*

If my father were president, he would sit in the Oval Office and

---

Temple Chizuk Amuno
1243 Parkside Avenue • Brooklyn, New York

Charles Banks
227 West 94th Street, Apt. 14–A
New York, New York

Dear Charles:

Thank you for your generous invitation to attend Joseph's birthday gathering. However, my wife and I keep a strictly Kosher home and I'm afraid a supper club is a little out of our league. But I'm sure it will mean a great deal to Joseph.

Of course I know you're not going to convert. Thirteen-year-old boys have been attempting to hoodwink me since 1919, and there are few such scams I have not encountered before—though I must admit that this one earns high marks for originality. But let's allow him to think he's getting away with it.

Don't be alarmed by Tuesday's lesson, for I am confident that Joseph will do well. I suspect he is merely testing you—and winning. Of course, you could always find a way to turn the tables on him; however, I am willing to wager a Kiddush cup that he is even more stubborn than you are.

Good luck. This is shaping up to be quite a contest.

Respectfully,
Rabbi Morris Lieberman

INTERVIEWER: Donald M. Weston, Ph.D.
SUBJECT: Joseph Charles Margolis

A: It was the best birthday I ever had. Charlie and Hazel took us to Delmonico's for dinner. The whole *world* was there. Aunt Carrie even got a kiss from Robert Montgomery.

Q: I'll bet that changed her mind about Charlie, huh?

A: Not all the way. She doesn't call him a shagitz any more, but every time she starts to call him Charlie her mouth gets stuck. This is gunna take a little work.

Q: Did you see Winchell's column?

A: Yeah. He spelled my name wrong, though. And he said we live in Queens, not Brooklyn. He's a troublemaker.

Q: How so?

A: Ethel Merman was at the next table and he kept trying to start a fistfight between her and Hazel. Then Charlie tripped him and he went away.

Q: Good for Charlie. Hazel's too much of a trouper to fall for that anyway.

A: No she isn't. She talked to the waiter for a long time and gave him some money, and somehow Ethel Merman wound up with a Diet Special instead of steak and a baked potato. You could hear her on Madison Avenue. Boy, she screams loud.

Q: Some people call that singing. I never understood it myself.

A: Then we went to Tuxedo Junction. Hazel sang "My Funny Valentine" right to me, and then I went on the stage with her and we did the "I Like New York In June" song just like Mickey Rooney and Judy Garland do it in *Babes on Broadway*. We practiced it for a whole week so we could surprise everybody. Smokes, me and my Mom signed more autographs than Charlie did.

Q: Did you get a lot of presents?

A: You bet. My mother bought me a watch with an aviator dial and Aunt Carrie got me a black zipper jacket that says GIANTS on the back and Craig got me The Shadow's Secret Code Book and Hazel gave me a little Victrola with all of Glenn Miller's records, especially "String of Pearls" and "In the Mood."

Q: What about Charlie?

A: He asked me what I wanted and I told him *Citizen Kane* at the Radio City Music Hall, but he said he could do a lot better than that. Just between you and me I think he's gunna buy me a saxophone because he hates it when I get spit all over his.

Q: I could be wrong, but I'd look out for a different kind of surprise if I were you.

Dear Joey,

Me and Stuke and Mel Ott and Burge Whitehead and Mickey Witek stayed up all night listening to the War News on the radio. Maybe your right after all. Adolf and His Singing Assholes are lining up on the Russian boarder, the Brits knocked 26 Messershmits out of the sky, the Two Little Pigs kicked us out of Berlin and Rome, and Ickes stopped selling our oil to Japan. Now Gehrig is gone. Go figure it. Hitler has already killed a million people but he's still alive. All Iron Horse ever did was play in 2130 straight games but he isn't. It makes your guts feel kind of funny on account of thinking that it's all getting ready to hit us at once. You better make sure your pal in the White House is on the ball and not playing hooky at Hide Park or etc., and that Mrs. R gets her ass out of the strip mines or having tea with some little Suzy Glutz so she can go back home to Washington and make sure the 4-flusher she is married to is doing his job and not just walking the damn dog. For better or for worse we are stuck with him now, and for the long haul too. But come to think of it, maybe Willkie was not such a hot idea after all.

The radio keeps making me think about Noah. "And God said The end of all flesh is come before Me, for the earth is filled with violence." I hope this does not mean you and me and Hazel and your Mom and Aunt Carrie and Craig and Stuke, on account of what did *we* do? And that reminds me Iron Fists. We only have 3½ more months and we are way behind where we are suppose to be. The Rabby even bet me that we would not be able to pull it off in time. If we win I get a kiddish cup, whatever *that* is. If we don't, I will probably lose my shirt on account of Stuke and the boys found out about the bet and are buying pieces of the action like they were Brandy Bottle Bates or Scranton Slim or somebody. This could cost me alot of $$$$$$$. So you better come up swinging Bucko. Your suppose to know it better than *me,* and not the other way around.

Charlie

P.S. Our bat-boy got a 16 year old girl pregnant. Counting backwards we figured out that it happened in our locker room in Saint Louis. What a guy. We never thought he had it in him. But they got rid of him anyway due to not being good for our image, which shows you what a bunch of heads they are in the front office. Everybody knows that kids are *suppose* to make mistakes or else they would not be normal. Sometimes you can even be proud of it like when I was 15 and got in a contest where you were suppose to drink 4 beers and see who could piss the farthest. I was the only one who could hit the mayor's Stutz on the other side of the road, except nobody told me that the mayor was in it with the window down. And even though he tried to run me over, the other guys looked at me like I was a king or something. (Come to think of it this is all a lie—so maybe you will just have to take my word for it.)

P.S.2. Oh, yeah. We have a backup kid in NY but his old man will not let him travel with us. That means until we find a new one, we will need another bat-boy for our next road trip. Know anybody?

Dear Charlie,

Please please.

Joey

TOP SECRET

The Green Hornet
C/O Craig Nakamura
3rd Floor

He had it planned all the time. His birthday present was a Giants uniform. God, to open something like that just when you're about to get into your pajamas. A 13 year old can't have a stroke, can he?

TOP SECRET

The Shadow
C/O Joey Margolis
4th Floor

What's the catch?

TOP SECRET

The Green Hornet
C/O Craig Nakamura
3rd Floor

He says if I don't know my Torah by heart after we play the Cubs, he's going to make me hitch-hike home from Chicago.

149

TOP SECRET

The Shadow
C/O Joey Margolis
4th Floor

Why do they always have to hang things like that in front of us? Smokes! Turn on your radio. DiMaggio just tied Willie Keeler's 44 game streak off the Red Sox. When do you leave?

TOP SECRET

The Green Hornet
C/O Craig Nakamura
3rd Floor

Two weeks.

TOP SECRET

The Shadow
C/O Joey Margolis
4th Floor

I'll try to hold off Mrs. Aubaugh by myself. But if you come back and I'm dead because she garrotted me, it's your fault.

Dear Joey,

That is the last time I ever let you pick the movie. Even at the Radio City. Or maybe I missed something. He starts a newspaper then grows a mustashe and screws everybody except his wife. That took 2 hours. And the only thing we find out is that he called his sled Rose Bush? Your taste is in your ear.

Some things to remember.

1. Mister Terry only has one rule but with 4 parts in it. No drinking, no gambling, no late hours and no women. This goes double for you. *All* of it.

2. You get ten per and cakes. This is player talk and it means two fins per game and barley. Come to think of it, this is player talk too and it means $10 and eats. I can not spell it out any better than that. You can have $2 of it but your mother gets the rest.

3. Your job is to hand us our bats and shut up. Last night at the Radio City you did not talk for almost 10 minutes so I know you can do it.

4. A couple of times a day I will ask you such questions as "What did God say to Noah?" and "How many floors were in the Ark?" and etc. If you know the answers in both languages you can go out with us after the game. If you don't, your grounded at the hotel.

5. If you get homesick just tell me and we can call your Mom and Aunt Carrie. It does not mean your a baby or anything like it.

6. The sleeper to Boston leaves at 11:00 in the P.M. on Sunday night. Craig can come to the Pennsylvania Station with us but only if he does not sneak on the train. I will check your suitcases right after All Aboard just to make sure he is not in one of them.

7. For the next 2 weeks your a NY Giant. Don't forget it.

Happy birthday again.

Charlie

P.S. They stopped writing about Stuke's triple play on account of DiMaggio. So Stuke started a hitting streak of his own. Right now it is up to 2 games.

Dear Charlie,

The cat's out of the bag. Rabbi Lieberman called our house today to find out if you had a talus and a yarmulke already or if you wanted to buy one from the Temple just in case. But my Mom was out shopping for pillowcases so Aunt Carrie answered the phone instead. And even though she sometimes does boneheaded things like make gefilte fish for Pistol Pete Reiser, she's no dummy and it didn't take her long to put two and two together. First she told my Mom she was going to open a vein, and then she said she was going to stick her head in the oven. But instead she called Edith Snyder and they went to Gimbel's Tea Room for lunch. That always gets her back to normal. And Robert Montgomery kissing her probably helped you out too. The last thing she said to my mother before she closed the subject was, "All right, Ida. A man who's willing to learn the Torah can't be all bad even if he is a Gentile. But if my nephew marries a shikse, let it be on your head." So I think you're winning.

I'm bringing my crystal set with me on the road because Craig says that in Boston you can pick up signals from Berlin. I think he's full of shit but what if he's not?

Joey

DiMaggio Stopped at 56; Giants Hit the Road

NEW YORK, July 17. Indians hurlers Al Smith and Jim Bagby joined forces in a front-line assault on Joltin' Joe DiMaggio at Cleveland tonight, and ended the Yankee Clipper's unassailable hitting streak at 56 consecutive games—the longest in baseball's history.

"At least we won the game," DiMaggio told his teammates when it was over. "Now let's get out there and win some more."

Behind the formidable pitching of Lefty Gomez, New York held Cleveland to four hits and one run before threatening in the ninth, when fireman Johnny Murphy put out the blaze for good. The final score: Yanks 4, Redskins 3.

DiMaggio was retired three times and walked once.

Meanwhile, Bill Terry's fourth-place New York Giants begin a two-week road trip that will take them to Boston, Cincinnati and Chicago. Whether they can gain any ground on the seemingly unstoppable Dodgers and Cards depends largely upon Carl Hubbell's arm, Charlie Banks' bat, and Jordy Stuker's glove. Skipper Terry is hoping that the injury-plagued lineup will be able to repair itself in time for the next

──────────○──────────

Dear Hazel,

Right now I am stuck in a compartment all alone on The Patriot Limited looking out of the window at Connecticut trees in the dark, and I can't get out because Charlie won't let me. I'm very sad. I thought this was supposed to be a birthday present, but as soon as we got here he turned into General MacArthur or somebody. And the only thing I did was show my best friend Craig what a peachy keen train this was and after he left I played a couple games of Old Maid with Stuke and Mel and Burge, even though I kept losing. But Charlie yells at me for *every*thing. Even when I was hungry and went to get a hamburger.

Could you please tell him to lay off? Just a little bit? Smokes, I'm only a boy. And maybe I'm also sort of scared because this is my first time away from home. Thanks.

Love,
Joey

Dear Toots,

I think you better learn how to bake cakes with such things in them as files and saws and etc. because after I kill this kid I will be doing a long stretch in the Jug. Right now he is locked in our compartment on the train and the only one who has the key is the porter who is not allowed to open it up for anybody but me. But that does not stop him from trying to bribe whoever he hears walking outside. Mel Ott almost said yes for $20.

This road trip is only 2 hrs. old and I already feel like I just played 3 double headers. I should of seen it coming before we even left the Pennsylvania Station. Him and the Japanese kid were wearing the exact same shirts and pants and shoes and socks on purpose so that if you looked at them real fast and did not notice such things as eyes and etc. you would think they were the same brat and get mixed up in the head, especially if you were a conducter. The railroad had to throw Craig off the train 3 times while we were still in the station and the 3d time was because they caught the 2 of them in the diner eating burgers and shakes and charging it to the NY Giants. So I booted Craig out the door, put Joey in the compartment, and told him not to move until I got back. This was on account of his family on the platform who were not finished with me yet. The mother gave me a bag of more pointy coconut things which I should of never told her I liked due to there being enough of them to feed Massachusets and part of Road Island, and also a briskit with directions in writing about heating it up and gravy and etc., like I would know what to do with an oven even if they gave us one which they don't. Then it was the Aunt's turn to give a speech about Joey's teeth. I always thought there was only one way to do it. You put the powder on the damn brush and then stick it in your mouth and call it a ball game. But she had enough instructions to build a B-17 bomber, and then finished by telling me that if I did not keep him away from the bad element, let it be on my head. What a laugh. He *is* the bad element. Then we left. But when I got back to the compartment the kid was gone. Where he was was at the other end of the smoker with Stuke's dice and the whole team around him, rolling 7's and saying such things as "Aunt Carrie needs a new girdle" and etc. By the time I got there he was in the middle of a joke that started with Superman flying over the beach and seeing Wonder Woman lying there on her back naked with her legs open and ended with Wonder Woman saying "What was that?" and the Invisible Man saying "I don't know but my asshole sure hurts." And when the little shit said asshole there was a space in the middle. After that I locked him up.

Before you read in Winchell that the police are looking for me, remember that you thought this was a good idea too.

I love you.

Charlie

P.S. If you want to take the mother and the Aunt out to lunch while we are gone, let it be on your head. But do not do it because you think they miss him. If I was them I would pack up and move before he came back. And don't think your going to get anywhere with the Aunt.

156

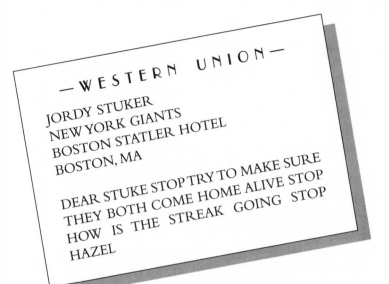

— WESTERN UNION —

JORDY STUKER
NEW YORK GIANTS
BOSTON STATLER HOTEL
BOSTON, MA

DEAR STUKE STOP TRY TO MAKE SURE
THEY BOTH COME HOME ALIVE STOP
HOW IS THE STREAK GOING STOP
HAZEL

Dear Hazelnut,

Don't worry. Me & the guys got together & decided we'll take turns looking out for Sprout. We have to. That kid's got all our money.

We beat Boston 5-4 in tonight's opener. It took him a little while to get the hang of things—I guess when you're 13 & all of a sudden you find yourself in a dugout at Braves Field wearing a Giants uniform, it hits you pretty hard. But once he finally got it, it sure happened fast. Buddy Hassett was up on a 3-0 count when Sprout started calling out things like "No batter, no batter. Take three & sit down." Mister Terry thought we should shut him up, until Hassett struck out. After that they didn't stand a chance. By the way, I snapped a couple of great shots before the game—your boyfriend was showing the kid how to grip a bat. They looked like Mutt & Jeff.

I read in Photoplay that Ingrid Bergman likes khaki. Since we're going to wind up in this damn war anyway, do you think if I enlisted now I'd have a better shot at her? The paper says we only have 500,000 men in uniform. I can compete with that. 10 million I can't. If you know her, tell her I'll do whatever she wants.

Stuke

P.S. And how come Carole Lombard never returns my calls?

P.P.S. The first three streaks were only for practice. This one's the real thing. 4 games now.

New York Giants

BATBOY: __Margolis__   PARK: __Braves Field, Boston__

— CHECK LIST —

ALL ITEMS MUST BE COMPLETED ONE HOUR PRIOR TO GAME TIME.

	SUN	MON	TUES	WED	THUR	FRI	SAT
22 Bats				√			
2 Boxes Bullpen Baseballs				√			
2 Boxes Dugout Baseballs				√			
10 Bullpen Towels				√			
30 Dugout Towels				√			
Bandages				√			
Antiseptic				√			
Water Cooler Filled				√			

NOTES:

1. How many kids did Noah have?

   Two.

   3.

   That's what I meant. He had two. And then he had another one.

2. How long did it rain for?

   40 days. Everybody knows that.

   Tough luck Bucko. 40 nights too.

   That's not fair. Even Solomon wouldn't have pulled a fast one like that.

3. How old was Noah when God gave him the job?

   76.

   600.

   Says who? And how come God thought an old fart like that could build a boat? He'd be lucky if he could still pee.

4. How do you say "Noah walked with God" in Hebrew?

   Es-haw-elloheem something.

   Es-haw-elloheem hees halech Noach. Like this is suppose to do *me* any good.

159

Joey,

Me and Stuke and some of the boys are going to eat at the Union Oyster House and after that see the new Cagney picture in Cambridge if we can get in. I will be back by 11:30. You can have dinner downstairs whenever you want and I already told them in the dining room the things your not allowed to eat such as ice cream Sundays instead of peas and etc. Also Charlie MacCarthy is on the radio tonight or instead you can go and listen to the piano player in the lobby. But the doorman knows your not suppose to leave the hotel so don't get any ideas.

Charlie

TOP SECRET

Dear Hornet,

The Brown Shirts are holding me prisoner at the Boston Statler Hotel. This place is crawling with them and now they've got me cornered.

Charlie stranded me here even though the whole team went to see *Strawberry Blonde* with Cagney in it. What a spoil sport. Just because I didn't know all the answers yet. What a sap. I tried to climb down the fire escape because there's a vaudeville house next door, and they're always easy to sneak into when you make your eyes cry and tell the usher that you lost your parents in the crowd and you need to get in and find them. But the doorman from the hotel was waiting for me on the pavement because Charlie already tipped him off. What a goop. The only thing to do here is count the squares on the ceiling (128) and the windows with lights on in the building across the street (211), or go downstairs and listen to some no-nothing piano player who never heard of anything newer than "Alexander's Rag Time Band" for Pete's sake. Even Bergen and McCarthy stunk on the radio.

But there was a brawl today, and I was in it. How it happened was this. Jim Tobin was pitching for Boston and Phil Masi was catching. When Stuke came up in the 6th he was looking for a long ball, but he must have been looking too hard because he kept leaning all the way over the plate and Tobin brushed him back on his butt twice. So Stuke got up and gave the four-finger signal to Tobin which in case you don't know means "One more time and the bat goes up your ass." Then Masi said to him "Aw, pipe down and act your age." Then Stuke said to Masi "How's your wife and my kid?" Then Masi said "Fuck you, shit-head." Then Stuke pulled Masi's mask all the way out and let it snap back on his face. Then Masi said "Ow" and everybody ran out of the dugouts and bleeding started. I got right in the middle of the whole pile and I was kicking Paul Waner on the leg when all of a sudden a hand reached in and grabbed the back of my belt. I thought I was finally going to get to tap somebody on the conk, but it was only Charlie. What a sour puss. He yanked me into the dugout in one yank and put me in a broom closet until it was over. But I still got poked in my right ribs by Babe Dahlgren's elbow and it hurt like Hell. It was *great*.

It's only 9:15 and I'm still wide-awake and I need to

find something to do. Smokes, he won't even let me go to Fenway Park and get Ted Williams' autograph. What a dope.

The Shadow

P.S. But Stuke has a new hitting streak. One game.

P.S.2. You *are* full of shit. I can't get Berlin from here. I was lucky I could get Connecticut.

IF MY FATHER WERE PRESIDENT
BY JOSEPH MARGOLIS

I think my father's presidency would be the kind of an administration where

If my father were president he would be too busy to take me places but guess what? He doesn't anyway. Ha-ha.

If my father were president he would be a Republican and there would probably be another Depression as soon as he

If my father had Fireside Chats but threw Nana Bert in the fireplace first,

If my father were president

Dear Toots,

Me and Stuke just spent 2½ hrs. sitting in a bar and killing time until 11:30 so the kid would think we were really eating lobsters and seeing Cagney without him and etc., and maybe he would get down to brass tax and learn his part so we would not leave him out again. But the bar had a juke box in it and I heard you on it 4 times. Including "Small Hotel". Do you remember? You had on black with the silver crisscrosses and you sang the whole thing to me even though Gary Cooper was there too. That was the first time I knew you were going to say yes. So I guess you can say that Joey wasn't the only one who got reminded of something tonight.

Right now he is fast asleep and it is tough to figure out from looking at him with his eyes closed where somebody that little comes up with so much moxie. Even when he is conked out you can see that his head is still working (which come to think of it is a little scary). All it makes me want to do is knock his old man's block off.

Today he made a big click with the Bees (or Braves or whatever in Hell they are calling themself this year). The ump behind the plate was Jocko Conlan who is the kind of square-off-the-shoulder guy that if he said the earth was flat, I would probably have to figure that it was C. Columbus who did not have all his dogs on the leash. So in the 3rd inning I swung on a 2 and 2, which was the first thing Harlan taught me I should never do off a puffin like J. Tobin. But I did it anyway. The ball was down here and I was up there and Conlan said "So long

Charlie." But before I could throw my bat on the ground, there was Joey (who maybe comes up to Conlan's ankle) saying such things as "Hey you ump. What kind of a call was that?" and "Where are your glasses?" and "Do you need a cane too?" and etc. So Conlan put his hands onto his hip-bones the same way he does when he is *really* sore and he pointed a finger at Joey and said "Say you. One more word like that and it is time for the showers." By now they were belly to far-head and the Bees were laughing so hard we could of walked a bunt into a slam. But Joey was really hot under the coller, so he kicked the dirt two times and said "Don't let it happen again or you'll be in Very Serious Trouble." And when he got back to the bench and punched the wall, the Bees gave him a big hand.

Then in the 6th, Stuke was up and started another scrap due to saying such things to P. Masi as "I fucked your wife" and etc. Before I could get to Joey, he was in the middle of that too. But P. Waner for the Bees was keeping an eye on him just in case and he even let the kid kick him a couple times until I got there. Then he handed him off to me.

He better get on the ball soon. I didn't tell him yet but there is a Glenn Miller show in Chic. that I want to take him to. I hope I do not have to leave him in the room and pretend I went without him.

It's 2:43 and I can't sleep because I am still hearing "Small Hotel" in my head.

Charlie

New York Giants

BATBOY: <u>Margolis</u>   PARK: <u>Crosley Field, Cincinnati</u>

— CHECK LIST —

ALL ITEMS MUST BE COMPLETED ONE HOUR PRIOR TO GAME TIME.

	SUN	MON	TUES	WED	THUR	FRI	SAT
22 Bats	√						
2 Boxes Bullpen Baseballs	√						
2 Boxes Dugout Baseballs	√						
10 Bullpen Towels	√						
30 Dugout Towels	√						
Bandages	√						
Antiseptic	√						
Water Cooler Filled	√						

NOTES:

1. What were the names of Noah's kids?
   Shem, Ham and Jor-El.
   You almost got me on that one. It's Japheth. Jor-El was Superman's old man (like you did not know). Good try though.

2. Where did the Ark end up after the Flood?
   Mount Ararat.

3. What kind of wood was it made of?
   Gopher. But reinforced steel would have worked better. Ask the Queen Mary.

4. "Noah was a man righteous and whole-hearted" in Hebrew.
   Noach ees tzadeek tawmeem haw-yaw.
   You forgot "bodoro-sov" at the end. Oops.

Joey,

Mickey Witek got us some tickets to the Andrews Sisters show tonight at the Palladiam, though I cannot figure out why they would want to sing in a shit-hole such as Cincy. Since we do not have a game tomorrow, Mister Terry says we can stay out til 1:00 in the A.M. but I want you to be asleep when I get back. I will try not to wake you up.

They have 2 different places to eat in this hotel so take your pick. The one with the skelaton over it is called The Pirates Cove and their steak is the best in Cincy. Which is not saying much. There is also a news-stand downstairs in case you want a Detective Comic or something.

                         Charlie

Riverfront Hotel, Cincinnati.

Dear Hornet,
   This one has 88 squares on the ceiling and no fire escape. And I don't even *like* the Andrews Sisters.
                 The Shadow

P.S. I can play "String of Pearls" on Charlie's saxo-phone and he can't. Serves him right.

US POSTAGE

The Green Hornet
c/o Craig Nakamura
236 Montgomery Street
Brooklyn NY

<u>TOP SECRET</u>

166

Dear Goodlookin',

You and Joey made the front pages of the *Mirror,* the *Telegram* and the *Trib.* He's sliding into third, you're tagging him out, and Conlan's calling him safe. (The papers didn't say whose idea it was, but it has Stuke written all over it.) Go on, admit it—the real game wasn't nearly as much fun. You fraud. If Winchell ever found out what a softy you are, he'd run you out of town. By the way, when is somebody going to admit that you haven't lost a game since you put the kid in a uniform? Or is that one of those superstitions that girls aren't supposed to understand? I was listening to the third inning between shows and they said Derringer seemed a little rattled. Whose choice was that—his or Joey's?

Mayor LaGuardia took the First Lady to see *Panama Hattie* tonight and afterwards he invited the entire cast to the club. Including Merman. As usual, that braying jackass wouldn't shut up until somebody asked her to sing—which I could have lived with if she hadn't snapped her fingers at me in front of Mrs. Roosevelt and said, "Miss, can you bring me a Horse's Neck?" Anything you wish, dearie. They're not usually made with cayenne pepper, but they were tonight. One verse of "I Got Rhythm" and they had to call a broomstick for the old bag.

I'd tell you there's a crescent moon outside that reminds me of the first walk we ever took together, except that it's been raining for six hours and if this keeps up we may need a few pointers from your friend Noah.

So close your eyes and pretend I just kissed you. Because that's what I'm doing.

-H-

P.S. I decided that Ida Margolis needed a new summer dress—whoever sold her that green thing should have been shot. So we spent most of the afternoon on Fifth Avenue and had high tea at the Plaza. Did you know that her father was the mayor of a Russian village until the pogroms forced them out? And incidentally, Aunt Carrie is a dream. Anyone who says otherwise just doesn't know how to talk to her.

Dear Carrie:

I can't thank you enough for helping me pick out the broach. I have no courage at all when it comes to jewelry, and if I'd been by myself I probably would have chosen pearls again.

I hope you didn't mind my asking your advice on how to handle Charlie, but he speaks of you constantly. If I can only learn how to keep him in line the way you do, maybe you'll be helping me choose a wedding ring instead.

Fondly,
Hazel

Dear Charles,

Whatever you could be thinking, you should cut your tongue out for it. To leave a lovely girl like Hazel alone in a place like New York is a sin. And to let her work for a living even. So what's in Cincinnati that you haven't got here? A ball game? You listen to me. When you're ten years old and you want to play third base it's cute. At your age it's not so becoming.

I'm not going to bring it up again. You won't hear another word from me. But a young lady of quality doesn't come along very often. You think God doesn't have better things to do than wait on line until you're satisfied? 48 years I'm here and I can promise you one thing: if you lose her, let it be on your head.

The subject is closed.

Aunt Carrie

Dear Hazelnut,

This afternoon Charlie started singing "There's a Small Hotel" in the shower. We thought it was an air raid. Marry the guy already, would you?

Stuke

P.S. The streak is over. Guess I showed DiMaggio. He only had one of them. I had eight.

New York Giants

BATBOY: <u>Margolis</u> PARK: <u>Wrigley Field, Chicago</u>

— CHECK LIST —

ALL ITEMS MUST BE COMPLETED ONE HOUR PRIOR TO GAME TIME.

	SUN	MON	TUES	WED	THUR	FRI	SAT
22 Bats					√		
2 Boxes Bullpen Baseballs					√		
2 Boxes Dugout Baseballs					√		
10 Bullpen Towels					√		
30 Dugout Towels					√		
Bandages					√		
Antiseptic					√		
Water Cooler Filled					√		

NOTES:

1. How big was the Ark?
300 cubits by 50 cubits by 30 cubits.

2. How did God promise that he would never pull such stunts as drowning everybody again?
He gave us a rainbow. And every time we see one we're supposed to remember.

3. Dummy Hoy played center field for the Red Stockings in 1895. How come they called him Dummy? Was he deaf or was he stupid? (This one is a freebie.)
Neither. They called him Dummy because he had this little piece of string hanging out of his back and when you pulled on it his mouth would go up and down. I wasn't there. How would *I* know?

4. "And Noah begot three sons. Shem, Ham and Japheth." Your turn.
Vyo-led Noach sh'low-shaw vawneem. Es Shaym, es Chawm, v'es Yawfess.

170

Rabby Morris Lieberman
Temple Chizuk Amuno
1243 Parkside
Brooklyn NY

Dear Rabby,
    The kiddish cup should be in the big size for such things as beer and etc. Pay up.

Charlie

P.S. Is Solomon one of your guys or one of ours?

The Windy City Swings to Glenn Miller
—WITH—
DOROTHY WALKER
TEX BENEKE
THE MODERNAIRES
—AND—
The Glenn Miller Orchestra
THE PARADISE BALLROOM
1128 WABASH AVENUE, CHICAGO
8:00 P.M.

TONIGHT ONLY

Dear Toots,

We have a question that nobody knows how to answer, even Stuke. If Photoplay had to pick a picture of either Eleanor Roosevelt in a bathing suit or Betty Boop in one, who would it be? Betty Boop, right?

Tell him he's wrong. First of all Mrs. Roosevelt is married to the President so she's more famous. And second of all Betty Boop is a damned cartoon. She's not even real. And they don't put cartoons in Photoplay.

He keeps forgetting the most important part of it. Who in Hell wants to think about E. Roosevelt in a bathing suit leave alone see her in one?

Like Betty Boop is somebody you would want to kiss either. At least if you smooched Mrs. Roosevelt you wouldn't get ink all over your mouth. Hazel, guess what? We beat the Cubs today 5-2 and I got injured right in the middle—

He didn't get injured. It was the 8th inning at Wrigley with a tie score and the bases full of Cubbies. I had D. Marantz on mine who I use to room with in Springfield and for some reason he thinks this is suppose to make us buddies or something even though he must of forgotten that we hated each other. (He snoared and always pissed on the toilet seat.) Then B. Sturgeon came up for Chic. thinking he was going to play The Hero by parking a haymaker in the lake, though even the Cubs know he cannot cross the street without getting lost first. So what happened was—

I called him a weenie-head and he tried to kill me. Then I had brain surgery. They sawed off the top of my skull and—

He got hit in the ass by a foul ball. And it served him right on account of showing off for some little 12 yr. old tootsie in the stands instead of doing his job. Afterwards they took our team picture and they wanted him to sit in the front row on the ground, though he will probably not be sitting *any*where until at least Tuesday due to B. Sturgeon picking a bouncing curve to glim him with.

I even got to hold Charlie's sax in the picture. And by the way—last night I learned how to play "Moonlight Serenade" on it and Charlie still can't finish "In the Mood".

Two things. (1) Yes I can. And (2) If that was Moonlight Seranade how come the hotel called up and said they would throw us out if he ever played it again? You know what a fake he is. If you took even $1/4$ of anything he says serious—

Look who's talking. You know what *he* did? In Cincy he said that him and the team were going to eat spaghetti and see the Andrews Sisters but that I couldn't go—and just because I answered the Jor-El

question wrong. But when I went downstairs and got a paper to see if there was a Bogey movie I could sneak into, I found out from page 18 that the Andrews Sisters were in Detroit that night. He made it all up, even the spaghetti part. Him and Stuke were really in Mickey Witek's room listening to the radio and dropping things out the window on people, including guava jelly sandwiches. Smokes, what a phony.

But guess who knows his Tora inside and outside now? So ha ha. For a present, me and the team took him to see Glenn Miller tonight. Even Mister Terry went. They have a new song I like called "I've Got a Gal in" someplace I never heard of but—

"Kalama-zoo-zoo-zoo-zoo-zoo-zoo-zoo."

Stuke tried to buy a High Ball for Dorothy Walker who sang it, but by the time it got there he changed his mind and drank it himself by telling Mister Terry it was sasparilla. (D. Walker did not sing so hot anyway.) We would not let Joey have anything but ginger ail all night but somehow by 11:00 in the P.M. he was walking sideways and saying "excuse me" to such things as chairs and etc. So Stuke followed him around and found out that what he did was wait until people would get up from their table to dance and then snitch their glass before they even made it to the floor.

Old ladies were the best. They don't walk real fast, so you have more getaway time. And they all drink Slow Gin Fizzes.

So after he got good and soaked and danced the jitter bug with Dorothy Walker 3 times (which you should of seen, due to his head not even coming up to her you know whats), he had a long talk with Mister Terry saying that if Stuke gets drafted he should put Burge at 1st and move Witek to 2d and then bring Demaree in from Center. We were all waiting for Mister Terry to say "Who gave you permission to think?" like he always does, but instead he got some paper and wrote it all down. I don't get it. If I tried something like that, he would chop my head off.

Aunt Carrie called us three times today.

Yeah. One time to talk to Joey about such things as teeth and etc. and the other two times to tell me I should cut my tongue out due to God not waiting on line. How come she always says "You will not hear another word from me" 20 mins. before she stops talking?

Maybe if you listened to her instead of—

We can finish this when we come home. I just looked at the clock and saw what time it is. Say goodnight Joey.

Goodnight Joey.

We love you.

Charlie

P.S. I finally got him to sleep. That only took 3 hours. Tomorrow there is no ball game so I am taking him to Racine, which I have not been back to since I left. I don't even know why I'm doing it.

P.S.2. Between you and me, when I saw that foul ball heading for him it was only the 2nd time in my life that I almost pissed in my pants.

P.S.3. Maybe we *should* listen to her. Aunt Carrie, I mean.

P.S.4. I love you. (This time it's just from me.)

Dear Hazel,

Right now I'm hiding out in the baggage car on the Empire Limited coming back home from Chicago, even though Charlie asked me to play poker with him and Stuke and Mickey in the smoker so they could have one more chance to win their money back. But instead I told him I was sleepy from the 12 innings at Wrigley which is a lie. And the only reason I'm in between suitcases and foot lockers is so he won't catch me writing to you.

Yesterday we went to Racine and saw all of the places Charlie grew up in, like his house on Candleberry Wood (where I wanted to ring the bell and go inside but Charlie said no) and the field where Harlan taught him how to play (which has two-foot weeds now but we still threw a ball around until we lost it) and the ammo factory that used to be his school. I could tell he wasn't having a good time because while we were eating tuna fish at a hash house in Monroe, FDR came on the radio and Charlie didn't even call him a lunkhead. So I tried to piss him off on purpose by drawing a picture of Eleanor naked, but all he said was "Wipe the mayo off your face." Maybe he was practicing getting sad because after that he dropped me off at the library downtown so he could go visit Harlan at the cemetery. And that's when I started thinking. How come he sometimes says that Harlan was killed by a pitch and other times it's a foul ball? But the Bureau of Vital Statistics was downtown too, where Elsie McKeever still thinks my name is Joseph Margolis

Banks. And since she is a better stool pigeon than Ratsy and Mole and all the rest of those Cagney squeaks, I went there to see if I could get her to spill the beans again. This time it only took her a minute and a half to do it. When she came back upstairs from a secret room under a trap door, she was holding an envelope with two clippings in it from 1933 and all she kept saying was "You poor poor dear." Which didn't scare me yet because she's the kind of old lady who would say the same thing just because it was raining. But then I read them. And when her telephone rang and she turned around to answer it, I put them in my pocket and left. I don't ever want anybody to see them again except you. That's why I'm sending them.

Something is screwy. His baseball card says that his father was a Vice President. And read the part about Harlan. No wonder he gets sore so easy. Smokes, the worst thing that ever happened to *me* was that Delvecchi held me on the ground while Bierman cut my face with a Coke bottle. Big deal. It healed, didn't it?

How come Charlie always takes care of me but nobody ever takes care of Charlie? Boy, what a sap I am.

Love,
Joey

Dear Joey,

Don't ever let me hear you call yourself a sap again. I never would have been brave enough to do what you did. The rabbi thinks you won't be a man until October, but he's wrong. You've already made the team.

Charlie once told me that his father was a salesman, but when I asked him what he sold, all he said was "Things." I guess that should have tipped me off. And I always suspected there was more to the Harlan story than he was letting on. Now I know why. He probably thinks it was his fault.

Joey, this is something that stays between us. If he ever decides to tell us the truth, he will. But it's got to come from Charlie. By the way, who says he doesn't have anybody to take care of him? You and I aren't exactly chopped liver, you know. (I got that one from Aunt Carrie.) We just have to make sure that we stay on the job. And we will.

Love,
Hazel

Dear Charlie,

In the package is the picture of you and me and Conlan from Cincy. Mom and Aunt Carrie bought the frame.

Happy Birthday!

I'm still working on your *real* present, but it's going to take a little while.

Happy birthday from your buddy.

Joey

INTERVIEWER: Donald M. Weston, Ph.D.
SUBJECT: Joseph Charles Margolis

A: My Mom made him his favorite dinner—orange chicken and potato pancakes. He even remembered to call them latkes because Rabbi Lieberman was there.

Q: Was your mother wearing her new dress?

A: You bet. And Hazel got there early to do her hair. Now she looks like Greer Garson.

Q: How did Charlie like the shindy?

A: He got a big bang out of the cake. That was Aunt Carrie's idea. She made it with Hazel. There were 24 sparklers on it for his age, and the one for good luck was a Shabos candle. It was supposed to be a joke, but Rabbi Lieberman didn't know whether to laugh or have a hemorrhage.

Q: I can imagine.

A: Later on me and Charlie recited our Torah for him, but we did it the way Cab Calloway would, including the Hi-De-Ho's. Then Hazel put a record on the Victrola and sang "Embraceable You" right to Charlie. Smokes, even Aunt Carrie cried—and after that she took him into the kitchen so they could have a long talk.

Q: Know something? You told me a year ago that all of this was going to happen and I didn't believe you. I guess that makes me a dope, huh?

A: Yep. Only kidding.

Q: So what's your *real* present going to be?

A: I'm not telling.

IF MY FATHER WERE PRESIDENT
BY JOSEPH MARGOLIS

~~If my father were president, he would never let Hitler get away with~~
~~If my father were president, Yom Kippur would probably wind up being a national holiday because~~
~~If my father were president there wouldn't be any more~~
~~If my father were president~~

Mrs. Eleanor Roosevelt
The White House
Washington, D.C.

Dear Mrs. Roosevelt,

I hope you don't mind, but I had to make a couple of changes. Please tell Mrs. Hicks that it's okay.

Very truly yours,
Joey Margolis

Alexander Hamilton Junior High School

To: Herb Demarest, Principal
From: Janet Hicks
Re: Margolis Essay

Herb:

What am I supposed to do with this? As usual, he didn't follow instructions—not even Mrs. Roosevelt's. I certainly can't send it to the White House this way. Should I have him redo it properly?

Janet

Alexander Hamilton Junior High School

To: Janet Hicks
From: Herbert Demarest, Principal
Re: Margolis Essay

Janet:
Bear in mind the following:
1. When pushed to the wall, our allies consist of the Board of Education and, in a pinch, Supervisor Meylan.
2. The boy's personal arsenal includes the National League, the entire Democratic Party, and God only knows who else.

In other words, dear, he's got us by the balls.

Send it to Washington. Let *them* handle it. If we're lucky, maybe they'll draft him.

HD

Dear Charlie,

Rachel's mother is letting her wear toilet water now. It's supposed to be violet, but it smells a lot like the stuff that my Mom waxes the floor with. I noticed it during History class, and when Mrs. Hicks asked me who was the first Secretary of the Treasury, I couldn't remember. Smokes, even our *school* is named after him. But guess what? Rachel turned around and looked at me.

After that I followed her for most of the afternoon, and even though I tried to hide it I'm pretty sure she knew that I was sniffing her. So I wrote a letter to put in her lunch bag, but I'm not so sure it's going to work. Should I change it?

> Dear Rachel,
>
> In case you haven't noticed, I spent a lot of time this summer growing up. But even when I was on the road with the New York Giants or dancing with Dorothy Walker of the Glenn Miller Orchestra, I thought about you once or twice and how maybe I shouldn't have put the caterpillar in your tapioca or the toad on your raisin bread. But smokes. Until you smacked me in the mouth and told me to Go To Hell, I didn't even think you knew what my name was.
>
> Craig doesn't understand why I waste my time on you, but I tell him that it's like Louis Armstrong says about jazz. "Brother,

if you can't feel it, I can't explain it." I'm
not saying that we have to get married or
anything, or that you even have to let me
kiss you. But if I say Hi to you in the hall,
could you at least say Hi back?

Love,
Joey Margolis

Oh, yeah. One more thing. Last night I fell asleep thinking about the way she smells. Then I woke up at 3:30 in
the morning and everything was kind of sticky. Charlie,
if a guy falls in love *before* he can ejaculate, does it count?

Joey

Dear Joey,
    Which came first, the chicken or the road? Think
about it.
    Parts of the letter will do the job but other parts
are going to come back and bite you in the ass if your
not careful. So we better take a good look at it and figure out where to put the fix in.
    **"In case you haven't noticed, I spent a
    lot of time this summer growing up."**
First of all, no you didn't. And second of all, if you have
stopped putting vegetables in her hair such as broccolli
and etc., she already knows this.

> "But even when I was on the road with the
> New York Giants"

You bet. Let's see her find another 13 yr. old boy friend
who can say the same thing. Also tell her about making P. Cavaretta and B. Hassett strike out. I will back
you up on such things if you need me to.

> "or dancing with Dorothy Walker of the
> Glenn Miller Orchestra"

Be careful. Getting her jealous is OK but you do not
want her to think that you like girls who are 25 or
worse. Make sure she knows that you and D. Walker
were just friends and that nothing serious happened.

> "I thought about you once or twice and how
> maybe I shouldn't have put the caterpillar in
> your tapioca or the toad on your raisin bread."

You just jinxed the dirt again. You will only remind her
of things that she might of already forgot. Say something instead like "maybe I shouldn't of been a dumbbell like Tom Sawyer" (who we know she does not like
and it shows that you pay attention to the things she
says in class).

> "But smokes. Until you smacked me in the
> mouth and told me to Go To Hell, I didn't
> even think you knew what my name was."

Good. This will make her feel sad and sorry. I use it on
Hazel all the time (which you are never going to tell
her, right?).

> "Craig doesn't understand why I waste my
> time on you"

186

What kind of a cement head are you??? Do you really think she wants to know this???

"but I tell him that it's like Louis Armstrong says about jazz. Brother, if you can't feel it, I can't explain it."

This is my favorite part. But make sure it was L. Armstrong who said it because I think it might of been Satchmo.

"I'm not saying that we have to get married or anything, or that you even have to let me kiss you."

Nope. Now your rushing it. "I am not saying that you have to let me buy you an ice cream soda or anything." See?

"But if I say Hi to you in the hall, could you at least say Hi back?"

Keep it. This is another one that Hazel falls for. Especially if I stick my bottom lip out too. When they think we are going to cry they make us dinner and take their clothes off.

"Love, Joey Margolis"

Not yet you don't. You cannot give it all away like that. Maybe try something like the Rabby does. "Respect-fully, Joey Margolis". Come to think of it, that's even worse.

And whatever you do, don't tell her about the ejaculating part. That's a guy thing and they don't need to hear it.

Charlie

P.S. What's "toilet water"? She doesn't stick her head in the crapper, does she?

P.S.2. We lost 8 out of 10 on our last road trip of the season with our new bat-boy. How did you swing *that*? Mister Terry says he is ready to offer you a 5-yr. contract due to being our good luck charm but don't take it serious. Our previous good luck charms were a picture of Mel Ott's mother, some chop-sticks from Saint Louis, and a pair of Stuke's old sox that he did not wash for 9 weeks and that broke in half when he dropped one on the floor.

P.S.3. You do not know as many things as I thought you did. Maybe you should think about some more of the big questions and I'll see if I can answer them.

Mrs. Ida Margolis

and

Mrs. Carrie Gettinger

request the honour of your presence

at the Bar Mitzvah of their son and nephew

Joseph Charles Margolis

on Saturday, the 25th of October, 1941

at 10:00 a.m.

Temple Chizuk Amuno

1243 Parkside Avenue

Brooklyn, New York

RECEPTION TO FOLLOW

THE FAVOUR OF A REPLY IS REQUESTED

189

Dear Charlie,

There are only eight questions I never found out the answers to, and what if I have a son and he asks me some of them? So here they are.

1. How come dinosaurs croaked?
2. Are there people on places like Mars and Saturn?
3. Why won't God let us see Him?
4. Where do we go after we die?
5. How does a radio work?
6. If there really is a God, how come Jews in Europe have to wear yellow stars and Hitler can get away with starving Leningrad and the *Titanic* sunk?
7. Who was the best baseball player ever (and not Matty just because you like him)?
8. Could a cyclone really blow a house over a rainbow?

Joey

P.S. I just found out that my Cousin Sammy is coming here all the way from San Diego for my Bar Mitzvah. Gulp.

Dear Joey,

When you ask questions you do not fart around, do you? But I will try anyway.

1. I don't know.
2. I don't know.

3. God lets us see Him all the time. He looks like Hazel and Rachel and Harlan and babies and etc. You should of known that already.
4. I don't know.
5. A radio works by turning it on and Jack Benny comes out. Is this suppose to be a trick?
6. I don't know.
7. The best baseball player ever was Ty Cobb though nobody likes to say so because his sole was made out of dog shit on account of beating up cripples and linching Negroes and etc. But the other best ballplayer ever was Joe Jackson, who even though he should of known better than to pal up with crooks in 1919, still got a raw deal anyway. Nobody could swing a bat the way Shoeless Joe could. So tell your son it was Jackson.
8. I don't know.

Okay so maybe I do not have all of the answers. But at least you learned *some*thing.

Charlie

P.S. And what do you mean "Gulp"? Your not getting cold feet on me are you?

P.S.2. Stuke just got me 2 tickets to Game #4 of the W. Series which he will not go to because he's not in it. I wonder who I am going to take with me.

Dodgers Snatch Defeat
From Jaws of Victory

Game 4 Upset When
Mickey Owen Drops Strike 3

BROOKLYN, Sunday. Ask 33,813 shell-shocked Dodger fans and they'll tell you it could not have happened. But it did. And this is one for the books.

Struggling to even the World Series at two games apiece, it looked like the Brooklyn nine had it all sewn up by 4:35 this afternoon at Ebbets Field. Leading the Yanks 4–3 at the top of the ninth inning with two away and nobody on, Brooklyn hurler Hugh Casey let loose with a perfect breaking curve to Yankee right fielder Tommy Henrich, who swung on strike three—and whiffed. And that should have been the ball game. But the Brooks' usually topflight catcher Mickey Owen had other ideas when he missed the ball entirely—and by the time he'd retrieved it from the Dodger dugout, Henrich had made himself at home on first. But that was only the beginning. DiMaggio singled, then Keller and Gordon doubled, and when nightfall settled over Ebbets Field the Yanks were long gone—with a 7–4 victory in their hats.

New York Yankees

	ab	r	h	tb	2b	3b	hr	bb	so	sh	sb	po	a	e
Sturm, 1b	5	0	2	2	0	0	0	0	0	0	0	9	1	0
Rolfe, 3b	5	1	2	2	0	0	0	0	0	0	0	0	2	0
Henrich, rf	4	1	0	0	0	0	0	0	1	0	0	3	0	0
DiMaggio, cf	4	1	2	2	0	0	0	1	0	0	0	2	0	0
Keller, lf	5	1	4	6	2	0	0	0	0	0	0	1	0	0
Dickey, c	2	2	0	0	0	0	0	3	0	0	0	7	0	0
Gordon, 2b	5	1	2	3	1	0	0	0	0	0	0	2	3	0
Rizzuto, ss	4	0	0	0	0	0	0	1	0	0	0	2	3	0
Donald, p	2	0	0	0	0	0	0	0	1	0	0	0	1	0
Breuer, p	1	0	0	0	0	0	0	0	0	0	0	0	1	0
aSelkirk	1	0	0	0	0	0	0	0	0	0	0	0	0	0
Murphy, p	1	0	0	0	0	0	0	0	0	0	0	1	0	0
Total	39	7	12	15	3	0	0	5	2	0	0	27	11	0

aBatted for Breuer in eighth.

Brooklyn Dodgers

	ab	r	h	tb	2b	3b	hr	bb	so	sh	sb	po	a	e
Reese, ss	5	0	0	0	0	0	0	0	0	0	0	2	4	0
Walker, rf	5	1	2	3	1	0	0	0	0	0	0	5	0	0
Reiser, cf	5	1	2	5	0	0	1	0	1	0	0	1	0	0
Camilli, 1b	4	0	2	3	1	0	0	0	0	0	0	10	1	0
Riggs, 3b	3	0	0	0	0	0	0	1	1	0	0	0	2	0
Medwick, lf	2	0	0	0	0	0	0	0	0	0	0	1	0	0
Allen, p	0	0	0	0	0	0	0	0	0	0	0	0	0	0
Casey, p	2	0	1	1	0	0	0	0	1	0	0	0	3	0
Owen, c	2	1	0	0	0	0	0	2	0	0	0	2	1	1
Coscarat, 2b	3	1	0	0	0	0	0	1	2	0	0	4	2	0
Higbe, p	1	0	1	1	0	0	0	0	0	0	0	0	1	0
French, p	0	0	0	0	0	0	0	0	0	0	0	0	0	0
Wasdell, lf	3	0	1	2	1	0	0	0	0	0	0	2	0	0
Total	35	4	9	15	3	0	1	4	5	0	0	27	14	1

Score by Innings

New York Yankees	1	0	0		2	0	0		0	0	4—7
Brooklyn Dodgers	0	0	0		2	2	0		0	0	0—4

Runs batted in—Keller 3, Sturm 2, Wasdell 2, Reiser 2, Gordon 2.

Earned runs—Yankees 3, Dodgers 4.

Left on base—Yankees 11, Dodgers 8. Double play—Gordon, Rizzuto and Sturm. Struck out—by Donald 2, Higbe 1, Breuer 2, Casey 1, Murphy 1. Bases on balls—Off Higbe 2, Casey 2, Donald 3, Breuer 1, Allen 1. Pitching summary—Off Higbe 6 hits, 3 runs, in 3 2-3 innings; French 0 hits, 0 runs in 1-3; Allen 1 hit, 0 runs in 2-3; Casey 5 hits, 4 runs in 4 1-3; Donald 6 hits, 4 runs in 4 (none out in fifth); Breuer 3 hits, 0 runs in 3; Murphy 0 hits, 0 runs in 2. Hit batsman—By Allen (Henrich). Winning pitcher—Murphy. Losing pitcher—Casey. Umpires—Goetz (N.L.), plate; McGowan (A.L.), first base; Pinelli (N.L.), second base; Grieve (A.L.), third base. Time of game—2:54.

Dear Charlie,

He had it in his glove. I saw it. Then he let go because he's a bonehead. Henrich got to first base fair and square—it's not his fault that Owen doesn't have hands. Smokes, *every*body knows that. So don't get cheesed off at *me*.

Joey

Dear Joey,

Maybe you need to get your eyes checked. You said it yourself that M. Owen had the ball in his glove. I saw that too. What I also saw was T. Henrich do some other things at the same time. Like (1) stick his big ass in Owen's face so he could not see and (2) kick Owen's arm so he could not hold on to it. Some "fair and square". Why don't you ask your buddy in the W. House to get Henrich a job in the War Dept.? What a laugh. He would probably pop the Queen of England on the noodle and then try to take London home with him by saying she dropped it. Your crazy.

Charlie

Mr. Peter Reiser
Brooklyn Dodgers
Ebbets Field
Brooklyn, New York

Dear Peter:

What a shame! And after the lovely year you had too. Let this be on Mr. Durocher's head for the rest of his life. What kind of an idiot puts a boy like Mickey Owen behind the plate after he's been out half the night with who knows what kind of people? I listen to the radio. I know.

Try not to read the papers for a few days—they'll only give you *tsouris*. But 48 years I'm here and I can promise you one thing: you'll get over it. Besides, you batted .343 and Mickey Owen didn't.

Carrie Gettinger

Dear Sprout,

It's only October 20, but there's already 2 feet of snow on the ground in this part of Kansas. It'll probably take me until spring training just to find my car keys.

I don't know how this whole Bar Mitzvah deal works and whether presents are supposed to be about God or something, but I figured you could get alot more mileage out of Spaulding's *Illustrated Baseball,* even if Noah didn't take it on the Ark with him. So here it is. (I'm on p. 418.)

Go get 'em, kiddo.

Your buddy,

Stuke

P.S. Personally I wouldn't give you 2¢ for Henrich *or* Owen, so I'm the wrong guy to ask. But it sure sounds like Owen blew it, huh? (By the way, I said the same thing to Charlie about Henrich. I'm no dumbbell.)

Presents

Mom ....a gold mezuzeh for around my neck

Aunt Carrie ....my own talus and yarmulke

Dad's secretary..check for $50

Rose and Ben Goldstein...........subscription to *Natural Wonders*

Morris and Estelle Goldman ....Ties

Edith Snyder...Handkerchiefs

Phyllis and Kenny Ellis...Socks

Gloria Liebowitz ....subscription to *Natural Wonders*

Aunt Ett ....4 shirts

Aunt Sheba..underpants

Cousin Sally..*Porgy and Bess* records

Cousin Jane ....*The Speeches of Franklin D. Roosevelt*

Grandma Hilda...Typewriter

Cousin Flossie ....Peanut butter cookies

Craig ....G-Man Ring With Secret Heat Ray

Alan and Barbara Sapperstein......subscription to *Natural Wonders*

Cousin Sammy ....GLASSIES!

Dr. Weston ....Joseph Margolis stationery

Stuke...Spaulding's *Illustrated Baseball*

Hazel ....Saxophone lessons

Charlie ....*The Complete Torah* with our
names in gold on the cover

Flatbush Clockmaker
Arrested by G-Men

BROOKLYN, Thursday—The FBI today dropped the net on a Nazi fifth column movement that has been operating out of Brooklyn for eight months, it is believed. Greta Aubaugh, 67 and a member of the German-American Bund, has allegedly been running a "safe house" for enemy agents under the guise of an antique clock establishment on Sullivan Street. Federal agencies have had Aubaugh under surveillance since March, when her ties to the Nazi party first came to light as a result of her active participation in the Bund's

TOP SECRET

The Shadow
C/O Joey Margolis
4th Floor

Burn everything. And if anybody asks, we don't know nothin. Smokes, Hitler probably has our address by now.

TOP SECRET

The Green Hornet
C/O Craig Nakamura
3rd Floor

You and your big mouth. Why couldn't we have spied on somebody safe like Mr. Schnabel at the deli? The only law *he* ever broke was leaving fat on corn beef.

TOP SECRET

The Shadow
C/O Joey Margolis
4th Floor

Look who's talking. You're the one who said she blew up
Warsaw. How many seats are you using tomorrow?

TOP SECRET

The Green Hornet
C/O Craig Nakamura
3rd Floor

89. Unless Cousin Flossie tries to kill herself again,
then 88. How come?

TOP SECRET

The Shadow
C/O Joey Margolis
4th Floor

I'm all sold out here. I could use at least ten more. Tell
your relatives that I need to see an invitation. Otherwise
it's $1.50. We ought to make enough to get our faces
changed in case Mrs. Aubaugh breaks out of jail.

Good luck tomorrow, Joey-San.

Temple Chizuk Amuno

SABBATH SERVICE

Saturday, October 25, 1941

on the occasion of the Bar Mitzvah of
Joseph Charles Margolis

Shabos Prayer....................................Rabbi Lieberman

Kiddush ....Cantor Rosenfeld

The Opening of the Torah.......Joseph Charles Margolis

Blessing Before the Torah ....Rabbi Lieberman

Torah Reading ....Joseph Charles Margolis
    Genesis VI, v. 9   Charles Linden Banks

Blessing...Cantor Rosenfeld

Haftorah Vayyechi ....Joseph Charles Margolis
    I Kings II, v. 1

"Today I Am A Man"..............Joseph Charles Margolis

Bar Mitzvah Blessing.........................Rabbi Lieberman
                              Charles Linden Banks

Kaddish...Cantor Rosenfeld

Sabbath Hymn ....Rabbi Lieberman

Temple Chizuk Amuno
1243 Parkside Avenue • Brooklyn, New York

Dear Charlie:

First, please allow me to thank you for making Joseph's Bar Mitzvah the success that it was. Outside of the High Holy Days, we have never before had to turn people away at the door. One would think that tickets were being sold.

I would also like to convey my deepest gratitude for the diligence and patience you have displayed over the past five months. I cannot imagine that facing the Cincinnati Reds could be nearly as difficult as keeping up with a thirteen-year-old boy whose attention span at any given moment is no longer than nine seconds, and whose sense of mischief often borders on the unlawful. When he pretended to forget the name "Japheth", you aged measurably. But I trust you saw the tears in his eyes when you and I blessed him.

I am enclosing a silver Kiddush cup which I took the liberty of having engraved with your name. The next time we do this, I will not be foolish enough to place any sort of bet with you until I am guaranteed even money in return.

Warmest personal regards,
Rabby Morris Lieberman

P.S. I'm afraid I can't quite agree with your position. Even a blind man knows it was Mickey Owen's fault—and he didn't need help from Henrich or anyone else. You're too young to remember Fred Merkle's bone-headed play of 1908. I'm not.

TOP SECRET

The Shadow
C/O Joey Margolis
4th Floor

Good news and bad news. We took in $211 but your aunt caught me red-handed and made me give it all back. If Mrs. Aubaugh sends the Gestapo looking for us, let it be on your aunt's head.

The Green Hornet

P.S. She didn't find the $10 that I stashed in my other pocket just in case. Want to go halfsies on a genuine G-man commission book and badge?

Alexander Hamilton Junior High School

— SEMESTER REPORT —

STUDENT: Joseph Margolis   TEACHER: Janet Hicks

ENGLISH	A
ARITHMETIC	A
SOCIAL STUDIES	A
SCIENCE	A

Neatness	A
Punctuality	A
Participation	A
Obedience	N/A

Teacher's Comments:

Either Joseph has too much free time on his hands or he is deliberately attempting to undermine the entire infrastructure of world literature. Thanks to his debatable oratory, my entire class now regards Stephen Crane, Sir Walter Scott, William Shakespeare, Samuel Clemens, Jane Austen and the Brontë Sisters as Communists, racists, anti-Semites, and—worst of all—rock-heads. For no just cause he has developed a particularly toxic loathing for Emily Brontë, a self-possessed and taciturn woman whom he is convinced was covertly working for a foreign government. (I suppose it serves her right for keeping the umlaut.) Fortunately, I have at least managed to secure his approval of Nathaniel Hawthorne—but for all the wrong reasons. "How come Hester only got one 'A'?" is not a question I was trained to answer.

He and Rachel have finally begun speaking to one another, though their conversations so far have been restricted to the following: "Hi." "Hi." However, these exchanges can occur as frequently as four times an hour; in fact, I have watched Joseph deliberately walk down the same hallway twice, merely for an opportunity to run into her again. I expect them to graduate to full sentences shortly.

Joseph has a mind of his own—but he will need to learn that he cannot expect to amount to much unless he does what he is told.

Janet Hicks

FINAL	**The Brooklyn Eagle**	TWO CENTS

VOL. CXII....No.2,254   WEDNESDAY, NOVEMBER 12, 1941   Sunny, mid-40's

PEACE TALKS WITH JAPAN STALLED; U.S. PLACED ON WAR FOOTING

CHURCHILL PLEDGES "WILL JOIN WITHIN THE HOUR"

BROOKLYN BOY NAMED CONTEST WINNER BY MRS. R

WASHINGTON, Wednesday. Joseph Margolis, 13, of 236 Montgomery Street in Flatbush, is one of ten winners named by Eleanor Roosevelt in an annual essay contest sponsored by her Committee on Child Education. Titled "If My Father Were President", this year's entries were submitted by over 5,000 students from schools across the United States. Winners and their fathers will be honored with specially struck medallions to be presented by the President and First Lady in a ceremony at the White House shortly after Thanksgiving.

In a curious twist, the youngster departed from the announced theme and invented a title of his own. However, it was the opinion of both Mrs. R and the judges that the boy's essay best captured the spirit of

Continued on Page Six

204

A: We found out about it at school. Right in the middle of equations.

Q: What did you do when they told you?

A: I threw up.

Q: You must have been pretty excited.

A: I guess so. Rachel didn't stop looking at me all day. One time she even smiled.

Q: Have you told Charlie yet?

A: Craig says she'll be a pushover now. I hope so, because I'm running out of different ways to say Hi and—

Q: Joey? Have you told Charlie yet?

A: No, but he came over for dinner last night and then he took me to see *The Maltese Falcon.* When we got back, he asked Aunt Carrie how come there were eight candles on the Hanukkah menorah. So she told him about the Maccabees and the lamp that burned for eight days, but he said he had a flashlight at home that wouldn't burn for eight *minutes* unless—

Q: Why haven't you told him?

A: 'Cause he's gunna get cheesed off at me again. Smokes, *you* know how much he hates Roosevelt.

Q: So what? Charlie's not the one who's going to the White House with you.

A: Oh, yes he is.

Q: What about your father?

A: There's something I forgot to tell everybody.

IF CHARLIE BANKS WERE PRESIDENT

BY JOSEPH MARGOLIS

I know this is supposed to be about fathers, but mine hasn't called me since my birthday and that one was from his secretary Molly. So even if he did get elected president, I'd probably have to read about it in the papers just like everybody else. But you know what? It's okay. And I can tell you why.

1.   When I was getting beaten up by bullies just because I was Jewish (which, as you know, is the same thing the Hitler Boys are doing in Europe), Charlie Banks was the one who came to Brooklyn and made them stop.

2.   When I almost couldn't have a Bar Mitzvah because my father wouldn't come, Charlie Banks was the one who learned the Torah with me, even though he is a Protestant and would not know Hebrew from a barn wall or a hole in the ground or Adam or etc.

3.   When my Mom didn't have enough money to send me to a summer camp that wasn't restricted to Christians, Charlie Banks was the one who made me a bat boy for the New York Giants and took me on the road with him.

4.   Whenever I do something I shouldn't do, like fib or not study or talk like a Big-Mouth, Charlie Banks is the one who tells me to knock it off.

And in case you think I am making any of this up just because he's famous, I have witnesses. If you want, you can ask my principal (Mr. Demarest) or my mother (Mrs. Margolis) or Hazel MacKay the singer (who is also famous). That's why I think

I should be allowed to get Charlie into the White House instead of my father. After all, the Constitution says that everybody has the same rights—including me and Charlie. And that's the law.

If Charlie Banks were president, the Nazis would have been gone a long time ago. Not from getting popped in the mouth (even though Charlie could do that too), but from going to Germany himself with police and the Army and throwing Hitler and Goebbels and Goring in jail until: (1) all of the Jews got to take off their yellow stars and (2) the lights went back on in London so Edward R. Murrow could come home and get a job. Then Charlie would find an old man with a white beard like von Hindenburg to run Germany the right way while Hitler cleaned toilets and made license plates.

If Charlie Banks were president, he wouldn't have time for biscuitheads like Father Coughlin or Representative Rankin who think that just because the Declaration of Independence was written by white guys like Jefferson and Button Gwinnett, nobody else should get in on the deal too. Instead, he would go in front of Congress to make a new law and if any of them gave him a hard time about Negroes or Orientals or whoever, he would point his finger and say, "You and you and you. Get out." Then when they were gone he would tell the rest of them, "Now let's have a bill."

If Charlie Banks were president, kids wouldn't get beaten up any more because all they would have to do was mail a letter to the White House and Charlie would send Cordell Hull or Frank Knox or Henry Stimson to wherever the boy lived so they could say to the bullies, "Hey. You'd better cut it out unless you want the president to come here himself." And they would stop because they'd know that Charlie would do it.

If Charlie Banks were president, Mrs. Roosevelt would never have to go into the coal mines again because Charlie would just shut them all down until they were safe.

And if Charlie Banks were president, kids without fathers would know that they still had somebody to take them to places like Steeplechase and Luna Park, and to yell at them whenever they had it coming.

That's why I would vote for President Banks.

Dear Charlie,

It was the birthday present I told you I was still working on. I guess I forgot about it. Besides, how did *I* know I was going to win?

Anyway, at least I didn't tell them about when we put the jelly in Carl Hubbell's shoes in Cincy or you asking the Rabbi what cigar box he came off of, or me winning $32 from you in stud poker. So it could have been worse.

Joey

P.S. We can take the Morning Congressional from Penn Station and stay at the Mayflower. It's close to the Washington Monument in case we go there.

Dear Joey,

What kind of a birthday present is *that?* I get to meet Oatmeal-Mouth. Oh boy. How would you like it if I made you eat dinner with Hoover?

Before I even think about saying yes (which I am warning you don't hold your breath) there are some things we will need to get square.

First of all, I do not even want to hear one word about Eleanor in a bathing suit or being naked or her bosoms while we are in the W. House. The way she runs around all over the place, she could be standing right behind us. And the next thing you know we will both be getting shot at sunrise.

Second of all, if we get introduced to her husband and he asks me such questions as "Did you vote for me?" or "What do you think of my New Deal?" or etc., you better step on my foot. Because unless there is something else for me to pay attention to (such as pain) I will tell him.

Third of all, your allowed to read your essay and say thank you. That's all. When they give us our medals or whatever in Hell they are, shake their hand and sit down. I will handle the rest myself. And if you get cornered by such people as Mrs. R or the Vice-President or whoever else they keep there, pretend you are Charlie Banks 3d Base and only say back to them such things as I would say myself. You should try to be more like me anyway.

Last of all, the elevator guy in my building (name of Pete) says he also saw Henrich stick his big ass in Owen's face. So I'm not the only one.

Charlie

P.S. If you do not mind, *I'll* decide what train we will go on and where we will stay and etc. And the only way I'll take you to the Washington Monument is if you promise to jump off. But don't worry. I will probably be right behind you.

P.S.2. I wouldn't of had to toss Hitler's ass in jail, on account of already pulling off his arms and legs and throwing the rest of him into yesterday's garbage. But you were right on the money about everything else. Even though I only read it once.

P.S.3. Except for the FDR part, thanks.

Dear Joey,

This morning I caught him standing in front of the mirror and saying, "You and you and you. Get out." He's a bigger fake than either one of us.

I heard somewhere that Mrs. R has always slept on satin sheets, even during the Depression. Of course I never pay attention to that kind of Republican gossip—but as long as you're going to be there anyway, see if you can find out.

Love,
Hazel

P.S. Charlie says he's going to tell the President to stick the Atlantic Charter up his ass. Make sure he doesn't.

— WESTERN UNION —

JOEY MARGOLIS
236 MONTGOMERY STREET
BROOKLYN, NY

DEAR SPROUT STOP YOU MADE THE KANSAS CITY PAPERS STOP GOOD JOB KIDDO STOP TRY TO KEEP CHARLIE AWAY FROM FDR STOP THIS COUNTRY'S IN ENOUGH OF A JAM ALREADY STOP YOUR PAL STUKE

Dear Charles,

Better you than his father. Better famine and pestilence too.

Make sure he eats everything Mrs. Roosevelt puts in front of him. From what I hear, the things that go on when that woman gets near a kitchen shouldn't happen to a dog. But he's young, he'll survive. He should only start an international incident yet.

He's been up since 4:30 this morning. Even God isn't awake that early. Don't let him get overheated on the train—it's cold, he could catch his death. And don't lose your muffler again. So you hit 43 home runs—you see how impressed I am? You can get sick too, just like the rest of us.

Not that the President should ask, but let him know that I voted for Willkie. And if he thinks I should be struck down for saying so, tell him I haven't been yet.

Aunt Carrie

Dear Aunt Carrie and Mrs. M,

We have not even gotten to Philly and he is out like a light. I think he wore himself out from telling everybody on the train that we are going to meet the President. Some of them even believed him.

Hazel did some nosing around and found out that there are 19 million kids in the U.S. of A. Only 10 of them are going to the W. House today. You can do the math yourself on account of I would not get near long division with a 10 ft. pole. But if you tell people that he is one in a million, you will be pretty close to the mark.

Once in a while I give him a hard time just because it is my job. But nobody ever thought I could run a country before. Half of the time I can't even dial a telephone.

Charlie

P.S. Thanks for the pointy coconut things. Everybody on the train says thanks too.

P.S.2. He already knows what he is not allowed to say to Mrs. R and Noodlehead. And I will make sure he eats everything that is on his plate. So don't worry.

Dear Hazel,

Whatever Charlie tells you, it isn't true. This is the way it really happened.

They started everything off with a little party for the winners, but with punch and cookies instead of Slow Gin Fizzes. And the first thing FDR did was roll up in his wheelchair to Charlie and say, "I could certainly use you in Europe, young man. I listened to that game in Pittsburgh. The way you clobbered that thing, I thought it would never come down." But Charlie didn't call him a Muffin Head or a Biscuit Mouth or anything like it. Some tough guy. Instead, he right away thanked him for inventing the Civilian Conservation Corps and getting us out of the Depression and beating Landon in '36 and telling Hitler to piss off. Smokes, what a marshmallow. Even when FDR said it was Mickey Owen's fault.

Then Mrs. R showed up and Charlie didn't know what to say to her. Probably because he was shaking so bad that he spilled juice all over his shoes. But he tried to talk to her anyway and wound up telling her that he liked what she did with the White House because it was a good color for the place. Since that was all he could come up with, I whispered that he should thank her for the 21st amendment but he kicked me so hard he almost broke my leg. The only reason he didn't get us into any more hot water was because that's when we went into the East Room to read our essays and get our medals and have our pictures taken by the newspaper guys. Then we ate lunch and left.

And that's the truth. So help me God.

Joey

P.S. If Charlie says anything else happened too, remember that he told me I should be more like him. So it was his idea.

P.S.2. I tried to get upstairs to find out about satin sheets in Mrs. R's bedroon, but they caught me on the second floor. Maybe it's a state secret or something. But in case you need to know, they wipe themselves with blue toilet paper.

P.S.3. And guess what? There was one more surprise we didn't know about. Mrs. Roosevelt named Charlie "Father of the Year". How's that for a pisser?

Dear Toots,

They made me Father of the Year. How's that for a pisser? If they only knew what I was planning to do to this kid they would of given it to Hitler instead.

You want a list? Try this.

1. We were not even in the door yet before we almost got run over by FDR (who by the way is not half bad once you get to know him). At first Joey kept his mouth shut like I told him to, but then Roosevelt asked him if he ever thought about running for President himself (which is maybe the worst idea I ever heard in my life) and Joey said back, "Why not? If a muttonmouth like Washington could get elected I guess anybody could." Then he looked over at me like saying it was *my* idea. It is a good thing that FDR thought he was kidding or else I would be writing this from Sing Sing. He said "This is a young man who says what is on his mind." No shit. You want to keep him?

2. Mrs. R was next. She thanked us for coming and then waited for me to say something back. Well what in Hell was I suppose to talk to her about? Jock itch?

216

In the meantime, Joey was whispering all of these clues about amendments and etc. which only made me look worse, and then he got sore because I kicked him in the shin. What I was trying to do was cripple him for life. So he jumped in and asked her if she wanted to go to Lincoln's Memorial with us like she did not already have Poland and Austria to worry about.

3. Then she took us into the East Room (which is big enough for her to play ice hockey in if she ever gets bored) where they had a stage and chairs and etc. for us to go on while the kids read their essays. Joey was the last one on account of his was the best, and when he was finished they all clapped and she gave us our medals. But instead of shaking her hand or crying or etc. like the other 9 kids did, he instead winked at her and said "Thanks Toots." I thought I was going to shit on the floor. Even worse was the 200 chowderheads with newsreel cameras and lights, on account of every one of them got it on film. But instead of sending us to the Electric Chair, all she did was wink back at him and wiggle her ass a little like she was either doing a hoochy koochy or else she just broke her hip. (With her it is hard to tell.) They ate it up. Everybody always said that Mrs. R was a good sport from such things as digging oil wells and riding tractors and maybe they are right. We're still alive, aren't we? Then she threw me a ringer by giving me Father of the Year. I guess she figured out by then that Joey's big mouth happened way before I met him.

4. After that they gave us lunch in a dining room that had 3 gold forks at every plate. Joey got stuck next to Henry Stimson which was a mistake, especially when they got into a fight about Europe. Remember that night at the club when we were talking about a safe place for people in France to go to until all of this blows over, and Joey said Switzerland on account of being neutral and I said what Switzerland needed to get was a pair of balls? Well now Henry Stimson knows it too. Then later on a band played music and Joey did a rumba with Eleanor. But I can't even talk about that.

This was the longest fuckin day of my life.

Charlie

P.S. He wants me to take him to the place where Lincoln got shot, even though he is asking for trouble since it will only give me ideas. So if you hear a loud bang tomorrow, it will probably be me.

WAR EXTRA!

The Brooklyn Eagle

TWO CENTS

VOL. CXII....No.2,286   SUNDAY, DECEMBER 7, 1941   Bitter, 20's

JAPANESE ATTACK PEARL HARBOR BY AIR; U.S. PACIFIC FLEET REPORTED SUNK; HEAVY LOSS OF AMERICAN LIFE FEARED

THE WHITE HOUSE

Dear Joey:

Thank you for your most recent letter. Although I am unable to "sneak you into the Army" per your request, there are plenty of important jobs here at home that will require someone with your persistence—such as selling war bonds, collecting scrap metal, and perhaps donating some of your time to the USO and other service organizations. Naturally, praying would be helpful, too. And try not to worry more than the President. Though we were unprepared for the attack on Hawaii, we are quite ready for war.

It was a pleasure meeting you after all this time. However, before your next visit, you and I will have to discuss the concept of protocol. Among other things, it is not appropriate to ask the First Lady to dance. I'm aware that I don't have much of a leg to stand on, given the fact that she accepted your invitation (twice)—so perhaps you'll just have to trust me on that score.

Congratulations to you and Charlie. You both deserve it.

> Cordially as always,
> Stephen T. Early
> Press Secretary

DEAR JOEY,

Me and Hazel got an early Christmas present. Stuke. When we opened the door he even had a ribbon around his neck.

Anyway we sat up all last night and talked about what they did to us at P. Harbor and I guess you can tell what is coming next. If you do not see us playing with the NY Giants for a while it is on account of we will be wearing a whole different type of uniform instead. Those son of a bitches started this thing

Eight days and eight nights did the lights burn for Judah Maccabee.

Wishing you the same joy.

Happy Hanukkah.

and now it is up to us to finish it. But before we do, I am going to need you to grow up a little faster than we thought because your the one who will be taking care of your Mom and Aunt Carrie and Hazel until we get back. Is this OK with you? Because I won't go unless it is. Even though I really want to.

Happy 1942. We had a good year, huh?

Charlie

P.S. We figured out that it should be the Marines. They know how to kick ass better than anybody. McArthur doesn't even know how to order lunch. And screw the Navy. Who ever heard of winning a war in white pants???

P.S.2. And I still do not see how one damn light could burn for 8 days. Tell Aunt Carrie that somebody is pulling her leg.

DEAR CHARLIE,

I got a letter from Steve Early at the White House and he thinks that you should stay right here because there are lots of more important ways you can win the war than just fighting. Like what if instead of enlisting you signed baseballs to sell War Bonds? I'll bet you could make at least a million dollars. Or you could go around the country to all of the boot camps and play exhibition games with the guys who are training there. It would get them in a really good mood before they shipped out.

*Wishing you all the happiness
that only Christmas brings.*

Anyway, I think Steve Early is right. So can you at least think about it? Roosevelt likes you. If you say you don't want to go, he won't make you do it.

Joey

P.S. Smokes, what if I get somebody pregnant or start drinking whisky or smoking cigars while you're gone? I can get in a lot of trouble if I'm by myself, you know.

P.S.2. 1941 was the best year of my life. 1942 stinks already.

P.S.3. If I can figure out a way to get in the Marines, can I go with you? Remember they have bugle boys, and I already know how to play your sax. I promise that I wouldn't get in the way and I'd do everything you told me. I'd even blame Henrich. Please?

Dear Charles,

So all of a sudden you're Sergeant York? It's not enough you play baseball, now this. What's next—cowboys yet?

Guns are dangerous. What do you know about loading one? I read the papers. How many accidents do you think are caused by people who don't know from *bupkis?* All of them. And the Marines yet. Watch them send you to the Philippines. I've heard what passes for food there. You want diarrhea until you're 95? Already you're too thin.

You won't hear another word from me. The subject is closed. Don't worry about Joey and Hazel, we'll keep them busy until you get back. But 48 years I'm here and this I can promise: if anything should happen to you over there, you won't hear the end of it.

Aunt Carrie

⚾ 1942

Alexander Hamilton Junior High School

To: Charles Banks

From: Herbert Demarest, Principal

Re: Joseph Margolis

Dear Charles:

I write at this time to express my deep concern for Joseph's well being. I have been a school principal for 25 years and I have never seen a student in such terrible shape. He has lost at least 10 lbs. in the last two weeks, he does not speak very often any more, and he is failing all of his subjects. Also, his mother tells me that he stays locked in his room with the lights off most of the time, except when he is out late with his new friends The Scavengers, a group of 17 year old boys who carry knives and pistols. He probably won't even get into college now. What a pity. Such a promising lad too. I would be surprised if he lived to see 16.

Charles, after you finish boot camp in South Carolina, maybe you can ask the USMC to transfer you to their Headquarters in New York. That way you can serve your country and keep your eye on the boy at the same time. Lord knows somebody better. I fear for him, Charles.

Sincerely,
Herbert Demarest
Principal

Parris Island, SC
Jan. 6, 1942

Dear Joey,

"He does not speak very often anymore"???? What a laugh. Bucko you would still be talking if you were knocked out cold and in a comma.

Couple of hints for next time. (1) Your principle calls me Mr. Banks not Charles. (2) He never signs his whole name but his initials, HD. (3) If he has been a principle for 25 years, then I am May West. (4) Now give him back his stationary and cut it out. What do I look—stupid to you?

We only got to Parris Island 4 days ago and I already have been gigged twice. Once for scratching under my arm pit without getting permission and the other time for saying "No" when some picklehead who says he is a drill sargent asked me "Aren't you a piece of shit Private?" Was I suppose to tell him yes??? He can kiss my ass first. Then they lined us up so they could yell at us some more and Stuke asked if he could go to the crapper but they wouldn't let him. And then they wondered where the fart came from.

I read your changes on the contract a couple of times on the bus and I am only letting you keep 2 of them in. So don't get any funny ideas about forgetting to sign it or saying that a dog pead on it or etc. I will be back for 10 days between boot camp and when they ship us to Pendleton in Calif. We can do alot of things in 10 days such as the Radio City and dinner

and ice skating and everything else we can think of—
but only if I have your John Hancock. Otherwise you
can forget it. Come to think of it, I even heard about
G. Cooper in "Pride of the Yankees" playing by then.
Stuke is all ready to go with me in case you can't.
(They have a word for this and it is called "blackmale".
If that pisses you off, tell it to the Marines.)

Pvt. Charlie

P.S. TO CONTRACT
FROM DEC. 1940

Mine

11. You will remember that we lost over 2000 boys at P. Harbor, some of them not much older than you. If you think that going on a road trip with me is more important than that, you are a chowderhead. And if I sometimes think "I wish I was with Joey at Coney Island instead of here" (which happened to me twice today), then I am one too.

12. You will write to me at least one time a week even if your sore at me or if you do not have anything to say (fat chance). I will do the same thing. You will also keep a glim on the NY Giants and tell me what place they are in and what kind of a knucklehead they got to play 1b and 3b without me and Stuke on the team.

13. You will remember that you are my buddy and even a World War can't change that. When all of this is over we will be back at the Polo Grounds and Saint Louis and saying such things as "They cannot bean Carl Hubbell on account of his halo gets in the way" and etc. just like before.

14. On Oct. 25 me and the Rabby said a Blessing to you and turned you into a man. I am going to hold you to that. Your not allowed to act like

a kid anymore except once in a while since your still only 13. The fake letter from your principle used up your ration through Feb.

15.   You will remember that in a few more months I may be on some island with K's and J's and W's in it such as Kwajalein, which we just heard of and thought it was somebody pulling our leg on account of it sounds like what they give you when you have clap. And suppose I am in a fox hole some night and I maybe get a little scared (which they told us happens to everybody no matter how big their balls are)? Who do you think I will tell? Not Hazel, on account of girls like to hear such things as "Dear Toots, The weather is good and so is their food and I just washed my own sox" and etc. even though I may be pulling a hand grenade out of my ass while I am writing it—and not Stuke who will probably be right next to me in the same fox hole and pissing in his pants too. So your the one who is elected. "Dear Joey, It is 4:00 in the A.M. and we can hear them a mile off, but instead of getting the shakes I was just thinking about that night in Chic. when you got soused and danced a jitter bug with D. Walker." I need to know I can count on you for this.

15. ~~If I can figure out a way to get smuggled onto a troop transport and I wind up on Guam or someplace else with you, you won't get sore at me.~~

16. **If I get into trouble, you'll come back.**

    Okay, but this has rules in it:

    If your sick, your Mom and Aunt Carrie will take care of you the same way they always do.

    If you are having girl problems with Rachel or etc., Hazel will handle it. I already have cleared this with her and she is ready.

    If you get hurt, I will find a way to be there myself.

17. ~~You can't call Roosevelt any more names until the war is over.~~

18. **If you get wounded or anything, you'll come home for good and tell the Marine Corps to kiss your ass.**

    I will even let you tell them for me.

—————————————   —————————————

Charlie Banks   *Joey Margolis*

P.S. But I don't have to like any of this, Charlie.

    Neither do I Bucko.

TOP SECRET

The Shadow
C/O Joey Margolis
4th Floor

You're not really going to sign it, are you?

TOP SECRET

The Green Hornet
C/O Craig Nakamura
3rd Floor

He's got me cornered. I don't think I can fight this one. Why the hell did he have to bring up Kwajalein?

TOP SECRET

The Shadow
C/O Joey Margolis
4th Floor

Because he finally got smarter than you. I <u>knew</u> this would happen. You gave away too many secrets, Shadow.

Here's my Gangbusters anti–spy gun. Guard it with your life. Especially if they smuggle a new leg to Mrs. Aubaugh and she blasts her way out of the clink with it.

TOP SECRET

The Green Hornet
C/O Craig Nakamura
3rd Floor

Maybe you don't have to leave. What if your mom and pop go to California without you, and you move in with us? We can fit your bed in my room easy and then we'll have our own headquarters. What do you say, Craigy?

TOP SECRET

The Shadow
C/O Joey Margolis
4th Floor

No dice, Joey-San. Pop says the window was one thing. My nose is a whole other deal.

TOP SECRET

The Green Hornet
C/O Craig Nakamura
3rd Floor

Where's Santa Monica?

TOP SECRET

The Shadow
C/O Joey Margolis
4th Floor

On the left of Los Angeles. My aunt and uncle have a hotel there. And there's even a garden in the back so Pop can grow his tomatoes.

TOP SECRET

The Green Hornet
C/O Craig Nakamura
3rd Floor

Are you coming back?

TOP SECRET

The Shadow
C/O Joey Margolis
4th Floor

I don't think so. But so what? They'll never be able to split us up, right?

UNITED STATES MARINE CORPS
Semper Fidelis

RECRUITING OFFICE   3156 EMPIRE BOULEVARD
BROOKLYN, NEW YORK

Mr. Joseph Margolis
236 Montgomery Street
Brooklyn, New York

Dear Mr. Margolis:

We are unable to process your enlistment application
for the following reasons:

1. You do not meet our height requirements;
2. You do not meet our weight requirements;
3. We do not accept library cards as proof of age—
   especially when they have been altered.

Check with us again in five years, son.

Very truly yours,
Capt. Hank Brunner
United States Marine Corps

Dear Charlie,

Craig is gone. People kept throwing bricks through their window and painting "Dirty Japs" on the fruit store, and then some kids from Crown Heights who we don't even know ganged up on him and broke his nose and his collarbone. So they went to California to live with his uncle. Five things I hate more than anything else in the world:

> Hirohito
> Brooklyn
> Pearl Harbor
> Hitler
> Emily Brontë

And by the way, you're a pretty chintzy sport too. You and your damned contracts. I checked the Business and Professions Code and it says "No written agreement shall be considered valid or binding if either party has been forced to affix a signature under duress." "Duress" means Gary Cooper and Radio City and etc. So here it is anyway. Signed, sealed and delivered. I'll see you in Court.

Joey

P.S. My Mom says I can go and visit Craig in Santa Monica when I'm 15. That's over a year. Smokes, what if he finds a new best friend by then?

Dear Joey,

Craig will find other regular buddies and that is the way it is suppose to be. But a best friend can only happen one time in his life and your it. So don't worry. You are safe on that score.

Bucko I really need your help with something important. All around the base guys are getting married right and left to everything from school sweeties such as Millie and Poopy and Dolly and Pissy or whoever the Hell, to dance hall girlies they just met yesterday and do not even know their name yet. That is why I have been thinking about Hazel and how she could of been Mrs. Charlie Banks 3d Base by now, but she isn't. I guess it serves me good and damn right. I knew which side my bed was made on and now I have to lie in it. But it is too late to ask her anymore. What if she says yes just because I might get shot at and she thinks that saying no will make me sad while I am ducking? So I need you to help her come up with the idea on her own on account of nobody in the whole world does that better than you do. But watch your step. She is alot smarter than either one of us and she can smell a con cooking all the way to S. Carolina. Think of it like a mission. And do not take any prisoners.

Today they showed us how to pull a rifle apart and put it back together again, like this is something we are going to get in the habit of doing in the middle of an air raid. They also cut all of our hair off and stuck a flashlight up my ass and made us run most of the way to N. Carolina only so we could turn around and run right back. Then we had lunch. The tray they gave us had three compartments in it. In the middle was green stuff and on the top left was white stuff and on the top right was brown and yellow stuff. During the usual grabass, Stuke threw up on the tray and nobody could tell which was the food and which was the vomit.

Stuke and Shiloh are teaching me how to talk Marine, which is an important thing to learn on account of some muck-a-muck (who I didn't know was a sargent) telling me "The old man wants a muster" and me saying back "So?" on account of not knowing what the hell he was talking about and getting to wash toilets for 4 days while I figured it out. So far I have learned that an Asshole is anybody in the Air Corps (this is one that I made up myself due to Wendell Bodie, who I will tell you about if he does not wind up being my first kill) and that "Semper Fi Mac" either means "Fuck you, I'm all right" or "Tough shit and handle it yourself" or "Hell no!" or "Glad to see you buddy" or "Hang in there on account of help is coming." I think it also means "Heil Hitler", but so far this is just scuttlebutt and has not been confirmed yet.

Now how am I suppose to remember all of these things and aim a gun at the same time?

Charlie

P.S. I just got a box of pointy coconut things in the mail. Are they going to follow me to the S. Pacific too?

P.S.2. Guess who turned up in our outfit? D. Marantz from Springfield and the Chic. Cubs. And he still pisses on the toilet seat.

P.S.3. Shiloh's name is not really Shiloh, it's Garth Puckett and he's from the Shiloh part of Tenesee. We figured we would give him a new moniker so the other guys wouldn't keep calling out such things to him as "Oh Garth. Federal men comin up the hill. Better hide the possum gizzards and git the moonshine out of the still" and etc. He swears he is 17 but he will probably not start shaving until 2 yrs. after you do.

P.S.4. Did you hear what Jello-Head in the W. House just said? "I think it would be best for the country to keep baseball going throughout the war." *Now* he tells me.

P.S.5. And who in Hell is Emily Brontë? Some new cutie who is giving Rachel a run for her money? Tell her if she took the damn dots off her e, maybe you would like her better.

Dear Charlie,

Emily Brontë wrote *Withering Heights* or maybe it was her sister. They were both working for the Gestapo anyway, so what's the difference?

Want to hear some top secret war news? The Marine Corps can go to Hell. When they wouldn't let me join I told them I wasn't leaving until they changed their minds, so Capt. Brunner made me an honorary private first class—which means that I get to bring him coffee and say "Next" to the guys who are waiting in line for physicals. Who does he think he's kidding? That was the same kind of job they gave to Mammy in *Gone With the Wind* and she sure as Hell was no Pfc. What a pudding-mouth. And if he calls me "son" one more time, I'm gunna knock his block off. But I think I found out some things you need to know, so pay attention.

Marine	*English*
Playing possum hockey	shooting the breeze (the bullshit kind)
The day the eagle shits	payday
Shower of shit	the bombs at Pearl and others like them
Wakey-wakey call	reveille

Nervous in the service?	You're supposed to answer with "Well, I sure ain't crackin' up from shackin' up" but nobody knows how come. What a bunch of dopes.
Jam it, cram it, and ram it	This already sounds like something you would say.
Dugout Doug	MacArthur, from still sitting on his butt.
Snerp	Any "ass hole" who gets made Father of the Year by Mrs. Roosevelt and then skips out on everybody just so he can go shoot people he doesn't even know.

They also say snafu, tarfu and fubar, but Capt. Brunner won't tell me what they mean. Maybe it's classified. Or maybe he's just a chowdermouth like you.

Pfc. Joey
USMC

P.S. I already went to work on Hazel, so don't worry. First I sent her a rose with your name on it, then I showed her pictures of Cousin Jane's wedding, and

240

then last night at the club I asked her to sing "Dat Man of Mine." I think it really got to her.

P.S.2. Guess who just learned how to play "Elmer's Tune" on the sax? I'll give you a hint. It wasn't you.

P.S.3. By the way. I outrank you. So when I tell you to toe the line, you do it.

Dear Joey,

When you tell me to toe the line, you better be 2 miles in front of me and moving.

We just got issued our 782 gear which we thought was going to be more pants that do not fit. (Mine are so short that you could paint targets on my calfs and Stuke's are so big that he could have four dicks in them and nobody would notice.) Instead it turned out to be our combat hardware. We got 1903 bolt-action Springfields and real bullets and K-Bar knives. They told us not to play with them until we had training, so as soon as they left us alone we played with them anyway. Marantz accidentally shot Shiloh in the ass but it was only a flesh wound. Not even worth the candle. That reminds me. SNAFU means Situation Normal All Fucked Up, TARFU means Things Are *Really* Fucked Up, FUBAR means Fucked Up Beyond All Recognition and FTA means Fuck The Army. So me and Stuke started making up our own. When our top kick gives us a hard time, we say such things back to him as "SYCKMA, Sir." Since we are saluting when we say it, he does not ask any questions. If he finds out that it means So You Can Kiss My Ass, they will probably hang us for treason.

So far I am the only boot in our outfit to get my marksman rating, even though the whole thing was an accident. At first it did not look like I was going to cut the mustard at all on account of our rifle range is at the bottom of this big hill with a road on the top, and I kept aiming too high and blowing out the tires of Jeeps and etc. Meanwhile the rest of the squad was at least hitting the targets by pretending they had Hitler or Tojo on them, but that still did not work for me—I almost killed the guy who was driving the bread truck. Then Stuke told me to pretend it was Paul Derringer's face on the target instead. After 11 bullseyes in a row they gave me a ribbon. Stuke thinks he should get part of it. I don't.

Charlie

P.S. Are you sure Hazel isn't wise to us yet? Your laying it on pretty thick.

Dear Goodlookin',

Headlines from the Home Front: our trumpet player eloped with a cigarette girl (between shows), the follow spot blew in the middle of "Bewitched, Bothered and Bewildered" so it sounded like I was singing the damned thing from somewhere in the hereafter, Cole Porter says he's writing a new musical for me called *Something for the Boys* (which I'll believe when I see it), and Ethel Merman's favored to win the Triple Crown—they've thrown a saddle on the bitch and called her Whirlaway. Want to switch places? You can hunt for nylons on the black market and I'll go live in a barracks with 75 naked men.

Joey took me to see four movies in three days: *Once Upon a Honeymoon, They All Kissed the Bride, For Me and My Gal* and *I Married an Angel*. I should have known it was your idea—he's not usually that subtle. During the first double-feature, Cary Grant kissed Ginger Rogers and he whispered to me, "Doesn't that make you stop and think?" So I whispered back, "It sure does. Do you suppose Cary Grant is still available?" He wouldn't speak to me for two hours. Later he suggested that we stop by Tiffany's on our way back to Brooklyn—a detour of a mere six miles— "just to see what's in the window." (Between you and me, this kid researches his assault tactics better than Eisenhower does.) There were only two items on display—diamond V-For-Victory broaches (a steal at

$5,000) and assorted wedding bands "for the soldier in a hurry." It'd serve you right if I chose the broach.

Before you boys gang up on me again I'll give you one hint, you coward. On bended knee, by candlelight, or in the middle of Yankee Stadium, I'll still say yes. (I'd even be willing to settle for flowers and candy, but you don't have enough ration points.) One condition: when you ask me, make it romantic. Otherwise it's Cary Grant's turn.

–H–

— WESTERN UNION —

HAZEL MACKAY
311 WEST 89TH STREET
NEW YORK, NY

DEAR TOOTS STOP HAVE ONLY GOT
$1.94 SO I NEED TO PROPOSE IN 5
WORDS OR LESS STOP TOO LATE
STOP CHARLIE

P.S. ROMANTIC ENOUGH?

— WESTERN UNION —

PVT. CHARLES BANKS
USMC
PARRIS ISLAND, SC

DEAR GOODLOOKIN STOP WHY
DIDN'T SOMEBODY TELL ME CARY
GRANT ALREADY ENGAGED STOP
GUESS I WILL HAVE TO ACCEPT STOP
MRS. BANKS

P.S. YOU OLD SMOOTHIE

— WESTERN UNION —

JOEY MARGOLIS
236 MONTGOMERY STREET
BROOKLYN, NY

TO MY BEST MAN STOP I KNEW YOU
WOULD COME THROUGH FOR ME
STOP AM GETTING YOU OUT OF
SCHOOL ON THE 23RD SO IT CAN BE
YOU AND ME AND STUKE AND HAZEL
AT CITY HALL STOP IT IS STILL
SUPPOSE TO BE A SECRET SO KEEP IT
UNDER YOUR STETSEN STOP THANKS
BUDDY STOP CHARLIE

245

Dear Charles,

Mazel Tov! A mensch yet! Whatever gave you the idea?

City Hall is for goniffs. We'll have the whole thing right here. Selmon's Delicatessen agreed to cater, even when they found out it was for you. (Selmon follows the Yankees, he can rot in Hell.) Invite whoever you want but try to keep Jesus Christ in the hall. I'm sure he was a very nice boy with a lovely mother—but we let him in the door, we kill Rabbi Lieberman.

If they send you overseas before we choose your silverware pattern, I'll need to know where I can wire you.

Aunt Carrie

Dear Sprout,

No fair. Foul ball. Kill the umpire. How come you get to be his best man all by yourself & I get stuck in second place? I scored the first unassisted triple play in 21 years, didn't I? I had 8 hitting streaks, right? And so far I'm the only one in South Carolina who's willing to tell him that it wasn't Mickey Owen's fault even though it was. But all Charlie says is, "Ask Joey. It's his call."

So here's my plan. Let's make him the only guy in history who ever had 2 best men at his wedding. Sort of like co-captains. One of us can hold the ring & the other one can give it to him. One of us can make the toast & the other one can drink it. One of us can invite people to the bachelor party & the other one can go to it. Sound like a sweet deal?

Everything here is AOK and OSIAS (Our Sergeant Is A Shit-head). They showed us *The Road to Morocco* last night until Marantz fell asleep at the projector and the film melted. So what's the griff on Dorothy Lamour? Is she or isn't she? Will she or won't she? Could you nose around a little and find out? I figure if I can't ask my co-best man, who *can* I ask? (And if she wants to come to the wedding with me, tell her yes.)

Semper Fi, Mac.

Your buddy,
Stuke

P.S. Charlie decided it was time to learn a different song on his sax (which we could have told him a year ago, huh?). So he picked "Elmer's Tune". Know what? The way he plays it, it sounds just like "In the Mood". And he couldn't play that either.

P.S.2. Deke Marantz has a bucket full of stories about rooming with Charlie in Springfield, so now we get the other half of it. Deke finally chickened up and admitted that maybe he did piss on the toilet seat a couple of times, but it was better than Charlie who missed the whole toilet and pissed on the floor.

Dear Charlie,

Me and Hazel went to Tiffany's on 5th Avenue and bought the wedding bands (we used your ring from Springfield to get the right size). They cost a lot of dough and since you probably can't swing it on a buck private's pay, we lent you the money ourselves (I put in 3 smackers). While we were there, we saw Ethel Merman buying a big green necklace and she said to Hazel, "He looks a little young to me, dear." So Hazel said back, "Who doesn't?" Then we left.

Rachel's been letting me buy her milk and eat my lunch with her, but I still couldn't think of anything to talk to her about. Then I had a great idea. So yesterday in the middle of chocolate pudding I said, "I need your help. My buddy is getting married and I'm one of the best men, but I've never done it before and I don't know what I'm supposed to wear. What about my blue pants and the shirt with stripes?" And she said, "Oh no. You have to wear a suit." Well smokes—of *course* you have to wear a suit. Even a blockhead knows that. But she didn't know that I already knew. So now we talk about different kinds of ties and shoes and etc. One question. How do I get her to change the subject? We're almost down to underpants.

Joey

P.S. They're building Dauntless dive bombers at the Navy Yard and they needed helpers but they told me I was too short. So I snuck in under the coffee wagon and wound up on the assembly line until they threw me out. I even put in a rivet.

Dear Joey,

There's more than one way to skin 2 cats with a stone. But your on the right track. The best way to get girls going is to ask them something you already have the answer to. Then they will think you are dumb and they are smart, and as long as you don't tell them the truth you can get away with murder. But be careful. What if she had even lousier taste than you do and told you to wear yellow pants or etc.? Because if you didn't do it, you would be right back where you started, only worse. See what I mean? It can get dangerous out there. And don't worry about how to keep them talking, on account of that is the one thing they always do better than we do. It comes with the turf like long hair and girdles. So when you run out of ideas just say the first word that comes into your head—even if it is "uranium"—because they can do at least 20 minutes on just about anything. Oh yeah. They also like it when we use colors to talk about their body parts, such as "your eyes are as brown as" or "your teeth are whiter than" and similar types of crap. But this routine has 6 or 7 rules that go along with it and if you do not watch yourself it can be like walking through a mine field. So don't try it until we practice and I say your ready.

Last thing. Never try to win a fight with them. They are always right. If they say that Abraham Lincoln was Chinese, they are right. If they say that Babe Ruth played for the Cardinals, they are right too. Get use to saying "Smokes, *I* didn't know that." Otherwise you will never get laid as long as you live.

I need to hit the sack. We have another run tomorrow in the early A.M., I think to Colarado. We finally figured out that they only do such things to us to see who croaks and who doesn't. They probably have money on it. But there is a word for this now. TUMBS. The Usual Marine Bullshit. The only reason I have time to write this at all is on account of we were suppose to see your buddy Citizen Kane tonight but when they opened the can the middle reel was somehow gone. Rose Bush my ass.

See you next week.

Charlie

P.S. They said that Capt. Colin Kelly sank the *Haruna* all by himself. What did I tell you? This thing is practically over already.

| FINAL | The Brooklyn Eagle | TWO CENTS |

VOL. CXIV....No.2,811   FRIDAY, FEBRUARY 20, 1942   Sunny, 18–26

EASTWARD HO!
FOR WEST COAST JAPS

WASHINGTON, February 19. President Roosevelt today signed into law Executive Order 9066, authorizing the military to designate strategic areas from which any and all persons may be excluded in order to maintain national security. The move was prompted by the widely felt belief that many of the 110,000 Japanese-Americans living on the West Coast are engaged in sabotage and other fifth column activities designed to weaken the nation's defenses against Imperial Japan. Although no actual or overt acts of espionage have yet been uncovered, California Attorney General Earl Warren stated, "The absence of any domestic sabotage shows just how devious their plotting really is, and provides almost certain proof of their guilt."

It is expected that all Americans of Japanese descent now residing in the coastal areas of California, Oregon and Washington will be required to move inland for the duration of the war. At present, there are no plans to evacuate the area forcibly or intern U.S. Japs in detention camps—although Gen. John L. DeWitt has indicated that the only way to protect American citizens against the Yellow Peril is to "lock them up and throw away the

251

TOP SECRET

The Green Hornet
C/O Craig Nakamura
Baywater Hotel
1756 Ocean Avenue
Santa Monica, California

Dear Hornet,

Guess what? The *Normandie* caught fire and burned up while it was still tied to the harbor, and nobody knows how it happened yet but they think it was spies. By the time Charlie and I got there it was lying on its side with steam still coming out of it, and the stacks were so big they almost reached the George Washington Bridge. Smokes, it was keen! The only clue I found was a wooden leg on the dock that had gunpowder on the foot. And you know what *that* means. Let's not tell anybody though. We're in enough hot water with her already.

Me and Stuke had a Bachelor's Party for Charlie last night at the Metropolitan Club even though they made me go home before the naked girl got there. (Her name was Darla and she called me honey after they found me hid–

252

ing in the closet.) There was an open bar but they only let me drink Coca Cola and water until I remembered that vodka looks just like water too. (It also makes you puke a lot faster than Slow Gin Fizzes, but I didn't know that yet.) The only bad part was that Mel Ott brought Leo Durocher with him, who I've maybe swapped two words with in my whole life and both of them were fuck you. But Charlie said that if he could stomach FDR for 3 hours then I could handle shooting the breeze with Durocher for crying out loud. So I got you his autograph. It says "To My Best Friend Craig" and I had to spell "friend" for him. I *told* you he was a dope.

One other thing. Since Rachel started trading her peach cobbler for my peas, I figured it was time for "Love Hate Marriage Friendship." But look what happens.

ʝΦ¢ʏ ɱɅʏ₲ΦⱢɪ₴
ʏɅ¢ʮΦⱢ ₱ɅɱɪⱢⱢ

FRIENDSHIP

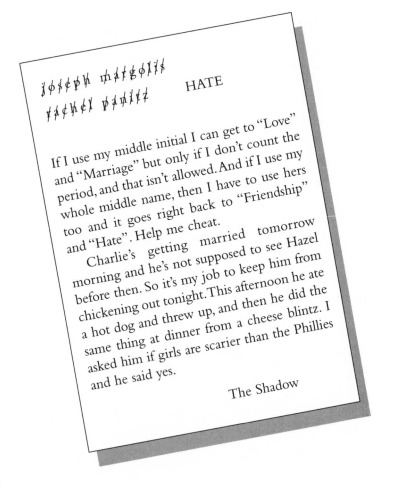

JOSEPH MARGOLIS   HATE
RACHEL PANITZ

If I use my middle initial I can get to "Love"
and "Marriage" but only if I don't count the
period, and that isn't allowed. And if I use my
whole middle name, then I have to use hers
too and it goes right back to "Friendship"
and "Hate". Help me cheat.

Charlie's getting married tomorrow
morning and he's not supposed to see Hazel
before then. So it's my job to keep him from
chickening out tonight. This afternoon he ate
a hot dog and threw up, and then he did the
same thing at dinner from a cheese blintz. I
asked him if girls are scarier than the Phillies
and he said yes.

                              The Shadow

254

Man About Town
by Winchell

====○====

Banks and MacKay—
Double Play!

Loose lips sink ships, but the lid's been blown off the military's hottest secret since Mata Hari batted those luscious lashes and stole France. Private Charlie Banks, the former muscle behind the New York Giants who's now playing ball with Uncle Sam, surrendered his post to curvy charmer Hazel MacKay with a hush-hush ceremony in Brooklyn yesterday. And it only took him two years to pop the question. Who'd'a thunk it? So what happened, Charlie? Finally get over those cold feet? Guess after this the Japs'll be a breeze.

====○====

Dear Winchell,
    Like you would know. Why aren't you in the Army you deadbeat?

                        Chas. Banks
                        USMC

Q: I never saw anybody shake so much in my life.

A: Smokes, I was nervous. What if I dropped the rings?

Q: You did.

A: Only Charlie's. I got more sweat on his than Stuke got on Hazel's so it slid easier.

Q: What did you whisper to him when he forgot the vows?

A: "Japheth." It was a private joke. That's how come Rabbi Lieberman started coughing. He was the only one who got it except for me and Charlie.

Q: You know, I've told three people that I met Charlie Banks and Hazel MacKay but nobody believes me.

A: Now you know how it feels.

Q: And why were you so worried about Aunt Carrie? She was a champ.

A: You weren't looking at her when the minister said "To live is Christ." If she'd squeezed her hands any harder she would have broken her fingers.

Q: She certainly fed him well enough.

A: No, she didn't. He got the smallest matzoh ball and no lox. Charlie bet me 25 cents that she was going to make him eat in the bathroom.

Q: By the way. Why didn't you try to sneak on the honeymoon? I thought for sure you'd take a stab at it.

A: I did. But they were wise to me. Before the train left for Niagara Falls they checked all the cabinets. I need to come up with a couple new tricks.

Q: That shouldn't be tough for an old pro like you.

A: Then how do I keep him from going to Camp Pendleton tomorrow?

Q: You don't.

A: How come? I got him to take me on a road trip, didn't I?

Q: This is different.

A: Yeah. I know.

Q: Joey, do you remember when he stood up for you at your Bar Mitzvah?

A: Smokes, like I wouldn't?

Q: Well, now it's your turn to do the same for him.

A: You don't think he'll forget about me, do you?

Q: Joey, *nobody* could forget about you. Especially Charlie.

A: Maybe I better make sure. Just in case.

OPEN THIS ON THE TRAIN

Dear Charlie,

In case you don't remember, this is my Check List from that first game in Boston when I didn't even know how many sons Noah had for Pete's sake. I guess it isn't much of a going-away present but there are two reasons for it. First of all, if you put it inside your helmet before the fighting starts, maybe you can pull it out between bullets and it will make you laugh. And second of all, it will remind you of the brawl with the Bees when I kept Paul Waner from poking you in the nose. (If I hadn't saved your ass he would have knocked your head off.)

> Your buddy and
> your best man,
> Joey

P.S. So far Tommy Henrich hit three home runs in spring training and Mickey Owen didn't hit any. Also Bill Terry is gone so they asked Mel Ott to manage the Giants and play third base at the same time. Aunt Carrie really let him have it because she thought they were punishing him or something. She said "So next you're selling peanuts too? Why don't you put your foot down?" I don't think she gets it yet.

Dear Joey,

You have got something up your sleeve and it must be big on account of I can't figure out what it is. We just crossed the boarder into Arkansaw and I already have lost $41 in poker to Stuke and Shiloh and Marantz and Sgt. Block due to wondering when your going to pop out of a duffle bag or get dropped from an airplane onto our caboose or mail yourself to Camp Pendleton in a cardboard box with holes in it. I knew something was fishy at the Pennsylvania Station when I had half of the USMC stationed in every door to make sure you would not dress up like a foot locker or etc. and smuggle yourself onto the train. That took alot of work—and you did not even try. And what about when we left? Hazel cried. Your Mom cried. Even Aunt Carrie cried for Christ's sake. And then there is you. "Take care of yourself buddy." Oh yeah. And the hand shake. That's *it*? Aren't you even going to miss me??? I thought you would of at least turned up with a couple of diseases and a fake letter from your doctor saying you would croak unless I stayed. Whatever happened to hiding out on troop transports and showing up on Guam with me and enlisting with phony papers so we could ship out together and all the rest of those things I said I would kick your butt for if you even tried them? What are you—too old for that now? Well if this is your idea of growing up, forget that I told you to be a man. I don't think your ready for it yet.

I guess I am blowing off steam and it probably

should not be at you. So I'm sorry. But these are things you think about when you find out that Corregidor and the Phillipines are almost gone and you ask yourself "What in Hell did I get myself into?"

Charlie

P.S. Thanks for the up-date on T. Henrich. Make sure you tell me when his birthday is too so I can send him a greeting card.

P.S.2. There are 800 of us on this train and only one chow car. We had to start lining up for breakfast at 6:30 in the A.M. but by the time I finally got there they were calling it lunch. SABUS. (Screwed Again By Uncle Sam.)

P.S.3. Sgt. Block got assigned to our unit after the shmuck we had on Parris Island blew out all the vains in his throat and got sent back to his fish market in Baltimore. When we found out about it at Roll Call I said to the man next to me (who I never saw before) "I wonder who our new Asshole will be" and he said back "Me." But he does not look like a sargent, he looks normal. And he did not gig me for calling him an asshole ahead of time either.

Alexander Hamilton Junior High School

— SEMESTER REPORT —

STUDENT: Joseph Margolis   TEACHER: Janet Hicks

ENGLISH	A
ARITHMETIC	A
SOCIAL STUDIES	A
SCIENCE	A

Neatness	A
Punctuality	A
Participation	A
Obedience	B−

Teacher's Comments:

Three weeks ago we began reading *Julius Caesar* in class. Given the fact that, of all the Shakespearean heroes, this one actually *was* a Fascist, I had little hope of slipping it past Joseph without at least a preliminary fili-buster. Naturally, I was somewhat startled when nothing of the kind oc-curred. In fact, he requested the "Friends, Romans and Countrymen" speech for his own and promptly delivered it with the kind of aplomb normally associated with the Barrymores (the sober ones). The applause that resulted was well-deserved, and when I complimented him on his performance, he replied, "Thank you, ma'am." Thus emboldened, I even went so far as to compare some of Caesar's weaknesses to those of the current President of the United States—and when that too failed to elicit a rebuttal from Joseph, I merely assumed that I had lost my sanity. O, merry madness!

I suppose we have Rachel to thank for Joseph's abrupt turnabout. Sim-ply put, they cannot keep their eyes off of one another—although Rachel has managed to preserve at least a few shreds of practiced indif-ference, like a tattered flag fluttering in the breeze. They generally utilize Study Hall to pass a series of covert notes back and forth to one another whenever they assume I am not looking. It's hard to tell from where I sit exactly what the score is—but I think Rachel is losing.

Janet Hicks

Dear Charlie,

Could you please read these and tell me what they mean? I tried to figure it out six different ways and I still can't.

Dear Rachel,

Your pupils are bluer than marbles, your skin is whiter than the dawn, and your hair is browner than a field that somebody just plowed.

Love,
Joey

Dear Joey,

That's disgusting. And stop it. I'm trying to study.

Rachel

Dear Rachel,

What if I asked you to go to the movies? Would you let me take you?

Joey

Dear Joey,

~~I don't know.~~ No. Besides, boys don't like Barbara Stanwyck and I do.

Rachel

Dear Rachel,

I <u>love</u> Barbara Stanwyck. And I'm sorry about the time I threw the yellow snowball at you.

Joey

Dear Joey,

If you send me one more note, I'm going to tell Mrs. Hicks. But maybe.

Rachel

Maybe *what?* Maybe she'll tell Mrs. Hicks or maybe she'll go to the movies with me? And if she was really trying to study, how come she kept looking backwards to see if I was still writing to her?

This is a lot more complicated than I thought.

Joey

P.S. And Barbara Stanwyck is a pain in the ass. Maybe if somebody threw a pie in her face she would learn how to lighten up a little for Pete's sake.

P.S.2. I dressed up like a Western Union Boy and took a fake telegram to the Navy Yard so I could tell them I had a delivery for Leon Landey (a name I found in the Bronx Telephone Book). This time I was on the assembly line for 45 minutes before I got the boot. Know what? They even have *girls* working there.

Dear Romeo,

You do not even know what the word complicated means yet. Wait until she lets you hold her hand. Then you are going to need a road map and Craig's secret code book and a slide rule too.

This one is easy. What she is saying is "Your a pain in the ass but if you stop I will break your fuckin neck."

The big clue is ~~I don't know.~~ This is her way of dropping the hook in the water. Do not bite it or she will pull you up by way of your nose. That reminds me— let Hazel pick the movie for you. Such ones as "Mr. Moto" and "Confessions of a Nazi Spy" and etc. will not do the trick this time.

And didn't I tell you not to try the colors until we had a chance to work on them? This is what you did wrong.

1. "Your pupils are bluer than marbles." You make her sound like she has glass eye balls.
2. "Your skin is whiter than the dawn." Dawn means sunrise. The sun is yellow. Does she have malaria????
3. "Your hair is browner than a field that somebody just plowed." Know what makes it brown? Mud and cow shit. I am surprised she didn't stick a fountain pen in your ear.

It does not look like you did any damage (yet) but just in case, here is a list we can start with.

White	Clouds, stars, the moon and that bubble crap that comes on top of waves.
Red	A cherry is the best, but that has a whole other meaning we will talk about when your a little older. For now use ruby.

Brown	Chestnut ponys.
Yellow	I one time tried "egg yoke" on Hazel and it started a big fight that ended with me getting locked out of the apartment. But later she told me that girls are suckers for buttercups, so I guess this is from the horse's mouth.
Purple	A tough one. Try tulips or some other damn flower. They are all the same anyway.
Green	Most green things will only piss her off, such as frogs and boogies and etc. Grass is okay but you have to do something with it first. Like "grass after it got rained on".
Blue	Sky and oceans.
Black	The only things I can think of are "the night" and "a well-digger's asshole". So stay away from black. It can only get you in trouble.
Orange	You will not need this one on account of she is not suppose to have anything on her body that is orange. If she does then make sure she goes to a doctor.

We have been on maneuvers for 5 days in a row now and we are really turning into a crack outfit. They will not tell us where we are going after here on account of what if one of us knows Hirohoto and spills the beans at dinner with him. But since we keep practicing landing on beaches from Higgens boats and taking cover, you do not have to have ½ a brain to know that it will be the S. Pacific. Unless Germany just got an ocean that nobody told us about.

They finally gave us 24, so me and Stuke used ours by going to L.A. First we ate dinner at the Pig N Whistle and then we went to a place called The Hollywood Canteen where only service men are allowed inside and you get to dance with movie stars who also make sandwiches for you. Stuke got asked to mambo by Carol Lombard but instead of saying yes The Tough Guy fainted on the floor. They had to sit him up in a corner and put smelly things under his nose until he woke up—but as soon as he saw that the one who was waving the smelly things was Lucille Ball he was out cold again. I knew it. All talk and no action.

Charlie

P.S. Promotions are next week. Stuke thinks he is going to make Sgt. and I'm not. It better not happen. He would be the first noncom to get his ass kicked by a private and have to say thank you for it.

P.S.2. Your still cooking something up, aren't you? Whatever it is, do it and get it over with. I cannot live like this.

P.S.3. Bringing up the yellow snowball was just about the dumbest thing you ever did in your life. Remember that they always keep score about such things—and at the rate your going, she will probably not let you kiss her until your 32.

Alexander Hamilton Junior High School

To: All Eighth Graders

From: Mrs. Hicks

Re: Vacation Assignment

The robins are chirping again, and it's time for another stab at "How I Spent My Spring Vacation". Perhaps it will come as a surprise, but I don't like reading them any more than you like writing them. However, the Board of Education insists. Papers should be 200 words in length and ready to turn in the day after vacation.

See if you can spend a little time doing something unusual; maybe it will make your compositions more fun to write. I doubt it—but it's worth a try.

Have a safe two weeks.

Mrs. Hicks

Dear Rachel,
    How about if we got married? Bet that would make a heck of a composition, huh?

Love,
Joey

Dear Joey,
    Leave me alone. And stop saying you love me.

Rachel

Dear Rachel,

But I do. "O, how ripe in show thy lips, those kissing cherries, tempting grow!" *Midsummer Night's Dream*. You can even have my kingdom.

Joey

Dear Joey,

I don't want it.

Rachel

Dear Rachel,

Can I at least take you to see *Mrs. Miniver*? Please, please?

Joey

Dear Joey,
  I can't. We're going to Atlantic Beach for two weeks. We rent a house there every year. But you can write to me.

  Rachel

Dear Rachel,
  Smokes, what am I supposed to do all by myself?

  Joey

Dear Joey,
  You heard Mrs. Hicks. Think of something unusual.

  Rachel

Dear Joey-San,
  I'm in a concentration camp. This isn't a joke. First the FBI put my father under hack because they said his tomato plants in the back yard pointed to an airplane

factory, and then they arrested my uncle for being president of the Santa Monica *kenjin-kai* which they said was getting ready to bomb Washington or some other kind of bullshit. Know what a *kenjin-kai* is? A bunch of old men who talk about radishes and play shogi. After that they gave us 24 hours to get rid of everything we owned except what we could carry, including my Mom's 200-year-old china (which went for two bits a plate) and my aunt's hotel. She had to sell the lease to some old fart for $750 even though her and my uncle put over $150,000 into it. Then they took us to a stall at the Santa Anita racetrack and made us stay there for three days (without cleaning the crap out first) until they had enough busses to take us to camp. So unless they decide to shoot us next, this is my address.

> Craig Nakamura
> Manzanar War Relocation Center
> Block 28, Barracks 3, Apt. 2
> Manzanar, California

It looks like a damn Army base here except with barb wire sticking you in the ass every time you turn around. There's about 100 long brown barrackses split up into apartments (that are maybe the size of our closets back in Brooklyn), and five of us are supposed to sleep in each one. Smokes, the walls don't even go up to the ceiling and you can practically hear the other three families we're sharing the joint with—especially the Fukudas. They have a 16-year-old named Kenji who calls me Puppet and an 11-year-old named Ichi who's weirder than you and me put together. He thinks he's the Hardy Boys. Both of them. And by the way, the bathroom is two blocks away and you have to wait in line to get in, even if you have the squirts.

Joey-San, do you think maybe Charlie could do something to get us out of here? Or at least find out where they're keeping Pop and Uncle Mits? I don't want to piss him off or anything, but he's the only famous person I know. You can even tell him I'm sorry I traded 6 of his baseball cards for one of Durocher.

> Your yellow friend,
> Craig

P.S. Whatever you do, don't put "Top Secret" when you write back. It can only get us in more trouble. They already took away my Shadow's Secret Code Book to see if there were any troop movements in it. Swear to God.

P.S.2. We found a rat under the oil-burner in our apartment. Kenji named it Earl Warren. Then he called me Puppet again.

P.S.3. But they have baseball teams here. The San Pedro Gophers are letting me play with them because I'm so short that the other pitchers don't know where my strike zone is. Guess where they put me? Third base. Banks can eat his heart out.

P.S.4. Tell your Mom and Aunt Carrie I said Hi. And Rachel and Mrs. Hicks and anybody else we know except Mrs. Aubaugh (unless she wants to lend me her leg so we can torpedo our way out of this place).

THE WHITE HOUSE

Dear Joey:

Thank you for your most recent letter. I wish there were an easy answer, but there isn't.

Craig will be quite safe at Manzanar—safer perhaps than on the city's streets, where attacks against innocent and loyal Japanese-Americans have reached inexcusable proportions.

I hope you will reconsider your feelings toward President Roosevelt. Dedicated friends are difficult for him to come by these days, and you have been among the most faithful. Try to remember that the right decisions are not always the popular ones—and only history can judge whether we have made a fitting choice or a regrettable mistake.

> Cordially as always,
> Stephen T. Early
> Press Secretary

Dear Goodlookin',

You'd better consider this a Joey Alert because something is definitely brewing. I haven't been able to get two words out of him all week, and you know that spells Big Trouble. Then this morning I telephoned to find out if he wanted to learn a new routine with me, but Aunt Carrie said he'd gone on a field trip to Delaware with some of his classmates. Apparently she's unaware that there's nothing to *see* in Delaware, or else she wouldn't have fallen for it. (I certainly didn't.) So keep your ear to the ground, Big Boy—because I'm a little worried about him.

Cole Porter stopped by the club yesterday to play one of my new songs from *Something for the Boys*. He calls it "By The Miss-iss-iss-iss-iss-iss-iss-iss-inewah" and I'm not making this up. Only Cole could concoct a title like that and get away with it—anybody else would have been hatched up on sight. I put it into the act during the second show tonight and it brought down the house. Wait 'til Merman gets wind of this. She thinks that Cole Porter is her personal poodle, and she hates it when he pees on the other side of the street. (Of course, they haven't exactly offered me the leash yet, but Cole says it's in the bag.)

I miss looking at you while you sleep. Come to think of it, I miss looking at you, period.

All my love,
-Mrs. H-

P.S. I managed to swing two weeks off at the end of the month and I intend to spend both of them hanging around your neck. So you'd better tell the Marines not to expect you for dinner. And if they give you a hard time, I'll set them straight. Who else is a bigger pain in the ass than I am?

UNITED STATES MARINE CORPS
Semper Fidelis

CAMP PENDLETON   OCEANSIDE, CALIFORNIA

To: COL. WILLIAM KOUTRELAKOS
From: SGT. ANDREW M. BURSTEIN
Re: THE MARGOLIS KID

WE STILL DON'T KNOW WHAT TO DO WITH HIM, BUT WE FINALLY FIGURED OUT HOW HE GOT HERE. APPARENTLY THE TRANSPORT VEHICLE WAS LEFT UNGUARDED IN THE LOADING BAY AT THE BROOKLYN NAVY YARD WHILE CPL. BUNTZ WAS MOVING HIS BOWELS ELSEWHERE. THIS GAVE THE KID JUST ENOUGH TIME TO HOP ON BOARD AND TUNNEL HIS WAY THROUGH 200 DUFFEL BAGS HEADED FOR PENDLETON. IT LOOKS LIKE HE HAD QUITE A SETUP BACK THERE—WE FOUND TWO STERNO CANS, A BOX

OF MATCHES, A FLASHLIGHT, A STACK OF SUPER-
MAN COMIC BOOKS, AND ENOUGH GROCERIES
TO FEED THE THIRD DIVISION FOR A WEEK. (CPL.
BUNTZ ADMITTED THAT HE SMELLED PORK
AND BEANS ALL THE WAY ACROSS THE COUNTRY
BUT ASSUMED IT WAS THE CARBURETOR.) WE
ALSO DISCOVERED A SMALL HOLE CUT INTO
THE CANVAS SIDING—PRESUMABLY THE KID'S
EMERGENCY BACKUP IF HE COULDN'T MAKE IT
TO THE NEXT REST STOP. SO FAR THE WEATHER
BUREAU HAS NOT RECEIVED ANY REPORTS OF
AMBER RAIN FROM CONFUSED MOTORISTS, SO
WE'RE PROBABLY SAFE ON THAT SCORE.

OUTSIDE OF ADMITTING THAT HE HAS ARMY
BUSINESS UP AT MANZANAR, HE INSISTS THAT
HE IS ONLY REQUIRED TO GIVE US HIS NAME,
RANK AND SERIAL NUMBER. (IN SUPPORT OF
HIS ARGUMENT, HE CITES THE USMC CODE OF
REGULATIONS AND *THE SHORES OF TRIPOLI*,
WITH RANDOLPH SCOTT. HOLLYWOOD IS
TURNING INTO A REAL PAIN IN THE NECK.)
THEN HE ASKED TO SEE PVT. BANKS AND PFC.
STUKER, BOTH OF WHOM ARE STATIONED HERE
AT THE BASE.

WE'VE CALLED THEM IN FROM THE FIELD AND
WILL KEEP YOU ADVISED.

277

Dear Mrs. Toots,

I *knew* he was going to pull something like this. Didn't I say he was going to pull something like this? Just like I know that my name is Charlie Banks 3d Base and I was born in Wisc. and I am 24 and I love you, I *knew* he was going to pull something like this. Do I know this kid or what?

We were in the middle of crawling through bushes and trees and shooting each other due to war games when they sent a Jeep for me and Stuke. Right away we thought the jig was up and we were getting court-marshaled on account of they figured out that "APSFY Sir" means AND P.S. FUCK YOU. Instead they took us to the CO's office and the first thing we heard in the waiting room was Joey's voice from inside saying "Do not be a biscuithead. You start with the Gilbert Islands and work your way up to Japan. Smokes, even a girl knows that." When they finally let us in, he was pointing to a big map on the wall and chewing out the Col. for Bataan and Singapore by using such words as "creepback" and "fringe merchants" and "working their bolt" and "aiming stakes", and if you didn't know he was only 13 you would of thought that Patton shrunk. Even the Col. did not know what in Hell he was talking about. So instead of finding out, he gave us 72 hrs. leave to get him off the base and make sure he never came back. Who does he think we are— Houdini? How are we suppose to fit everything into 72 hrs.???? These are only some of the places I want to take him. (1) Graumans Chinese and the footprints. (2) Brown Derby (which is shaped like one). (3) Arroyo Seco Pkway (where you can drive all the way to Pasadena without any stop signs). (4) Angels Flight Trolly (which goes up and down instead of back and forth). (5) Hollywood Canteen. (6) Bogey's house. (7) The "O" in the sign that says HOLLYWOODLAND, where you can sit at 6:00 in the A.M. while the sun is coming up and play "In the Mood" on your sax. And etc. It is a good thing I already started my list, because I *knew* he was going to pull something like this. Then we are going up to the Army Base at Manzanar to see what kind of trouble Craig has got himself into now, and to bring him and his folks home once in for all. Concentration camp my ass. The kids also said the old lady with the wooden leg was a spy.

We just got into L.A. and found ourself a room at the Biltmore. (Stuke gets to pay for it on account of he is a Pfc. and I'm not.) We wanted to take Joey to dinner at the Pig N Whistle but he is out like a light. He earned it. 3000 miles across the whole U.S.A. right under their nose and they never got wise to him.

Didn't I tell you he was going to pull something like this?

Love,
Pvt. Charlie

P.S. Thanks for squaring things with his Mom and Aunt Carrie. Maybe you can bluff them out of being sore at him by telling them that he forgot the difference between Calif. and Delaware. That happens to me all the time. Idaho, Nebraska, who gives a shit? Either way, we will make sure he is on the train by Thurs. so he will be home in time for school.

P.S.2. Oh yeah. He's suppose to write an essay about spring vacation now. I told him that if he puts me in this one I will cut his hands off. Otherwise they will probably make us go to England and eat with the damn Queen or somebody.

P.S.3. Can you believe that he put one over on the whole USMC and got away with it???? I can't even scratch my *ass* without getting gigged.

Romanoff's
Where the Stars Meet

To Charlie,
    Don't turn your back on *anybody*.
    Got that?
                    Humphrey Bogart

Ciro's

To Joey,
    So. A tough guy, huh? Let's see
you prove it.
                    Jimmy Cagney

MUSSO AND FRANK
A Hollywood Tradition

Dear Stuke,
    Sealed with a kiss.
                    Rita Hayworth

Dear Rachel,

Well, you said I could write to you in Atlantic Beach, so I am. Right now I'm in California with Charlie and Stuke, and I thought about you tonight because we had dinner with Barbara Stanwyck at Ciro's. (In case I forgot to mention it, she's a close personal friend.) I told her that she was your favorite, so just before she kissed me goodnight she came up with the idea of signing a menu for you. Here it is. It's supposed to say "To my dearest fan Rachel, thank you," except I got chocolate moose on "dearest". And in case you're wondering, underneath it is Clark Gable's. I don't even know if you like him, but he always gets sore when we ask Barbara to sign stuff for our friends and we don't ask him too. So does Mickey Rooney.

I guess it's a good thing that we didn't get married after all. Being out here made me realize that I still need to sew a couple more wild oats before I'm ready to settle down. But I hope you're having fun at the beach anyway. Your eyes are bluer than the breaking waves and your skin is as white as the froth-filled foam on top. I'll probably see you at school next week even though Clark asked me to make a movie with him at Metro. But my Mom always says No whenever that happens, so don't worry.

Love,
Joey

P.S. Oh, yeah. Judy Garland says Hi.

The Biltmore Hotel
Union Square
LOS ANGELES, CALIFORNIA

TO ALL GUESTS:

IN THE EVENT OF AN AIR RAID ALERT, PLEASE SWITCH OFF ROOM LIGHTS AND PROCEED QUIETLY TO THE LOBBY. COFFEE AND CAKES WILL BE SERVED UNTIL THE ALL-CLEAR HAS SOUNDED.

THANK YOU FOR YOUR PATIENCE AND COOPERATION.

—THE HOTEL MANAGER

THE HARLEM CLUB
at the heart of Central Avenue

NOW APPEARING

**LOUIS ARMSTRONG
PEARL BAILEY**

THROUGH SUNDAY

283

Dear Mrs. M and Aunt Carrie,

I am inclosing a photo I took at the Harlem Club that I figured you would want to keep in your scrap book. It shows Joey playing my sax next to Louis Armstrong playing the trumpet. (Joey is the short one.) He says he didn't mean to be a show-off, but you know how his head works. Stuke got us a table at the ring side even though it cost him $10 to do it (which is his job now on account of he is a Pfc. and I'm not), so we were close enough that when Pearl Bailey started singing "The Saint Louis Blues" and Joey winked at her, she could see it. Right away she stopped the song and said to the band "Hold it fellas. I think I got me a beau here" and asked Joey how old he was. (He said 22 and she pretended to believe him.) After that she wanted to know what he was doing all the way down on Central Ave. so he told her that he dropped in to see if he could give L. Armstrong a "couple of pointers on the horn". By then I could figure out what was coming next so I handed him my sax, which I always bring with me in case somebody asks me to toot with them (which they never do). Then Pearlie May said to Armstrong "You hear that Louie? You got competition" and the next thing we knew Joey was on the stage playing "Moonlight Seranade" with the rest of the band going along behind him. L. Armstrong even made a couple of trumpet mistakes on purpose just so Joey wouldn't be the only one. When they were finished, Louis said to Joey "How did you do that, man?"

and Joey said back "It's like you always say, man. If you can't feel it, I can't explain it." And Armstrong took the credit for it like he was the one who said it all along instead of Satchmo. Smokes, what a phony. Joey says he wants to be a Negro now, but I told him I can't help him with that.

In case you didn't know it already, this kid isn't afraid of *any*thing.

Charlie

P.S. I haven't clued him in yet, but I am giving him my saxaphone to take home with him on account of he will probably have better luck with it than I do anyway. He gets L. Armstrong and all I get is such things as boots and baseballs thrown at my head. Make sure he takes care of it though.

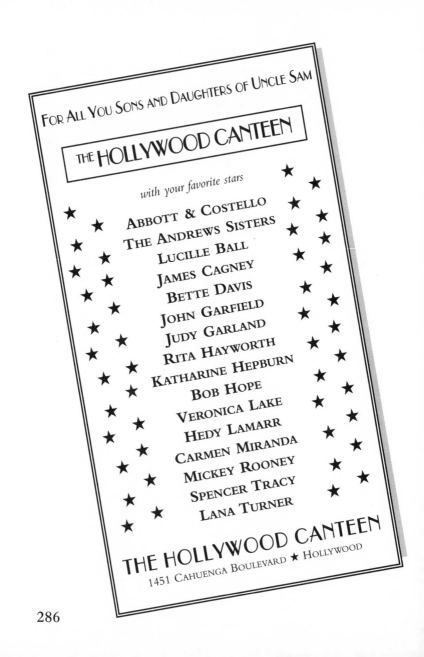

Miss Veronica Lake
c/o Hollywood Canteen
1451 Cahuenga Boulevard
Hollywood, CA

Dear Veronica,

In case you don't remember, I'm the Marine who danced with you nine times last night & asked you to marry him twice. And if that doesn't narrow it down, I was with another Marine & the 13-year-old kid who kept calling me "Dad." Anyway, I just wanted you to know that I'm only 22 & I'm not really his father, but my buddy put him up to it because he's still sore that I made Pfc. and he didn't.

Look, I know that you probably dance with a lot of guys & hear the same routines from most of us, but if I'd taken all the dough I blew on seeing you in *Sullivan's Travels* and *This Gun for Hire* and given it to Roosevelt instead, he could probably pay for the whole damn war with it. I guess this doesn't make me special, but what are the chances that you'd let me buy you a hamburger & a chocolate egg cream anyway? Or coffee & a donut? Maybe I could rack up some points by telling you that my liberty is up in 36 hours & you'd be my last date before I shipped out, but I'm not going to do that (even though it's true). Instead, I'm just going to tell you that I'm staying at the Biltmore in Room 714 on the off chance that maybe you'll call and say yes. Come to think of it, I'd even settle for walking you to your car.

Jordy Stuker

P.S. I don't know if it makes a difference, but in real life I play first base for the New York Giants. Honest. So I'm famous too. Sort of.

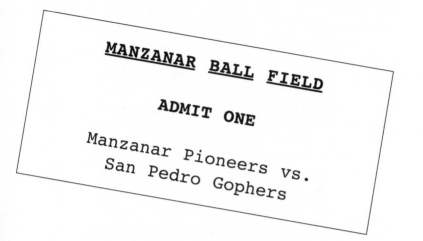

MANZANAR BALL FIELD

ADMIT ONE

Manzanar Pioneers vs.
San Pedro Gophers

Manzanar Free Press

VOL. I, No.32   MANZANAR, CALIFORNIA   APRIL 8, 1942

CHARLIE BANKS GUEST OF HONOR AT BALL FIELD

New York Giants slugger Charlie Banks was the surprise guest at this morning's American League game between the San Pedro Gophers and the Manzanar Pioneers, arriving just in time for the second inning. The acclaimed third baseman told the Free Press, "I heard that my buddy Craig Nakamura was playing third for the Gophers and I didn't want to miss it. This guy is going to be an All-Star someday." Nakamura, 13, was a temporary replacement in the Gophers' lineup but has since been made a permanent member of the team due in large part to the pair of doubles he smacked to deep

LEAGUE STANDINGS

	W.	L.	Pct.
Ramblers	5	0	1.000
Giants	3	0	1.000
Wonders	2	1	.667
Gophers	2	1	.667
Pioneers	2	3	.400
Mayors	1	3	.250
Yankees	1	4	.125
Senors	0	4	.000

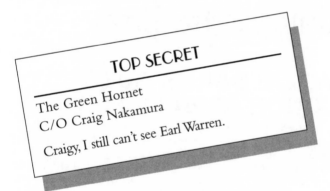

TOP SECRET

The Green Hornet
C/O Craig Nakamura

Craigy, I still can't see Earl Warren.

TOP SECRET

The Shadow
C/O Joey Margolis

That's because he hates people. Ever since Mrs. Fukuda started chasing him with a broom. So stay under the bed and keep looking at the wall behind the oil burner.

Guess what? We think Kenji sunk the Arizona but we don't have any proof yet. Want to stay here and help me find some?

TOP SECRET

The Green Hornet
C/O Craig Nakamura

Smokes, *can* I?

TOP SECRET

The Shadow
C/O Joey Margolis

Nah. You're not dangerous enough for the Army, Joey-San. You need to have pointy teeth and tails like we do.

By the way, thanks for the new code book. They've improved it since the old days.

TOP SECRET

The Green Hornet
C/O Craig Nakamura

Did they let you keep your crystal set?

TOP SECRET

The Shadow
C/O Joey Margolis

Only when they figured out that Yamamoto
wasn't listening on the other end. Last night we
turned it on and heard "You're A Sap, Mister
Jap" and "When The Cohens and The Kellys
Meet Those Little Yellow-Bellies". It was festive.
You think Charlie's having any luck with the
major?

TOP SECRET

The Green Hornet
C/O Craig Nakamura

He's trying. I *told* you that you should have
stayed in Brooklyn with me, you dumbbell.

TOP SECRET

The Shadow
C/O Joey Margolis

You rock-head. Quick! Look! There's Earl
Warren.

293

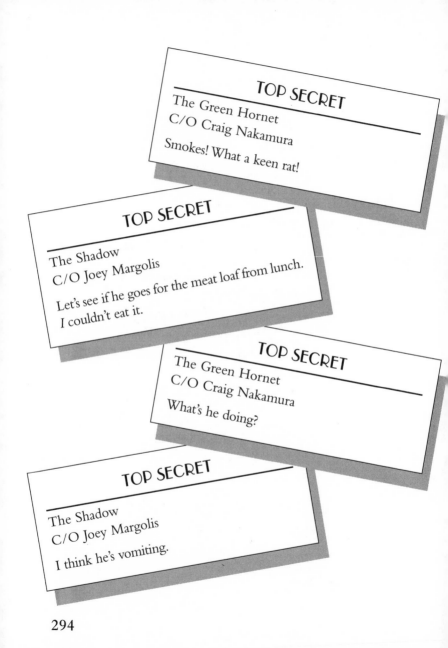

TOP SECRET

The Green Hornet
C/O Craig Nakamura

Smokes! What a keen rat!

TOP SECRET

The Shadow
C/O Joey Margolis

Let's see if he goes for the meat loaf from lunch.
I couldn't eat it.

TOP SECRET

The Green Hornet
C/O Craig Nakamura

What's he doing?

TOP SECRET

The Shadow
C/O Joey Margolis

I think he's vomiting.

TOP SECRET

The Green Hornet
C/O Craig Nakamura

Craigy, Charlie says a best friend only happens one time in your life. Do you believe him?

TOP SECRET

The Shadow
C/O Joey Margolis

You bet, Shadow.

TOP SECRET

The Green Hornet
C/O Craig Nakamura

Yeah. So do I.

Dear Hazel,

Charlie's right. The Army can kiss our ass and so can FDR. It turned out that they were holding Craig's father and uncle prisoners at some damned camp in Tule Lake while they decided whether or not to ship them back to Japan. Then those G.I. chunkheads found out that neither one of them had ever been to Japan in their lives, so they had to let them go and send them to Manzanar instead. At least they'll all be together now.

Toots, you should of seen this kid in action. Go on. Tell what happened.

You **tell.**

First I went to see the Major by myself on account of (1) being a Marine and (2) playing 3d Base for the NY Giants. But that didn't work on him due to (1) hating Marines and (2) hating the NY Giants.

Get to the secret weapon part.

I am. So I told him about some of the stunts Craig has pulled such as thinking he is the Green Hornet and selling tickets to Joey's Bar Mitzvah and saying "God Bless L. Durocher" before he goes to sleep and etc., just to prove that he is normal and not some Pearl Harbor sneak with big teeth and black glasses and TNT in his ear. But that didn't work either.

Don't forget the secret weapon part.

Would you keep your shirt on?????? Instead, the only thing the Major said back was "These people are a threat to our security" like Craig was going to chase Eisenhower across Germany with a pop gun or something. So when I saw that I was not getting anywhere, it hit me that I had a secret weapon.

And it was me!

Remember when he hoodwinked the Rabby into letting me stand up for him? And conned me into making him a bat-boy? Well at least me and the Rabby were a challenge on account of having brains. This Major was a whole other ball game. I figured Joey could use him for target practice just to stay limber. So I yanked him out of the barracks where him and Craig were lying under some beds and watching a rat.

Earl Warren was chewing his tail and taking a shit at the same time. It was festive.

Then I booted his ass into the CO's office and let him go to work by saying to him on the way in "Just start your usual riot." Well they did not know what hit them. First he took them to the mat about the father's tomato plants pointing to Lockheed by saying that they were also pointing to Brazil and so what? Then he said the whole Constitution out loud by heart just to prove that there was nothing in it about vegetables. And when it didn't look like that was going to do the job either, he started making up amendments.

Only the 19th. That one's about voting rights for women, which wasn't going to do us much good anyway.

What did you call it?

"Unlawful Detention. The right of the citizens of the United States to life and liberty cannot be taken away or restricted because of a person's national origin." If you didn't know it was me, wouldn't you think that James Madison wrote it?

It was like being in a train wreck when all you can do is watch it happen. I was never so scared stiff in my whole life. Joey wasn't. He just kept going. By the time he got to the part about Clarence Darrow being his uncle and taking him and Craig to baseball games, the Major was on the horn with Tule Lake and Craig had his family back. Isn't C. Darrow dead?

Who cares? Know what else, Hazel? Charlie got the Gophers to keep Craig in the lineup by telling the newspaper that he was going to be an All Star someday.

Just between us he could not hit a barn with a 40-ft. pumpkin, but how many knocks is one kid suppose to take????? And when you play 3b for the NY Giants they always think you know what your talking about.

Even Bogart.

Oh yeah. We were eating dinner at Romanoffs and we saw him at another table, so we flipped a coin to see who'd get to ask him for his autograph.

I won.

My ass you did. You were using Stuke's nickle with the 2 heads on it. But before we could do anything, Bogart came over himself and said "Say. Aren't you Charlie Banks?" Bogey knew who I was. *Bogey.*

He's making a picture with Ingrid Bergman about the war in North Africa, but he says we shouldn't waste our money and the only reason they made him do it was because George Raft said No.

But guess who said Yes? Veronica Lake. To Stuke. I would of thought he was snowing me but I answered the phone myself and heard her voice. He almost broke a leg running out of the shower with soap in his eyes.

We worked on the letter with him for two hours before we let him send it. Up until then she thought I was his son.

So did Lana Turner and Hedy Lamar and half of the other movie stars at the H. Canteen. Every time it looked like Stuke was going to click with one of them I would send Joey over there to say such things as "Pop it is past my bed-time" or "Can I have my allowance now?" or etc. It is a good thing Stuke did not have his K–Bar knife with him or else they would of been finding pieces of us all over Calif. for the next 7 yrs. But V. Lake let him take her to Mocambo.

Hazel, if he marries her we'll have two stars in the family—you and Veronica.

What about *me*?

Are you going to let me ship out with you?

Nope.

Then you don't count.

Chiseler.

Fake.

That does it. Sack time Bucko. We need to get you to the train early.

Stuke paid for the ticket. That's part of his job now since he's a Pfc. and Charlie's not.

Your stalling. Tell Hazel you love her.

I love you, Hazel.

Me too.

Joey and Charlie

P.S. Craig is going to be OK up there until all of this is over. I even told him I would be checking up on him once in a while just to make sure he is dotting his P's and Q's. But one of these days somebody is going to have to tell me how McArthur and DeWitt and etc. can get away with it. This stinks even for the Army.

P.S.2. Boy, when Joey decides to grow up he does not waste any time, does he? I sure hope I had something to do with it. But it got me thinking about not knowing what is going to happen in the S. Pacific or how long before they let us come home or etc., and what if he loses his way while I am gone? So I am inclosing something for you to give to him only if you have to (though I will probably be older than Noah by the time they ship us out).

P.S.3. Stuke just got in. She let him kiss her. You can tell because (1) he has a funny look on his face and (2) he just went into the closet to take a piss.

WAR BULLETIN:
U.S. Planes Bomb Five Japanese Cities

═══════○═══════

SUNDAY. In a dispatch that has electrified Allied nations around the globe, the White House today announced that sixteen American B-25 bombers, under the command of Lt. Col. James H. Doolittle, successfully attacked the allegedly "unassailable" Japanese homeland by air, scoring direct hits on Tokyo, Yokohama, Osaka, Kobe and Nagoya. With no U.S. airfields in the far Pacific, and a carrier-based assault impossible given the range limitations of the Mitchell B-25, the question remains, "Where the heck did our planes come from?" FDR was willing to offer but a single clue: "Shangri-La"—a tongue-in-cheek reference to the mythical Himal-ayan paradise popularized by James Hilton's novel *Lost Horizon*. The extent of the damage is not yet known, but it is believed that the losses to

Man About Town
by Winchell

THE BOYS GET TOKYO;
MERMAN GETS "THE BOYS"

With Jimmy Doolittle wrapping up production in the skies above Japan, Uncle Sam's about to get another shot in the arm. According to the beat on the Street, Ethel Merman's joined the war effort by signing with skipper Mike Todd to star in Cole Porter's new song-and-dancer *Something for the Boys*, coming in for a landing at the Alvin in early January. This time the Queen of Musical Comedy finds herself playing Blossom Hart, a Texas war worker who begins receiving radio signals through the Carborundum fillings in her choppers. (And we thought radar was the latest word!)

"It's Cole's best score since *Anything Goes*," gushed Eth at the Stork. "Wait 'til you hear a number he wrote for me called 'By The Miss–iss–iss–iss–iss–iss–iss–iss–inewah'. The minute he played it, I knew I had to say yes." And nobody crosses the Merm!

Dear Goodlookin',

I need to borrow your rifle for five minutes, but I promise I'll wipe off the prints before I send it back. And if you should happen to hear that they've misplaced the Queen of Musical Comedy, pretend you don't know anything about it. (Incidentally, I'm glad you think this is funny, you sadist. Wait until you find out that they've hired her to play third base for the Giants, too. Come to think of it, she's built more like you anyway.) Joey and I ran into her tonight at the Stage Door Canteen—she was boring the pants off of Gypsy Rose Lee (who wasn't wearing any). Talk about an unlikely pair. When was the last time anybody thought of Merman and Gypsy in the same breath?

Cole Porter dropped by the club on Monday to see if I'm still speaking to him (I'm not), but that didn't stop him from butting in while the kid and I rehearsed our Canteen number—a cute routine I swiped from *Pal Joey*. (Your little bat boy tried to convince me that he should have the bigger part because, after all, "they didn't call the show *Pal Hazel*." He has a bright future as an agent if he wants one.) Cole felt it was all wrong for us and recommended "They're Either Too Young or Too Old", which probably means he wrote it. I would have told him to go to Hell if it hadn't stopped the show, so maybe I'll let him off the hook—but not before 1950.

I just heard on the radio that the Japanese captured two of the Doolittle crews when they crash-landed in

China. According to Tokyo Rose, they'll be given a fair trial and then executed. (That one's going to take a little explaining.) Promise me something, you big bruiser. When you boys are sitting around bragging about who has the biggest you-know-what, don't let anybody talk you into joining the Air Corps. I like you best when all ten of your toes are on the ground. Besides, you're manly enough already.

Roosevelt says that the war could last two years or more. Remind me never to complain about a long road trip again.

Boy, do I miss you.

All my love,
-Mrs. H-

P.S. Joey told Rachel that her hair was as brown as My Friend Flicka. Was that your idea? I tried to explain to him that girls rarely appreciate being compared to livestock, but he won't listen to me—he still believes you're the last word on romance. (Come to think of it, so do I. Maybe I'd better shut up and quit while I'm ahead.)

P.S.2. By the way, Rachel's fallen for him hook, line and sinker—but he hasn't figured that out yet, and I'm certainly not about to tell him. That's the kind of thing you guys need to learn for yourselves after we've made you miserable for a few years.

P.S.3. And stop saying you want them to ship you out. Don't you read *Stars and Stripes*? It's dangerous over there. Personally I'm tempted to tell General Vandegrift that you're a Communist—I'd rather have you here in a prison stockade than in some mucky swamp with sore shoulders and nobody to rub them for you. So be careful what you ask for—you may get it.

WAR BULLETIN:

Corregidor Falls to Japan; "Sukiyaki" Comes Off Brooklyn Menus

WEDNESDAY. Outnumbered after prevailing over nearly insurmountable odds for six weeks, and following more than 300 air attacks, Gen. Jonathan Wainwright issued a terse statement of surrender from embattled Corregidor this morning: "The resistance of our troops has been overcome." With these words, 42,000 American and Filipino troops became the property of the Japanese, representing one of the worst defeats in U.S. history. Reports of atrocities against American prisoners, presumably in retaliation for last month's bombing of Tokyo and other Nipponese cities, are as yet unconfirmed.

Brooklyn, however, took the news in full stride. Overnight, sukiyaki disappeared from its menus, to be replaced by "noodle stew". Take *that*, Tojo.

═══════════○═══════════

UNITED STATES MARINE CORPS
Semper Fidelis

CAMP PENDLETON   OCEANSIDE, CALIFORNIA

To: ALL SECOND DIVISION MARINES
From: GEN. A. VANDEGRIFT
Re: EMBARKATION

BUSES LEAVE FOR P.O.E. SAN DIEGO AT 0600 TUESDAY THE 16TH. SHIP ASSIGNMENTS WILL BE HANDED OUT AT THAT TIME. WE CAN'T TELL YOU WHERE YOU'RE GOING, BUT YOU'LL BE HEADING IN THE DIRECTION OF THE RISING SUN.

GOOD LUCK.

Dear Charles,

I heard from Estelle Goldman that her boy in the service lost five pounds from what the Navy calls a decent meal, and the portions they serve on those ships wouldn't keep a snake alive. So look for a few packages from us before you leave, but don't expect a miracle. Ration points yet. Three for sugar, two for flour and who knows what's going to come out of the oven?

God forbid you should find yourself in the jungle, you'll boil the water before you drink it. They have diseases over there that should only happen to Hitler. And remember that your brains aren't in your *tuchus*, so use them and stay away from bullets.

Love,
Aunt Carrie

Dear Sprout,

Got your orders at mail call & I think we have the bases covered. But just in case I forgot anything:

√ I won't let him shoot off his mouth.

√ I won't let him stand up in any foxholes.

√ I'll keep him away from land mines.

_√_ I'll keep him away from mosquitoes, malaria, jungle rot, dengue fever, snakes, spiders, lizards, flies, crocodiles & tall grass with headhunters in it.

_√_ I'll make sure he writes.

OK, Boss? Remember, tho—he's 2 inches taller than me & most of that is muscle. If I can pull this off without losing any of my teeth, maybe I'll attack Japan while I'm at it.

Don't worry about us, Sprout. We're Marines. And one of us scored the only unassisted triple play in 21 years.

Your buddy,
Stuke

P.S. Am enclosing this week's issue of *Yank* with Veronica's pinup on page 16. I'm trusting you to take care of her until we get back.

P.S.2. I hear you've got a pretty jake love life of your own. How about a few pointers for a pal?

Dear Rachel,

In case you haven't heard, I'm performing at the Stage Door Canteen on weekend nights with Hazel MacKay, the world famous singer. Technically I'm not allowed to invite anybody who isn't a member of the armed forces, but I think I could probably sneak you in through the kitchen. This isn't something you want to miss. Last night after our set we were spooling spumoni with Mary Martin and Gertrude Lawrence and Noel Coward and Gypsy Rose Lee (who had clothes on).

So how about it, Toots?

Love,
Joey

Dear Joey,

Boys who go to night clubs where drinking happens are usually no good, and boys who eat ice cream with strippers like Gypsy are *always* no good.

And don't call me Toots. You're not exactly Mickey Rooney, you know.

Rachel

Dear Rachel,
    Do you like *any*thing about me?

                    Joey

Dear Joey,
    Your eyes are greener than Jefferson's face on a $2 bill.

                    Rachel

Dear Rachel,
    Do you mean it?

                    Joey

Dear Joey,
    Maybe.

                    Rachel

Dear Charlie,

Here's one you can use whenever you want. GAPITA. Girls Are Pains In The Ass. These are only some of the things I've done for her since you left.

1. Got her Barbara Stanwyck's autograph the week she decided she liked Myrna Loy better.
2. Put a rubber band around 25 dandelions and left them on her chair. She sat on them.
3. Stood under her window at 9:30 in the P.M. and played "Moonlight Serenade" for her on our sax. The landlady threw water on me.
4. Went through every color in the damned rainbow trying to tell her how pretty she is and all she said was "You spelled 'ocher' wrong."
5. Invited her to the Stage Door Canteen, which only made her call me a bum.
6. But now she says she likes my eyes. Smokes, do they do this to us on purpose?????

We heard about what the Japanese did to our guys on Bataan and how some of them tried to fight back but got marched to death instead. Didn't you say this was practically over? And that reminds me, Big Shot. I don't know what they're teaching you in the Corps, but this isn't some game with Cincy or the Cubs or etc., where all you have to do is slug P. Derringer if he gets you sore. Stuke said he was going to keep an eye on you, and if I find out that you did anything dumb-ass like jump out of a foxhole to pop Tojo on the chin just because he called you a Yankee Doodle Son-of-a-Bitch or whatever, you'd better hit the ground running because you won't get much of a head start. I mean it, Charlie. Don't let anything happen to you. And remember to let me know where you are when you get there.

Joey

P.S. Craig said to tell you that Earl Warren bit a corporal and then peed on his foot.

P.S.2. If you told the Marine Corps that my birthday is on Monday, would they let you stay back and take a different ship later? Maybe one that left in 2 years? It's just a thought.

P.S.3. I need to come up with a new way to sneak into the Navy Yard. Ever since they took away my shoeshine box, they're wise to all of my disguises.

Dear Joey,

Right before we got on the boat we found out how bad our boys shellacked Yamamito at Midway. That's the end of the ball game for Japan. Let's see how they like it when the shoe is on the other oar.

Deke Marantz got a letter from one of his buddies who just came back from Australia all browned off at the Army. (Who *wouldn't* be???) He says he wrote home asking his Mom to send him some India nuts but the damn sensors cut out the "India" part because it is the name of a place where some of our boys are stationed, and what if Hirohoto or somebody shoots down our mail plane and finds out. (Like they do not already know. We have been there for 4 mos. already.) Then he wrote to his girl in Penna. by starting it off with "Dear Pearl" due to it being her name and such, and they cut out "Pearl" on account of the Harbor with the same moniker and Dec. 7 and so forth. We think he is making it up on account of even the Army could not be that dumb. But what if they are? And what if the USMC is dumber? Part of the deal is that I want to make sure you know where I am all the time, just so you will not worry without a reason. And in case there *is* a reason, such as reading in the paper that our boys are getting their ass shot off in Singapore and that's where you know I am, you can tell Hazel I am on a beach at Tahiti drinking Slow Gin Fizzes instead. (I know I told you that you are never suppose to lie, but you are old enough to learn that lying to girls is a whole other catagory if you think the truth will make them cry.) So me and Stuke cooked up a plan. Whenever you get a letter from me, keep a glim on the second sentance. The first letters of the words there will spell out the name of the place they sent us to.

Dear Joey,

I can't tell you where we are but they think we are heroes here. <u>W</u>e <u>a</u>re <u>k</u>nown <u>e</u>very-where.

That's if we get sent to Wake. And this is the rest of our list so far.

GUAM — Getting up at midnight.

NEW GUINEA — Nobody ever wanted Germany until it nailed England's ass.

TARAWA — Those Aussies really are wicked artillerymen.

BATAAN — Bees are too angry at night. (This is one of Stuke's. Ever hear anything more boneheaded in your life? For my money it might as well have a big arrow pointing to it that says THIS IS A SECRET CODE.)

TOKYO — Turn over Kaiser, your out. (This is my favorite.)

And let's just hope that we do not get on a place like Einwetok or Ioribaiwa on account of I may miss the whole fuckin war. Meanwhile I will make sure that I put a little star at the top of the letter (*Dear Joey) in case one of these is in it, just so you do not waste your time looking on the map for a place called GISWOERP (though I would not be surprised if you found one there).

Smokes, are you a sucker. Rachel has got you on a string like you were a yo-yo. You should never of left the dandy lions on her chair on account of you might as well give her a dog coller and tell her where to buckle it on your neck. Do you want to set us back 50 yrs.???? Remember one thing—just because you have a dick does not automatically mean you deserve one. You need to earn it. The next time she gives you a rough time such as spelling the wrong colors or calling you a bum, take a sad breath and look into her face and say "Well I guess you do not want to see me anymore". Then turn around and walk away slow with your head down as far as it can go. And whatever you do, *don't look back*. This will scare the heck out of her due to making her think "The jig is over" or "It is put up or shut up time" or whatever in Hell goes through their head whenever they have just gummed up rest of their life by letting the right boy fly out the window. Between you and me, I have heard the scuttlebutt and found out she is crazy about you. So turn the tables and do not chicken out. I know you Bucko. You will wait 15 mins. and if she has not called yet you will write her a letter that starts "Dear Rachel, I cannot stop thinking about you" and boom, your behind the same 8-Ball again. Don't do it.

We have been on the *Farragut* for 3 days and my stomach is still in San Diego, but Stuke is doing the barfing for the both of us. (This is part of his job now on account of he is a Pfc. and etc.) Everybody is jealous of him because at least he is not hungry. With 2500 men on board and a mess hall that fits 300 of them (as long as they are skinny ones) we only get to eat one time a day. Yesterday Sgt. Block pointed to Shiloh's leg and said to Marantz "I wonder how that would taste with pickle relish on it." So Shiloh said back "Taint funny McGee" and hid until Taps behind the poopdeck or fantail or hornpipe or whatever in Hell the Navy calls that long fat gizmo on top. But I am cleaning up. Right now my pointy coconut things are going for 25¢ per.

They also only turn on the water for ½ hr. a day on account of not having alot of it, though you would think with a whole damn ocean outside they would figure out a way. Ever watch 2500 guys try to shave at 40 sinks in 30 mins.? Well I one time went to Macys with Hazel when they were having a sale of dresses, and women were lined up at the door like they were running the K. Derby and just waiting for the bell to go off. It is the same kind of thing.

We are stopping first at one of our bases in the S. Pacific to hook up with divisions coming in from

Norfoke and other places. I will write again when we get there.

Charlie

P.S. You need to polish the sax one time a week to keep it in good shape. I used Thursdays but you can pick whatever one you want.

P.S.2. During the day, they are drilling us on passwords we will need in the jungle in case we run into a Japanese spy dressed like a USMC. One of them was "Who lost Game 4 of the 1941 W. Series?" Half the guys said "Brooklyn" and the other half said "Mickey Owen" and the third half said "Tommy Henrich". Then some fist fights happened so they scrapped the question. But I told you so.

P.S.3. Hazel wrote to me about your birthday and "Andy Hardy" at the Radio City and etc. I wish I could of been there. You know that, right? Just think about it. When I first met you, you were a 12 yr. old Big-Mouth. Now your a 14 yr. old Big-Mouth except a little taller (but only a little). Can you believe it has been almost a whole year since we went on the road together?????

Dear Mrs. Toots,

I'm sorry I have not written to you in almost 2 hrs. but I got tied up on a long one to Joey. I told him not to send Rachel a love letter no matter what. That should do it. I figure he will probably have one in the mail to her as soon as he hears me say don't. Do I know this kid or what?

They are playing Taps so I need to make this short. I will write again at 11:30 after they think we are all asleep in our bunks.

Love,
Mr. Toots

INTERVIEWER: DONALD M. WESTON, PH.D.
SUBJECT: JOSEPH CHARLES MARGOLIS

Q: You sure about that?

A: Heck, yes. Anytime he wants me to do something, he always tells me not to. Then he pretends to get sore so I won't figure out he snaked me.

Q: What happens when you do what he says?

A: I get what I want.

Q: What happens when you don't?

A: I lose. 'Member how Pinocchio had a conscience and it was Jiminy Cricket?

Q: Uh-huh.

A: Well, I have one too. Know what? Craig was right. Charlie's a lot smarter than me after all.

Q: So what are you going to do about it?

A: What do I look—stupid to you? I'm gunna fall for it.

Dear Rachel,

There are a couple of things I think you'd better know:

Barbara Stanwyck didn't kiss me goodnight. The only time I ever met her was in the parking lot when I asked her to sign the menu for you.

I wouldn't know Gypsy or Gertrude Lawrence or Noel Coward from a hole in my head.

The only reason I told you about dancing with Dorothy Walker of the G. Miller Orchestra was to get you jealous.

I don't have any wild oats and I wouldn't know how to sew them even if I did.

If there was one thing in my whole life I would erase if I could, it would be the yellow snowball. I'm *really* sorry I did that.

There's no drinking allowed at the Stage Door Canteen except juice and Nehi and other soda pop, so don't worry.

I still want you to go there with me so you can sit at the ring side and watch me and Hazel sing our song, and everybody will think you're my girl.

I can't stop thinking about you, and not just because of brown hair and blue eyes and etc.

I love you.

I hope you don't get sore at me for writing this, but I can't even tell whether you like me or not. So this is my last try. Please, please?

Love,
Joey

WAR BULLETIN:

Rommul Gains in Africa; Giants Gain in Hub

BOSTON, Wednesday. With the news that Field Marshal Erwin Rommel has seized the port city of Tobruk and pushed his Panzer divisions 60 miles into Egypt, the unstoppable New York Giants have managed a similar feat in Boston, sweeping an improbable four-game series from the formidable Braves. Previously crippled by the departure of Banks and Stuker to the war in the Pacific, the Gotham Nine appeared to be headed for the cellar. But with Johnny Mize and Billy Werber settling in at first and third, respectively, the Big Boys' early season shakes seem to have vanished as quickly as fifth place turned into second place last night at Braves Field.

Dear Charlie,

Boy, are you lucky that you're in the S. Pacific and not at the Polo Grounds. The Giants just lost nine straight and they're only in last place because there's nowhere lower for them to go. I don't know whose idea it was to get Billy Werber at third base after you left, but they would have had better luck if they'd hired Aunt Carrie instead. Yesterday he let three balls fall on his head and four more go through his legs, and when he swung on a 2 and 2 (which even a rock-head knows you don't do off a puffin like H. Gumbert), he let go of his bat and almost brained Mickey Witek who was standing on first. I'll bet that when you and Stuke come back they give you a big fat raise before you even do anything. Smokes, will they be glad to see you.

I know you told me not to, and you're probably gunna get cheesed off at me again, but I tried really hard not to send an "I Love You" letter to Rachel, and for awhile I even didn't. Almost an hour. But then I started thinking about the way her eyes smile even when her mouth doesn't and the sound her laugh makes whenever Kathy Fine says something funny to her, and I couldn't help it. How come *I* can't make her laugh like that? But I'm sending you what I wrote to her anyway so you can chew me out.

Hazel has a surprise for you, but I'm going to let her tell you what it is.

Your buddy,
Joey

Dear Goodlookin',

It wasn't my idea to land on the cover of *Life* magazine, especially in coveralls and a welding iron. However, our little shyster decided he was going to help build dive bombers at the Navy Yard no matter what, and you know what happens when his mind is made up—air raid sirens go off all over Brooklyn. Apparently they caught him sneaking in through a drain pipe, so he cornered some Admiral Whozis and promised he could deliver "Hazel MacKay, the World-Famous Singer" if they'd let him on the assembly line. Well, what was I supposed to do?! You can't open a damned newspaper any more without reading about some little Tillie from Tallahassee who threw away her egg beater and picked up a rivet gun instead. "Woman Ordnance Workers—The Girl He Left Behind Is a WOW!" So the boys from *Life* unpacked their cameras and I managed to whip up a fuselage. Don't ask me how. I have enough trouble with omelettes.

I wonder where you are tonight. I hope it's someplace safe and snug.

I love you.

-Mrs. H-

P.S. And I promise—my pinup days are over.

*Dear Joey,

I can't tell you where we are, but at least I can tell you where we aren't. Not Ethiopia where zebras eat antalope legs and never dance. (If Stuke really thinks we are going to get away with this one, he is out of his fuckin mind.) There is nothing for us to do here except (1) cool our heels for 3 wks. until the other divisions pull in and we leave for the war, or (2) watch their movies which are so old that nobody talks in them and the people walk fast and jumpy. (Who in Hell is Clara Bow?) But Stuke got kicked in the ass by a kangaroo.

I read your letter to Rachel. What is it with you and the damn yellow snowball????? Are you going to give her one for a wedding present too? And who do you think your fooling anyway? "I know you told me not to, and you're probably gunna get cheesed off at me again" and etc. Bullshit Bucko. How long did it take you to figure out that I wanted you to send her one all along? 10 seconds? 9? 3? You use to be alot easier to trick. In Cincy you did not find out that I was putting one over on you until after you fell for it and learned the Tora. Remember? (Come to think of it, I guess I was no cracker-jack either. One minute I am telling you that I would never take you on the road with me, then all of a sudden I am chasing your ass 1/2-way across Chic. and trying to keep your face out of D. Walker's bosoms. How in Hell did you get me to say Yes?) It is a good thing that Rachel does not know you as well as I do or she would of put 2 and 2 together by now and learned that "This is my last try" only means "Until the next one". Nobody stays in the ring longer than you do.

Want to hear a pisser? I just found out that when we get to where we are going, I'm not allowed to go on the beach and fight with Stuke and Marantz and Shiloh and etc. Sgt. Block said The Word came from the Old Man (who could be anybody from FDR to Vandagrift to Moses for Christ's sake). "Washington does not want any dead All Stars on their hands on account of it screws up the news reels." Ever hear of anything more beef-headed in your life? It gets worse too. Where they are putting me is at a type writer in the Communications Room. What a laugh. They will have to teach me how to spell first. Whoever came up with *that* idea must of died from the neck up (which means it was probably FDR after all).

But I'm a little worried Iron Fists. Sometimes Stuke's brains are in his belly-button, especially when I'm not around to look out for him. If you don't believe me, ask the kangaroo who kicked him. So keep your fingers crossed. He means alot to both of us, huh?

Charlie

P.S. We found out from Armed Forces Radio that the Giants are really in 2nd place and not last. Also, Billy Werber is a good man (for an old fart). Thanks for telling me different though.

Dear Mrs. Hazelnut,

One of the bunk fliers in Easy Company had a bunch of pinups on the wall, and right in the middle of them was you on the cover of *Life*. You were stuck in between Chita, Rita, Lola and Roxie, who all together weren't wearing enough to diaper a kid with. Well, I thought about these things for awhile and when I was finished thinking, I bopped him on the conk. (I probably should have let your husband do it, but I'm a Pfc. and he's not.) So when you're scouting godfathers for Charlie Jr., remember who upheld your honor down here in the balmy South Seas.

Stuke

P.S. Keep a glim on Sprout. The way he's going, he could be a father before *any* of us.

Dear Joey,

I never knew a boy like you before. First you put food in my hair and boogies in my lunch and then you think I'm going to a night club with you. Well, I probably am and I don't even know why. Maybe because you're cuter than Mickey Rooney. But not by a lot.

My mother says I can stay out until 10:00 unless Gypsy takes her clothes off.

Rachel

P.S. But this doesn't mean we're getting married or that I'll kiss you. I don't think.

dear joet,

i am in thr communication shack on the voat. either there is something wrong with the fype writer they gave me or with the dingers on my left hsnd. also i cannot figure ouyt how to make big letters eben though i have tried almOST ALL OF THE KEYS EXCEPT THE ONES WITH MUMBERS. I GUESS ONE OF THEM WORKLED. NOW HOW DO I TURM IT OFF????

WE ARE IN THE MIFFLE OF THE S. PAVIFIC ON OUR WAY TO VISIT HIROHOTO,s boys. we will be there tomorrot. then we will have to ask them where we are on accoumt of they still will not tekk us.

rachel is a goner. the part that gives it aWAY IS "I NEVER KNEW A BOT LIKE YOU BEFORF". YOU DID A GOod job buckio. but when you puck her up to take her to the cxanteen make sure you vring her one of those shrively purple flowets that they like to pin on their dress. hezel will know what they are

caLLED. AND DONT GET NERVOYUS ABOUT KISSING HER. BITE THe bull by the horns.
   i will wrute again after we gert to the war.

charLIE

P.S. YOU NEVER TOLD ME ABOUYT THE BOOGIES IN HER LUNCVH. YOU ROCK-HEAF.

P.S.2. DON'T FORGET TO BRING UP THE YEL-LOW SNOWBALL. IT HAS BEEB ALMOST 2 WKS. SINCE THE LAST TIME.

Dear Charlie,
   I'm taking her to the Canteen on Saturday night at 7:00. That's 94 hours and 21 minutes. I was afraid I wouldn't be able to remember everything you told me, so I went through it again and this is my list.

   I won't say shit or fuckin or piss or chowderhead.

   I'll hold the door open for her.

   When I pin the orchid onto her dress I won't let my hand shake much.

If she says something boneheaded like "The capital of South Dakota is Philadelphia" I'll tell her she's right even if I have to bite my mouth off.

I won't fart.

I'll look at her and smile at least once when Hazel and I are singing our song.

I won't pretend I'm a Big-Shot.

If she wants to talk about uranium, I'll let her.

I'll keep our color list in my pocket in case I want to tell her how white her eyeballs are but I forget what comes next.

When I walk her home from the subway, I'll hold her hand. (I don't know about this one, Charlie. I haven't practiced it enough. And smokes, I'm only 14. Maybe we could wait for a couple of years, huh?)

You're a lot smarter than the USMC after all. They left the zebra and antelope line in your letter so I could figure out where you were. Then I looked at a map and I think I know where they're sending you next. It's on our Noah Check List from Braves Field which ought to be inside your helmet—the part where I said "Smokes, even So-and-So wouldn't have pulled a fast one like that." Well, they named a whole bunch of islands after So-and-So and that's where you're headed. Bet?

I think I need to start getting ready. It's 93 hours and 48 minutes.

> Your buddy,
> Joey

P.S. How's this for a pisser? Remember Lenny Bierman, the guy who used to kick the heck out of me and Craig until you wised him up? Well, guess who's paying me two bits a week to do his algebra for him? He even bought me a burger when he got an 83%. Boy, you sure straightened him out. Did I ever say thanks for that? If I didn't, I was a dope.

WAR BULLETIN:

○

Marines Invade Solomon Islands

○

GUADALCANAL, Friday. The United States Marine Corps today launched the first offensive of the Pacific war in an amphibious attack on the tiny island of Guadalcanal in the Solomons. Heavily fortified by Japanese troops, the Imperial stronghold has been targeted by the Yanks principally for its airstrip at Henderson Field, situated on the edge of Sealark Channel. Its capture by the Marines would establish an Allied footing in the South Pacific and cut off all supply lines to and from Rabaul, the primary Nipponese base in that sector of the globe.

Resistance was reported as moderate to light when the first U.S. Higgins boats landed on Green Beach early this morning. Outside of a few pockets of rifle fire, the Marines encountered little opposition, though it is believed that a counter-attack is presently being mounted by the War Ministry in

———○———

*Dear Joey,

I can't tell you where we are but this time it is the medics who are putting in the longest hours. Gee usually all doctors are lucky—camps and nurses and leaves. (It has taken me 2 hrs. to write this much. You know why.)

We lost Shiloh today. He was in the first landing party on the beach and they did not even let him get out of the boat before they chopped him. It turned out he was only 16. That's you in 2 yrs. Maybe this is why

I have not been able to stop thinking about you since I heard the news, and remembering the first letter you ever wrote to me and how we almost didn't get to be friends and how little you looked when you told me about your father and Nana Bert and etc. We have come a long way together.

Joey listen to me. Everybody gets handed a rotten deal sooner or later and your just getting it out of the way early. Want to hear a secret? The same thing happened to me too. My Mom was a waitress who died from the flu of 1918 when I was almost 2, and I only know from pictures that she was pretty and looked like my big brother. But my old man was a cheap hood who would of swiped the fleas off a cat if he thought he could of pawned them, and who croaked from being on the wrong side of a shootout in Madison when they brought him home horozontal. (I told you not to believe everything you read, especially baseball cards.) This is why Harlan was the only hero I ever had. He took me to school and made me supper and kept the bullies away from me and showed me how to play his sax and shaped me up and taught me everything I know about baseball. He was also the one who kept my father from beating the shit out of me on account of it use to happen all the time. Three days before my old man died he caught me playing with his jack-knife and came after me with a bat. But Harlan got in the way. When I took him to the hospital he was hardly breathing and blood was coming out of his nose. The rest of what I told you is true—he hung on for as long as he could. But it wasn't a pitch that killed him, it was my father. And I've never told anybody this in my life.

I want everything to go the right way for you Iron Fists. "Chapter One—I Am Born." Remember that.

Charlie

P.S. When Marantz radioed in for supplies Stuke asked for *Yank* with Hedy Lamar in it. So we know he's OK.

P.S.2. By the time this gets to you, I am betting that Rachel will of let you kiss her. So how did it go? I am putting my chips on you Bucko. You never lose.

Stage Door Canteen

240 WEST 44TH STREET
NEW YORK, NEW YORK

A Rookie and His Rhythm . . . . . . .Kay Kyser and His Orchestra

"The Package" . . . . .Edgar Bergen and
Charlie McCarthy

The Machine Gun Song .Gracie Fields

The Girl I Love to Leave Behind . . . . .Ray Bolger

Blow, Gabriel Blow . . . . .Ethel Merman

How About You? .Hazel MacKay and
Joey Margolis

Zip . . . . .Gypsy Rose Lee
I Can't Strip to Brahms

Bugle Call Rag .Benny Goodman and
His Orchestra

Sing For Your Supper . . . . .Nancy Walker

South American Way . . . . .The Andrews Sisters
Don't Sit Under the Apple Tree

My Heart Belongs to Daddy . . . . .Mary Martin

The Hut-Sut Song . . . . .Betty Comden, Adolph Green
and Judy Tuvim

By the Mississinewah .Ethel Merman

I Got Rhythm . . . . .Hazel MacKay

Buckle Down, Winsocki . . . . .Ray Bolger and
Nancy Walker

Dear Charlie,

I kissed her. I kissed her. I kissed her. I kissed her. I kissed her. I kissed her. I kissed her. I kissed her. I kissed her. I kissed her. I kissed her. I kissed her. I kissed her. Then I kissed her again. (The first time it was on her mouth, but the second time I missed a little. I think I bit her chin.) And guess what? Holding her hand was the easy part. I can't believe what a noodlehead I was.

These are the only things I did that would have pissed you off.

1. When I opened the Canteen door for her, my hand was so sweaty that I accidentally let go and hit Harpo Marx in the forehead.

2. When Hazel and I were singing, I looked over at Rachel at the ring side and I winked at her and I smiled at her and then I forgot all the words to the song. (Hazel said afterwards that she wanted to push me down the tuba.)

3. When we got back to Brooklyn, it was still early so we walked around the reservoir and I took her hand like it was something I was used to doing 8 times a day. Then I pointed to the water and told her I peed in it when I was a kid. I still don't know why I said that.

4. When it looked like it was getting to be kissing time, I took out our sax and tried to play "Moonlight Serenade" to set the mood, but I guess my mouth was already thinking about hers because it didn't come out so hot. Then a man opened a window and yelled out "Hey. Shut the fuck up." So I kissed her instead.

Charlie, this was all your idea and I want you to be my best man even if I have to come out there in a row boat and bring you back myself. (You'll do it, right? Because I'll wait for you if I have to.) Do you think that Mel Ott would let us have the wedding at the Polo Grounds? We don't even need the whole park. Just third base.

Joey

P.S. It's 4:25 in the A.M. but who the Hell cares? I'm never going to sleep again in my whole life. What if I miss something?

P.S.2. I forgot to tell you the best part. She even kissed me back.

P.S.3. The Giants just dropped to third place. This time it's the truth. I *told* you they'd stink without you.

P.S.4. How soon do you think they'll let you come home?

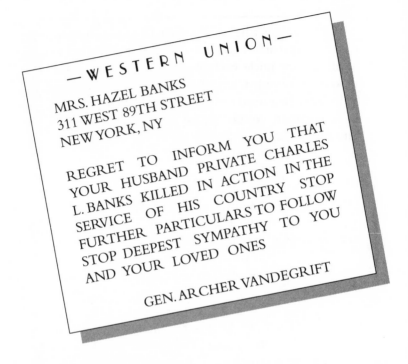

— WESTERN UNION —

MRS. HAZEL BANKS
311 WEST 89TH STREET
NEW YORK, NY

REGRET TO INFORM YOU THAT
YOUR HUSBAND PRIVATE CHARLES
L. BANKS KILLED IN ACTION IN THE
SERVICE OF HIS COUNTRY STOP
FURTHER PARTICULARS TO FOLLOW
STOP DEEPEST SYMPATHY TO YOU
AND YOUR LOVED ONES

GEN. ARCHER VANDEGRIFT

Dear Joey-San,

I just heard it on the radio and I thought it was that rock-head Orson Welles making suckers out of us again like he did with the Martians. But then Pop said it was true, and I *had* to believe it. Are you okay?

Joey-San, remember when my grandma died and I cried for three days until you got me the Hornet ring? Well, Uncle Mits said something to me that I'll never forget. He said, "Craig, if you think about all the happy times, you won't be sad anymore." And the reason I'll never forget it is because I tried it myself and found out that my uncle was full of baloney. I guess what I mean is that only Charlie could have stopped Bierman from ganging up on us, and only Charlie could have taken you on a road trip, and only Charlie could have made the Gophers think I was some kind of prize at 3d base even though I secretly stink, and only Charlie could have gotten Rachel to love you back. And he did all these things because he wanted to. So think about the happy times and when you start to cry anyway it's because you should. Charlie earned it.

As soon as they let us out of here I'm coming to Brooklyn to visit you, even if I have to walk. And you know I mean that.

> Friends forever,
> Craig

P.S. I'll give you back the Hornet ring too, if you think it'll help you feel better.

P.S.2. I didn't really like Mel Ott better than him. He knew that, didn't he?

Temple Chizuk Amuno
1243 Parkside Avenue • Brooklyn, New York

Dear Joseph:

Please allow me to express my sadness over Charlie's passing, and to assure you that our entire congregation shares your sorrow as well. He was a compassionate man who cared a great deal for you, and who never seemed to give less than he had. You can always be proud of him.

Kaddish will be said in his memory on Friday night, and yahrtzeit candles will be delivered to your home. Naturally, this is somewhat unusual given the fact that he was a Protestant; however, since we've already broken all of our remaining rules for Charlie Banks, we felt that this should be no exception.

Should you find your grief too difficult to bear alone, remember that I am always available.

Warmest regards,
Rabbi Morris Lieberman

340

Dear Sprout,

I guess this is what it must feel like to lose a leg or something, when you know you're never going to be in one piece again no matter how well they teach you how to walk. Charlie wasn't only my friend, he was the part of me that always knew the right things to do (like asking Veronica Lake for a date) & the wrong ones (like picking a fight with Phil Masi & starting a brawl that cost us the game with the Braves). But even when I gummed up the works, he never got sore. All he said was "See? Don't let it happen again." And I watched him do the same thing for you. That was our buddy, Sprout.

I wanted you to know how it happened because you were the one he was thinking about at the end. It was d-day plus 2 when me & a patrol of eight other guys got ambushed on the beach—they had us pinned behind a log on our bellies & there was no way for us to get out. So Marantz radioed back to the *Farragut* but they couldn't send in any reinforcements because the shell fire was too thick. Then Charlie found out about it. And when he did, he clipped a corporal on the chin, snitched a Higgins boat, and buffaloed his way through 70 tons of heavy artillery like he was dodging raindrops or something. When he finally rolled up onto the beach I asked him "What took you so long?" and he said "I couldn't find a place to park, move your ass." Just like when he used to bat me home from third so I wouldn't jinx the dirt. And all I remember about crawling back to the boat was thinking "I sure hope

Dorothy Lamour appreciates this" when from behind me Charlie whispered "Say Stuke? Whatever you do, don't tell Joey about this. Otherwise he'll want to try it himself." Then there were two shots and the ball game was over. But the rest of us made it back alive.

You had it figured right when you called him a hero. But you only knew the half of it. When you're old enough so that you & me can go out and get crocko together, I'll tell you the other half myself. That's a promise.

Your pal,
Stuke

Dear Joey,

I called your house twice, but your aunt said you couldn't talk to anybody. I guess I can understand why. Anyway, I just wanted to tell you how sorry I am.

Yankee Doodle Dandy is playing at the Kings, but I won't go unless you take me. Even if I have to miss it. So call me when you come home from Wisconsin. Please, please.

Love,
Rachel

Charlie Banks Laid to Rest

RACINE, WISC., Saturday. Charles Linden Banks, intrepid slugger for the New York Giants whom many felt was destined to become one of the greatest baseball players of all time, was buried with honors next to his brother Harlan in a simple graveside service here today. A private in the U.S. Marine Corps since Pearl Harbor, Banks was killed at Guadalcanal on August 9—two days after his 25th birthday—as he was attempting to rescue a squad of Marines who had been pinned to the beachhead by enemy fire.

Among those in attendance were his widow, singer Hazel MacKay, and representatives from each of the teams that both feared and respected him: Stan Musial of the Cardinals, Lou Boudreau of the Indians, Tommy Henrich of the Yankees, Phil Cavaretta of the Cubs, Early Wynn of the Senators, Mickey Owen of the Dodgers, Johnny Pesky of the Red Sox, Johnny Vander Meer of the Reds, Ernie

Dear Joey,

When I got home from Penn Station I found a condolence telegram from Ethel Merman, but I didn't think it could possibly be real—I was convinced that Charlie was putting one over on me from Up There. "Hey, Toots. How's this for a ringer? Just in case you thought I wouldn't be around any more." So I figured I'd call his bluff by inviting her up for tea. She said yes. Now I've got to go through with it. My husband is laughing his head off.

I don't know about you, but I can remember one or two occasions in the past when you and Charlie and I had a slightly better time than we did on Saturday. I thought I was doing pretty well in the tears department until Aunt Carrie read from Philippians. "So now also Christ shall be magnified in my body, whether it be by life or by death." Until that moment, I had no idea how much she cherished him. And of course your eulogy did me in completely—but that was no surprise. What on earth would have happened to him if he hadn't met you? The Charlie I fought with was the one who'd turn up every fifteen minutes with a black eye or a bloody nose. The Charlie I married was the one who learned the Torah and won Father of the Year. You made all the difference, Joey.

I told you once before that it was our job to take care of him—and we did it to the end. I'm so glad he's got his brother to look out for him now. He and

Harlan haven't played ball together in nine years, and now they've got all the time in the world.

Thank you for being there for him. And for me, too.

Love always,
Hazel

P.S. Just before you left California, Charlie sent me something that he wanted you to have in case this ever happened. So I'm enclosing it here. When you open it, pretend he's writing to you from a road trip. And in a way, he is.

Dear Joey,

I hope that you never get to read this because if you do it will mean that I lied to you when I said I would always be here. But nobody ever told me about such things as Pearl Harbor and etc., or else I would of put "maybe" at the end.

You do not have to worry about growing up anymore because the hardest part is over. There are only a couple more things you need to know before your ready to do the rest without me.

1. Your head and your heart are two different things. One of them can get you into trouble and the other one can't. It's okay to be scared when you can't tell them apart. That happened to me every day of my life. But nobody ever saw it except you.

2. Everyone has something worth it inside of them even if it doesn't show. Sometimes you have to look a little harder than other times but don't give up. Otherwise all your going to see is a sorehead who plays 3d base.

3. When you get famous or rich and maybe you think that you wish I was there to see it, remember that one way or the other I am.

The last thing you will always remember is the most important one. A long time ago I told you I did not know for a fact yet that you were somebody special. Now I do.

I love you Bucko.

Charlie

Epilogue

CHARLIE BANKS DAY 1977

SUNDAY, AUGUST 7, 1977

SCHEDULE OF EVENTS

10:00 a.m.   **Flag-raising at the
                                            Banks Gravesite**
                                            Park Cemetery, Racine

Guest Speakers

Jimmy Carter, *President of the United States*
Julian McKenna, *Governor of Wisconsin*
Joseph Margolis, *Author; Sportswriter*

12:00 noon   **Buffet Lunch**
                                            Veterans Hall

2:00 p.m.   **Waterford vs. Racine**
                                            (1977 County League Champions)
                                            Racine Baseball Field

TICKETS: $100

*Proceeds to benefit the
Charles L. Banks Scholarship Trust,
University of Wisconsin*

August 7, 1977. What would have been Charlie's 60th birthday. The Racine Chamber of Commerce collected almost $50,000 this time. That means that two kids are going to the University of Wisconsin who wouldn't have had a prayer otherwise. Go, Badgers—courtesy of Charlie Banks. Not bad for a guy who didn't know how to spell "Illinois."

Actually, I hadn't intended to participate; I've been turning them down for fifteen years, much like that Navy guy who was one of the Iwo Jima flag-raisers but hasn't given an interview since 1946. Some things hurt a little too much to bring up again. But then my nine-year-old sat me down for a heart-to-heart.

Chucky:	Was his glove in the Hall of Fame when you wrote him the letters?
Me:	Not yet.
Chucky:	Was his picture on shirts?
Me:	Not yet.
Chucky:	Did he take you to places?
Me:	All the time.
Chucky:	Did he show you how to do things?
Me:	Yes.
Chucky:	Did you love him?
Me:	Very much.
Chucky:	Then I think you should go.

That was when I opened the box that I sealed forever thirty-five years ago. The first thing I found was the Purple Heart, then the Oak Leaf Cluster. Both of them were stuck in the envelope with one of his allotment checks. I thought I'd be afraid to look in his wallet, because I still remembered what was inside—but then I surprised myself by suddenly wanting very much to see it. Yeah, it was there all right. Stuke snapped it at Crosley Field in

Cincinnati when we were both wearing Giants uniforms. (God, I was a shrimp! Where I came off having that loud a mouth on that small a body is a conceit I'd rather not pursue.) Charlie's hand is squashing down my cap, and I'm giving him a dirty look. He's just said to me, "If you were any shorter I could sign autographs on your head." And if it hadn't been quite so true, I'd have kicked him.

Then I found the letters. And you know something? I was right. Some things hurt a little too much to bring up again. Especially when your nine-year-old has just hit the nail on the head—when it turns out that the thing that's been haunting you for most of your life is wondering if he ever knew how much you'd loved him in return. But the first envelope proved to me that looking back had not been a mistake after all. *"I almost gave up on you. Guess I should of known better. Happy 1941. From your buddy."* He knew.

A couple of loose ends . . .

Hazel MacKay lives in a Manhattan townhouse designed by her husband, who's spent most of their twenty-six years together giving Frank Lloyd Wright a real run for his money. Upon turning fifty, she reluctantly conceded that her ingenue days were probably over and has since settled for a series of concert tours around the country, proving to her sold-out audiences that "for a middle-aged broad" she's still got what it takes to bring them to their feet. Oh, yeah. She finally buried the hatchet with Ethel Merman. In 1975 they were both asked to perform on a CBS anniversary jubilee—and for twenty minutes it was just the two of them side-by-side on a pair of stools, harmonizing their greatest hits together. No one who was watching will ever forget it.

Jordy Stuker became the only left-handed first baseman in National League history to land a date with Ava Gardner. Though the press made the most of it, nothing much ever came of the relationship. She thought he was Mickey Mantle, and he was under the impression she was Lana Turner. ("They don't make 'em like they used to.") In 1955 he hit the road with Jack Kerouac and never quite recovered from the experience. For the past twenty years he has taught Philosophy at a small college in New Hampshire, where his students are only permitted to call him Stuke. He made Hall of Fame in 1962.

My mother is still keeping a Kosher home at eighty-eight. I got her a housekeeper, of course, but there really didn't seem to be much point.

> *Me:* Mom, what are you doing?
> *Mom:* Waxing the floor—what does it look like I'm doing? The girl's coming tomorrow. Do you want her to think I live like a pig?

She never listened to another Giants game after Charlie died. When the team moved west, she shed no tears. These days she's into college football.

Aunt Carrie lived to see my first book published. She read the galleys, then asked me if my editor was a *shikse*. Of course. I remember Passover that year—the last Seder we shared with her before she gave in to the cancer that nobody but Aunt Carrie knew she had. Generally, I was in charge of the prayers, but on this particular Pesach my aunt requested one of them for herself. "Next year in Jerusalem," she said with a quiet dignity that we weren't able to appreciate until it was too late. A month later she passed away, and I still believe, with all my heart, that she completed her journey to the Promised Land.

Craig Nakamura is a civil liberties attorney in San Francisco, specializing in internment redress. One of these days he's going to convince the government to cough up what it still owes to 120,313 American citizens. The last time I visited him we drove down to Manzanar, figuring that time had erased all traces of what had gone on there and restored the land to the apple orchard it once was. We weren't quite so lucky—the guardhouses, the barbed wire, and the foundations were still all too visible. After a little rooting around, we found the spot where his barracks had been and the field where I'd watched him smack a pair of doubles to deep center. Then we both cried and we hugged each other. Sometimes that's all it takes.

My father passed away on March 12. There were only three people at the funeral, and Nana Bert wasn't one of them. A former business associate was overheard to say, "I just wanted to make sure that the son-of-a-bitch is really gone. I never did trust him." The rabbi couldn't find anyone to deliver the eulogy, so he volunteered to do it himself. After struggling with the text for three days, he finally threw in the towel, mumbled a couple of prayers from Ecclesiastes, and called it a ball game. It didn't much matter to me one way or the other. I lost my Dad in 1936. But I got a much better deal all the way around.

I started my own family in 1961. January 20th, as a matter of fact—the day Jack Kennedy was inaugurated. (God, how Banks would have hated him. "He did to the country what he did to Marilyn Monroe—only at least she got dinner out of it." And etc.) By the way, I married Rachel after all. Charlie always told me to stick with my instincts, and Rachel was a very early one. Chucky's got two older sisters—Sarah, who's eleven, and Jenny, who's fourteen. We live in a three-story brownstone in the Borough of Brooklyn, four subway stops from my old neighborhood. And if you paid me a million dollars, I wouldn't move anywhere else in the world. Know why? Because the way things turned out, Brooklyn was never about my Dad after all.

Brooklyn was—and still is—about Charlie.